The Detective Joanna Best Mysteries
Book 3

The Little Lady Vanishes

Cenarth Fox

The Detective Joanna Best Mysteries
Book 3
The Little Lady Vanishes

First published in 2018 by Fox Plays
www.foxplays.com
www.cenfoxbooks.com

ISBN 978 0 949175 20 5

Cover design by Oliviaprodesign

Some of the mainly Australian words/expressions found in this novel.

AFP - Australian Federal Police
ant's pants, the - high self-opinion, he thinks he's the ant's pants
barbie - barbecue, BBQ
bikkies - biscuits, cookies
brief - solicitor, attorney, lawyer (also a legal document)
clicks - kilometres
crook - ill, sick
dacked - trousers pulled down
Dorothy Dixer - question prepared for government minister
dunno - don't know
edhen - someone whose first and last names are interchangeable e.g. Colin Gregory (named after Sir Edward Henry, fingerprint pioneer)
fair dinkum - truthful, honest
fit as a Mallee bull - strong, healthy
jiffy - a short time
K - a kilometre
maisoncttc - duplcx, two adjoining houscs on thc samc block
merchant banker - rhyming slang for wanker (idiot)
mobile - cell phone
nowt - nothing
OIC - Officer in Charge
parma - short for parmigiana, veal or chicken dish served with cheese
patma - short for Pat Malone, rhyming slang for 'on your own'
peanut-gallery - cheap seats in a theatre
rabbiting - talking
Reg Grundies - rhyming slang for undies, underpants
rubbernecks - sticky beaks
shiner - a black eye
slab of beer - usually 24 bottles or cans of beer
smacker - a kiss
squiz - a look
ant's pants, the - high self-opinion, he thinks he's the ant's pants
U3A - University of the Third Age, adult learning
zip - nothing

For
Liz and Ken Launder
theatregoers, readers and friends

1

'HEY, BABE, HAVEN'T SEEN YOU HERE BEFORE.'

'It's my first time,' she said taking money from her wallet.

'Let me get that.'

'No, it's okay.'

He placed his hand on her wrist and smiled. 'I insist.'

His grip was firm and, being shy, the woman accepted the offer.

'Thank you,' she replied with half a smile.

He paid for her drink, and the creep Darren Sandilands was off and hunting. He treated women appallingly yet still managed to pull them. How? How do bastards impress women, seemingly with ease? Darren could. Mind you, his relationships never endured.

From his pathetic chat-up routine, Darren struck gold with the virginal Elisabeth Thorne. She was lovely, young, talented, attractive, and intelligent, but alas ignorant in the wicked ways of the world. Why did she even start to go out with Darren let alone stick with him? Ah, therein lies a tale.

She came from a religious family—Mum, Dad, Elisabeth and her older sister, Ruth. Good biblical names there, none of your Maddison, Midori, Ziva or Yaz. The parents were into regular church attendance, a sherry for Christmas, perhaps, and subtle but ironclad chaperone services for both their girls.

When growing up, apart from school and church, Elisabeth's main activity was ballet. She began as a child and progressed through the Royal Academy of Dance (RAD) syllabi. She was good, looked fabulous and her parents were thrilled watching their daughter pirouette on stage. Her teachers reckoned she was special and said so.

'Elisabeth must audition for the Australian Ballet School.'

Neither parent knew about the life of a professional dancer, even one in the corps de ballet. They assumed their daughter would marry and have children thus ending her life as a dancer. Ballet was good for fitness, for making friends, and staying out of trouble, especially with boys. So when she was finishing Year 12, it was time to consider a real career. They encouraged Elisabeth to consider teaching or nursing.

She adored ballet and dreamt of becoming a ballerina. But standing up to her parents was not an option. Did Mum and Dad realise their gentle pressure was paving the way for their darling girl to leap into the arms of the lecherous Darren Sandilands?

Obviously not.

After leaving school, Elisabeth gave up ballet and trained to be a kindergarten teacher. She graduated, went to a break-up party in a wannabe upmarket hotel—"don't tell my parents"—with fellow students and there she met the plumber from Oakleigh.

Darren Sandilands came from the other side of the social divide. His hedonistic family was the type featured in trashy tabloids with multiple marriages, sex, drugs and a Chiko roll. Their vocabulary was limited with every adjective starting with *f*.

Darren had two personalities. In public, he was gregarious and spent money on his birds. In private, he was possessive and controlling. 'You can't wear that ... Where do you think you're going? ... Give me your phone.' Meet Darren, aka Mr Control.

At their first meeting, Elisabeth gave Darren her phone number. She did it on a whim. She missed ballet, would rather dance than teach preschoolers, and wanted out of the church and chaperone set. Darren was her ticket to freedom, and she grabbed it. Inside, she felt turmoil.

She begged her sister. '*Please* don't tell Mum and Dad.'

Darren fancied her and told his mate, Jordan, 'I've never had a dancer.'

'What, a stripper? Yeah, we both have.'

'Nah, this is a ballet dancer; long legs and tight arse. And she's gaggin' for it.'

Darren was Elisabeth's first proper boyfriend, or rather improper boyfriend. She lied to her parents when she went out with Darren. She knew they would die if they knew. Darren was evil on two wheels. He never collected her from home. God no.

He had a motorbike, recreational drugs, and an "up yours" attitude to anyone in authority. Darren the rebel. Oh, but the sex was exciting. He wasn't sophisticated but had the experience to introduce Elisabeth to a smorgasbord of activities with the appropriate vocabulary thrown in. She became fluent in talking dirty.

Had Darren been in a position of influence, he would have been a starter for a #Me Too campaign but the flashy misogynist was a humble and unambitious plumber. Several betrayed and abused women knew him well but not so the world.

Darren enjoyed sex and giving orders. To him, a woman existed to satisfy his demands. He saw nothing wrong with treating women as a sex slave. "They love it", "I'm doing them a favour" would have been his response if asked. He was never asked.

When Elisabeth's parents discovered their "fallen" daughter, they despaired. Their older daughter, Ruth, was married and settled with a baby boy. But younger sister, Elisabeth had fallen off a cliff. She moved out of home and into Darren's squalid love nest.

Living in sin with a heathen was but the entrée. Drinking, smoking, having sex, and ignoring her folks, gave the parents a reason to pray longer and harder.

Wiser heads from their church urged them not to panic. 'She'll grow out of it,' said one. 'He'll get bored and dump her,' said another.

Hardly encouraging. Elisabeth's mother went to pieces. 'No decent young man will want her. She's ruined herself. What if she's pregnant?'

Mr Thorne tried to help. 'You did tell her about contraception?'

More woe for Mrs Thorne as the default position of blaming the woman (the mother) kicked in. Was she to blame for Elisabeth's fall from grace? No, but who better to blame?

In his ordinary flat, Darren began to throw his weight around. He could go out drinking with his mates but Elisabeth had to stay home. When they did go out, she wore her classy top and jeans but he thought it too tarty.

'You ain't wearing that, babe.'

'But I only bought it last month. I've never shown it off yet.'

'Get changed, bitch.'

And so Darren turned on his tyrannical nature. Elisabeth discovered his obnoxious side. Perhaps a combination of hormones, ignorance and a desire to rebel had blinded her at first.

In the bedroom, Darren demanded sex. He demanded it elsewhere as well, and then started to film the beautiful former dancer as they made love. She didn't like the idea but the smooth-talking Darren flooded her with flattery.

'Come on, babe, smile for the camera. Oh, that is so hot.'

She thought about leaving but feared his response. So Darren continued to plumb houses by day and his bird by night. She found a job in a kindergarten, and made a success of it from the off. The toddlers loved the leggy, blonde woman with the flashing smile.

At home, Darren reverted to type, making suggestions Elisabeth found frightening. He wanted to share his woman with his mates and one in particular. Elisabeth refused without hesitation. Darren persisted.

The situation turned nasty one night when Darren's mate, Jordan, arrived with a slab of beer. It was a prearranged visit with Jordan on a promise.

Elisabeth saw the true nature of Darren's pal and headed to the bedroom. 'I need an early night,' she said and disappeared. She made plans to leave.

Twenty minutes later the bedroom door opened and in came the two gentlemen. Gentlemen? Elisabeth discovered the truth. She was to entertain her boyfriend and his mate. Nightmare.

Trying to explain to them in a normal voice and using truthful comments didn't work. They ignored her protests. Darren used some hoary (horny?) old chestnuts to persuade his true love (his what?) to join the party. Are these lies passed down from lowlife to lowlife?

'Come on, babe, if you love me,' he slobbered.

Like millions of unwilling women before her, Elizabeth participated in the sex. Mentally she was shattered. Waking up in the wee small hours, she struggled to get out of bed. Darren snored as she wept in the bathroom wiping blood from her battered body.

The next morning at work, her kindergarten boss was so concerned she sent Elisabeth home. When there, she packed her suitcase and left. No note. No message, text or email. She fled.

Her choice of refuge was limited. She knew her parents would welcome her with open arms but her shame and guilt stopped her. Instead she took a cab to a Camberwell maisonette in which her sister Ruth, her husband and baby boy lived.

Ruth opened the door, holding baby Daniel. He was crying, Elisabeth was crying and soon Ruth joined the party. But joy slipped in as well.

Elisabeth didn't need to ask if she could stay. That was a given. But Ruth insisted her sister call their parents. This wasn't easy for the heartbroken young woman who knew she'd made a terrible mistake and caused her parents to suffer mightily.

'Hello, Mum, it's me,' said Elisabeth, who couldn't control her tears.

Ruth made a smart move by handing her son to his aunt and taking the phone. Elisabeth and the little guy fell in love there and then.

'She's here with me, Mum,' said Ruth. 'She's okay. She's going to stay but can we leave it a couple of days before we come over?'

'Of course. Your father will be over the moon.'

'We all are. I'll call tonight. But your little girl's come home.'

Ruth shed a tear but took delight in seeing her sister singing to her nephew. They made a great team and bonded for life.

Darren spewed. He came home reminiscing about last night's gleesome threesome. Jordan had texted his mate during the day thanking him for the photo of the bedroom activity which now settled on Jordan's phone. Elisabeth's unwanted fame was on the move.

Finding his flat empty annoyed Darren no end. He demanded his bird be home when he got home, and she had better have his meal ready or on the go. He shouted. No reply.

It didn't take long to search the apartment and discover he was on his patma. In the bathroom, her stuff was gone. He looked for her case and clothes. All gone. The truth dawned, and boy was he mad.

'That fucking bitch has dumped me.'

This was not on. Darren did the dumping. He swore revenge. He rang fellow pervert Jordan, and told him to meet in their usual pub.

'What's up, mate? Are we on again tonight?'

'Just be there,' snarled Darren and Jordan smelt the anger.

Over a pot and Parma, Darren explained the situation. Jordan looked at Darren and felt a sliver of fear. His mate was ropeable, and Jordan was doubly disappointed that a second serve of the ballet dancer was off. To try and pacify his mate, Jordan made a suggestion.

'You should stick a photo of the bitch on one of them revenge porn sites.'

Darren looked interested. 'What?' Jordan explained.

'Blokes put up photos of their ex-birds and get ratings. You can name and shame the bitch. That'll teach her for pissing off.'

Darren felt better. He got Jordan to help with internet coaching, and they looked at online revenge porn sites on their phones. They found one asking for women in Melbourne.

'This is the go,' said Jordan. 'Post that photo you sent me. Here, I'll show you.' He completed the task with a few clicks.

Ah, what a couple of kindly gents.

Ignorant Elisabeth settled in the bosom of her family. She still suffered from the brutal sex games—games?—but felt safe with her sister, brother-in-law and little Daniel. They had a lovely meal and were relaxing talking about anything other than the dreadful, ex-boyfriend.

Ruth's husband, Matthew, was tidying in the kitchen and Ruth was putting Daniel to bed. Suddenly the lounge room filled with a scream of terror. Matthew ran to Elisabeth and Ruth hurried out of the bedroom. They looked at their guest.

She turned white. She held her phone and froze, unable to speak.

Ruth and Matthew moved towards her. Elisabeth put up a hand to stop Matthew. He stopped. Elisabeth handed the phone to Ruth who gasped.

It was a text from Mr Wonderful. *Cop this, you fucking bitch.*

Accompanying the text was a picture of a naked Elisabeth Thorne, the kindergarten teacher, in full flight with two grinning perverts. Their faces were obscured; hers was not.

Elisabeth's suffering exploded.

2

SENIOR CONSTABLE JO BEST WAITED IN THE STREET. Detective Sergeant Deborah "Billy" Hughes was due in her role as Uber driver. She arrived.

'Good morning, Senior,' said Billy as Jo hopped into the car.

'Good morning, Sarge,' replied Jo buckling her belt. 'This is very kind of you. I could probably find my own way to Major Crime.'

'I've told you, it's only a temporary move. Once DI Steele cools down, I'll see you're straight back to Homicide.'

'Promises, promises,' said Jo. 'And it's not the Pope, it's you. You're worried I might pinch your job.'

They both laughed. Billy had pushed for Jo's transfer after she not only solved the murder of a journalist, and in the process was nearly killed, but also outwitted the boss of Homicide who tried to trap her as she led her double life as a criminal.

Now that last bit needs some explaining.

It's true, Detective Senior Constable Best had been involved in a scam or two but only to retrieve money, which had been scammed from innocent people in the first place. The fact that one of the people scammed happened to be her mother, certainly helped turn the cop into a crook. But that was in the past. Funds were restored, criminals captured, and all was well with the world.

Or was it?

Billy wanted to protect her brilliant young protégé. To do so, Billy arranged for Jo to work in Major Crime and on a particularly sad case. A 4-year-old girl had vanished, literally. Two weeks of almost non-stop police activity, intense searching and public appeals had produced zip. Not only had little Candy White not been found—dead or alive—but clues as to her fate were non-existent.

The two females arrived at Major Crime to be greeted by DI Patricia "Trish" Goddard, herself new to the section, and recently appointed as Officer in Charge to lead the investigation into the missing child.

Billy and Trish were old pals. Billy did the introductions.

The women shook hands.

'Welcome Detective,' said the DI. 'Your reputation precedes you.' Jo worried then realised her new boss meant nothing nasty or sarcastic. 'I'm looking forward to working with you, and if what DS Hughes has told me is true, we'll all benefit.'

A smiling Billy Hughes made her apologies and left. DI Goddard took Jo into the Incident Room and introduced her to the team—all five of them.

When the little girl went missing, there were a dozen officers assigned to the case with scores of police and hundreds of volunteers doing the physical search. The outdoor search had tailed off, and officers working on the case now consisted of DI Goddard, five others and Jo Best. Goddard began.

'Can we have a potted history please, as much for me as Senior Constable Best? Sergeant?'

DS Colin Gregory, an edhen, stood and addressed the group. As he spoke, he pointed to photos and a map.

'Two weeks ago, last Saturday, Candice White, known as Candy, aged 4, disappeared from the playground at Citizens Park in Church Street, Richmond. The Richmond Police Station is here, 100 metres from the playground. Candy's parents were at the park, the father, Gavin, on the adjacent oval watching a kids' game of football.'

'Why?' asked the DI.

'Gavin's mate, Steve Rumford's little boy was playing.' Goddard nodded. 'Candy's mother, Donna, was sitting beside the playground, here; talking to a woman she'd never met before. Candy was playing on the playground equipment with about 20 other kids and surrounded by several adults—parents and grandparents. Donna says she kept an eye on her daughter but, as we later learnt, she didn't. Candy was wearing a hat similar to a hat worn by another girl about Candy's age.'

'How similar?' asked Goddard.

Gregory pointed to photos of the two hats. They were similar.

'How long Candy was missing before her mother noticed is unknown. When Donna realised the girl she thought was her daughter was someone else, she panicked. She looked, and couldn't find Candy, and that's when the shit hit the fan.'

The DI kept asking questions. 'What was the length of time the mother didn't know her child was missing?'

Jo noticed her new boss didn't use people's names. Donna was "the mother" and Candy was "the child". Why? Was it to take emotion out of the case? There would be plenty of emotion to come as, after more than two weeks, this looked like the gut-wrenching death of a child.

Gregory replied. 'Hard to tell, ma'am. Donna reckons it was about two minutes but Kate, the woman she was talking to believes it could be as long as four or five.'

'Five?' queried Goddard. 'Two's plenty but five's an age in which to snatch the child.'

'Apparently the women hit it off and were talking animatedly so child watching was not as it might have been.'

'What were the women talking about?'

Gregory hesitated. That he couldn't remember. 'Sorry, ma'am, I'm not sure.' He looked at his colleagues.

Senior Constable Cathy Drew thought she remembered. 'They both have pre-school children and I think they were discussing the usual things about raising kids.'

Goddard fumed. 'Not good enough, Sergeant. Or the rest of you. "I think" must become "I know". Every detail is important and even the smallest bit of information could be the key to finding this child.'

'Yes ma'am.' Gregory grimaced and continued the briefing. 'We took statements from everyone in the playground, and no one remembers a girl leaving who was dressed like Candy.' He pointed to a map of the park. 'If she went this way, or this way, there are no fences. It she left via the childproof gate, she needed an adult to unlock it. But parents and grandparents with kids were coming and going. If Candy had been crying, screaming or struggling, you would think she'd be noticed. But if she went willingly then why would anyone remember her? It's a kids' playground, the weather was fine and there were about 30 kids in the immediate area coming and going.'

'You've done it again, Sergeant. "About" 30 kids is unacceptable. We need the exact number, their names and contact details of their parents. We could use child psychologists to interview the kids. We're dealing with a child's life here. No stone unturned. One exact piece of information could help solve this case. Please, no more guesswork, everyone, get *all* the detail and make it precise.' She paused looking at her team, including Jo. 'Is that clear?'

There were murmurs of assent. Some team members now knew the rumours were true. DI Goddard was a perfectionist who never accepted slipshod or even mediocre work.

Silence reigned. Jo had questions but decided to stay quiet, at least for now. The DI continued.

'So we still don't know if she wandered away or someone took her.'

'It's unlikely she'd wander away, ma'am,' said Gregory.

'True, but until we know otherwise, that possibility remains on the table, which leaves abduction by friend or foe and if so, both abductor and abductee have vanished into thin air.'

Jo wondered if someone could vanish into thick air.

'That's about where we're at, ma'am,' said Gregory.

'So, assuming it's an abduction, who are the suspects?'

Gregory pointed to photos of several people as he spoke.

'We ruled out the parents as both were obviously in view before Candy went missing.'

'Did you rule them out as part of a conspiracy?'

Gregory's collar prickled. 'No ma'am.'

'Everything's possible until we discover the truth.'

The DS nodded and wondered what his next mistake might be. He continued, now feeling under pressure.

'When interviewed together, the parents gave us nothing. When interviewed separately, both suggested family members or friends.'

'Charming,' said Goddard. 'And?'

Gregory indicated faces on the board. 'All have alibis and were nowhere near the playground on the day in question.'

'How's the marriage?'

Gregory looked at Senior Constable Connie Bryant who had been dealing with the Whites. 'Hard to tell, ma'am,' she said. 'On the surface it appears solid but there are issues, going back several years.'

'What issues?'

'Gavin was married before, and has a teenage son, Alex, who doesn't get on with his father. A former neighbour, Lawrence, once had a fling with Donna after she and Gavin were married. Gavin's stepfather, Gordon, has been described as a sex pest. And Donna's best friend, Kylie, was Gavin's girlfriend before he hooked up with Donna.'

The DI groaned. 'Great, it's the family from reality TV.' She took over and Gregory sat down.

'I'm sure you know the nightmare scenario. If it's not someone connected to the family, and all known sex offenders are in the clear, we are left with the child being abducted by a stranger who has, by luck or design, left us absolutely nothing.'

Again, the room fell silent. They waited for orders. Goddard was a planner.

She addressed Gregory. 'Sergeant, I want all statements checked again but only by someone who wasn't a part of the original interview. And alibis—each one is to be checked and double-checked, and again by someone not involved with the original interview.'

'Ma'am.'

'Sex offenders. What checks have been made?'

'Pretty thorough ...' He stopped. 'Very thorough, ma'am, and all known locals have alibis.'

'And non-locals?'

Gregory looked nervous. 'Do you mean interstate, ma'am?'

'Sergeant, this enquiry has been running for 16 days. Right now, we have no body, no witness and no suspect. To me, that means at the very least we need a bigger net, and possibly several bigger nets.' Goddard added a crescendo to her next sentence finishing with a fortissimo finale. 'If at first you don't succeed, think smarter, try harder and keep going till you fucking well do succeed.' The silence this time was very loud. 'Now, does anyone want to say something?' Silence. Jo decided to enter the fray.

'I'd be happy to check interviews and alibis, ma'am.'

'Thanks Senior, but as we're both new, you and I are off to the family home. Right, we meet again at 11.' She set off. 'This way, Detective.'

Jo followed and the rest of the team made faces at one another.

In the car, the DI got chatting without being chatty. 'You and I are in the same boat, Detective.'

'Ma'am?'

'We're the outsiders. We're the ones expected to find something new, anything to crack this case. It's called pressure. Are you good at handling pressure?'

Jo wondered if this was a trick question. 'I guess it depends on the situation, ma'am.'

'Well how about being tied up in a factory, ready to be pistol whipped, and having a dingbat of a detective fall through a skylight?'

Jo looked at her DI. She obviously knew about Jo's last adventure. The DI took her eyes off the road and smiled.

'You have an interesting history, Senior Constable, with what I gather is a nose for the truth.'

'I've made my share of mistakes, ma'am.'

'Good for you. Mistakes are great teachers.' For a while, they drove in silence. 'We're on a cold call. I haven't contacted the family. That may seem cruel but it's how I work. Of course I'm sympathetic to their situation but my job, our job, is to find that little girl. If we get emotional, we lose focus. Understood?'

'Yes ma'am.' More silence until the DI got personal. 'Have you got children?'

'No ma'am. I've been told a gentleman is required for that to happen.'

'God, believe me he doesn't have to be a gentleman.'

'Not necessarily in person of course.'

'Exactly. My daughter has no significant other but is keen to make me a grandmother and IVF is so bloody expensive. I told her a chicken baster would be a hell of a lot cheaper.' Jo didn't know what to say to that. 'Do you think that would still make me a grandmother?'

'Probably more of an old hen, ma'am.'

The DI liked the quip but stayed serious. 'Not so much of the old, thank you.'

They paused then laughed. Jo did some thinking.

I can see why the DI's a mate of Billy Hughes.

They arrived at the White house and rang the bell. Donna opened the door. DI Goddard was polite and did the introductions, explaining they had no news, were recent additions to the taskforce, and would like to ask some questions. They settled inside.

'My husband's not here. He's only gone back to work today.'

'We can chat to him later,' said Goddard. 'May I call you Donna?' Donna nodded. 'Please call me Trish and this is Jo.' The suffering mother struggled to provide a weak smile.

'We want you to know the police have brought in new officers to continue the search for Candy. How are you and Gavin coping?'

Jo saw a new side to her boss. She sounded genuine and her manner was gentle and concerned.

'It's so hard,' said Donna in a soft voice. Tears waited in the wings. 'It's the not knowing that's so hard. If we knew she was dead, at least we could cry and grieve and put her to rest.'

Cue the waterworks. Goddard said nothing. When she did, it was almost too soft.

'I wanted to ask you a favour, Donna.' The weeping mother wiped her eyes and looked at the inspector.

'Yes,' squeaked Donna, thinking this might be another of those dreadful press conferences.

'Please may we have a quick look in Candy's room? We won't disturb anything, I promise.'

The mother was relieved. 'Of course,' said Donna rising.

Goddard stood. 'Don't trouble yourself. I'd love a cuppa, and we'll be back in a jiffy.' She indicated the corridor. 'Is it this way?'

Donna was thrown. 'Yes, it's the last on the left.'

'Lovely,' said Goddard leading Jo to the child's room.

Jo watched Goddard look into each room they passed. They reached Candy's room. It had her name and photo on the door. It was closed.

Goddard paused and knocked quietly. Jo wasn't sure why. The DI opened the door and they entered.

It was tidy, too tidy, thought Jo. The bed was wrinkle-free and weighed down with dolls and soft toys. Mobiles with mermaids got in the way. Dust was banished from the house, and the dust police patrolled the corridor outside.

Goddard pulled out gloves and Jo copied her. Forensic officers had long ago examined the room but once a professional ...

'Look, observe and remember,' said the DI. 'Don't talk.'

Jo obeyed. Being kidnapped and threatened by criminals was pressure, but then so was this.

What am I looking for? And what if I find or observe nothing?

They worked independently. Jo sneaked a look at Goddard to see how she worked. After a few minutes, the DI pulled off her gloves.

'Let's go,' she said and led Jo to the kitchen.

Donna looked up. 'Tea or coffee?'

'Tea please,' said Goddard, 'black, no sugar.'

Jo requested tea with milk. Goddard pulled out a stool and sat at the bench in the kitchen. The three women settled and sipped.

'Even though we've only just met, Donna,' said Goddard, 'I can see you're being really strong, and I admire you greatly for that. I'm sure your husband and family are getting through this time thanks to you.'

Jo thought this was laying it on with a trowel. Donna didn't.

'Thank you,' she whispered.

Jo noticed Donna's tea struggled to stay in its cup.

Then came the switch. Goddard was polite then complimentary before she cut to the chase. Jo took mental notes.

'Going through your interview notes, Donna, I see you mentioned Gavin's father as being a bit creepy.'

'He is a creep.'

'How is he creepy?'

'It's Gavin's stepfather, not his father. Oh just the way he'd look at you. If we had a pool party, he'd stand really close to me. When he left, his hug was always too tight and his hands wandered.'

'Was he like that with Candy?'

Donna went white. 'God no.' She looked aghast. She never thought that lecherous behaviour translated to children. She stood, turned to the sink and vomited. Jo stood to help but Goddard stopped her with a raised hand and a look. The distressed mother returned. 'I'm sorry.'

'You're strong, Donna. You're the one keeping Gavin going.'

How does she know that, thought Jo? Or is she fishing?

She was fishing and paused, putting the pressure on Donna.

'He's started to blame me.' She looked at the police. Their silence encouraged her to continue. 'Does he think I wasn't watching? I told him. I thought I could see Candy all the time. It was only when the girl with the same hat and top came running towards me that I realised.'

Donna began to cry silently. Her life was hell.

Goddard continued. 'Tell us about the lady you met in the playground.'

'Kate ... I can't remember her other name.'

'Langdon,' said Jo, and Goddard was impressed.

'That's right.'

'Did you speak to her first?' asked Goddard.

'No, she spoke first. She asked me how old Candy was.'

'How did she know Candy was your daughter?'

'I think she saw me putting the hat on Candy.'

'You think or are you sure?'

Jo saw a pattern with her DI. *This woman hates guessing.*

Donna shook her head. Any question was too hard right now.

'Don't worry,' said Goddard rising. 'Look, we'll get going, Donna. Thanks for the tea, and thanks for being so helpful. We really appreciate it.' She looked at her colleague. 'Don't we, Jo?'

Jo was surprised but saw the method in the request.

'Yes indeed,' said Jo and smiled at Donna.

At the door, Goddard handed Donna a card. 'I want you to call me at any time, day or night, if have remember anything no matter how trivial, or if you have any questions, or even if you just want a chat. I mean it, Donna, call me.'

Donna's face displayed her gratitude. 'Thank you,' she whispered. 'And please find my baby.'

On the way back to the car, Jo couldn't help thinking she was lucky to have met DI Patricia Goddard.

3

'YOUR THOUGHTS, DETECTIVE, PLEASE?' Jo and Goddard were driving. 'The house, the child's room, the mother, her body language, her answers—everything.'

Jo felt pressure. 'I'm no psychologist, ma'am.'

Goddard snapped. 'Oh for crying out loud woman, this is not a quiz, there are no right answers. Just tell me your impressions.'

Jo got the point and let rip. 'Donna is clearly still upset ...'

'Call her "the mother" or "the woman"; don't use her name other than to her or her family.'

Jo got the point again. Remove emotion from the situation. 'The mother was a wreck emotionally. She was shaking, had been crying, and was suffering doubly because her husband now appears to blame her for the tragedy.'

'Why?'

'Why is the husband blaming his wife?' Goddard nodded. 'Because he wasn't there when the child disappeared, and she was.'

'Did the woman in the playground deliberately engage the mother so as to give the abductor time to take the child?'

Wow. That came out of left field.

Jo responded with a question of her own.

'And was the child in the similar hat, part of the abduction plan?'

Goddard smiled inwardly. 'And what about the creepy stepfather?'

'I think there are hordes of middle-aged men who are creeps but who would never remotely consider a child as sexual prey.'

'Interesting,' said Goddard pulling into a shopping centre car park. 'What do you know about carpet?'

'Ma'am?'

They hopped out and walked into the arcade and to a carpet store. A salesman approached. Jo thought she knew him.

'Mr White,' said Goddard discreetly showing her ID and introducing herself and her colleague. 'Sorry to trouble you at work. We've just come from your home.'

His face showed the strain. 'What's happened?'

'No news I'm afraid. My colleague and I have been added to the squad looking for Candy, and we wanted to say hello in person rather than over the phone.'

'You saw my wife?'

'We did.'

'How was she?'

'Under the circumstances, she's doing okay.'

He shepherded them to a corner of the store, and spoke softly.

'What did she tell you?'

'About what, sir?'

He hesitated. 'People, did she talk about people?'

'May we call you, Gavin?'

He nodded. 'Sure. But did she talk about people?'

'She did, Gavin.'

'Who? Did she talk about Kylie? I'll bet she never mentioned Lawrence. Did she mention him?'

'We didn't call to interview your wife just as we're not interviewing you. This visit is to allow you to meet the new detectives working to find Candy.'

That threw him. 'Okay.'

Goddard gave him her card. 'I gave my card to Donna, and urged her to call me at any time. The same goes for you, Gavin.'

He looked at the card. 'Right, thanks.'

'Is there anything you think we should know?'

He shook his head. 'Nah.'

'Anything you want to tell us … about anyone?' He shook his head. Goddard smiled. 'We'll keep in touch. Take care.'

She headed out of the store with Jo following. They passed a bakery and the Best nostrils came under attack.

Back in the car, Jo was ready when Goddard spoke.

'Your thoughts, Detective, please?'

'He doesn't seem as upset as his wife, and he was certainly worried about at least two people.'

'Why?'

'Why is he not as upset or why did he want to give us some names?'

'I think DS Hughes undersold your intelligence, Detective.' Jo had to think about that last statement. 'Plenty to investigate, Detective.'

'Yes, ma'am.'

'I haven't followed up on those two names Gavin gave us because, as yet, I don't know the background. Knowledge is power, and with it one can ask questions from a position of strength. We have some catching up to do, young lady. Now, can you be trusted on your own?'

'To do what, ma'am?'

'Chat up an attractive male person?'

Interesting.

'I hope so. Who and why, ma'am?'

'Dr Jack Carr is the family GP for Candy and Donna. I gather Gavin is a typical male who has to be dead before he'll visit any doctor.'

'And you want me to visit the GP on my own?'

'I'll be down the road at Candy's crèche. Now both the doctor and the childcare staff have been interviewed before but I'm hoping a fresh pair of eyes, and in your case, legs, may glean a previously unknown fact or two.

'I'm not sure what you're suggesting, ma'am.'

'Yes you are, and I like your booties.'

Many years ago, Jo learnt at least one thing from her mother. 'Now Joanna, if you work on your hair, makeup and clothes, and wear crappy shoes, you've wasted your time and money. Remember that.'

'Yes Mum.'

Jo looked at her short black boots with heels and inwardly smiled. 'Can I arrive without an appointment?'

'Hasn't DS Hughes told you about arriving unannounced? Haven't I? We just did that with both Donna and Gavin.' Jo looked blank. 'If you announce your visit, Detective, the person may scarper or bury the body. Surprise is a deadly weapon. Use it.'

'Yes, ma'am.' She had a vision of the GP climbing out of a window.

They pulled up outside a medical centre. Goddard pointed at the building.

'Call me when you're free.'

'Right,' said Jo to herself as the DI drove to the crèche.

The medical centre had a dozen or more GPs and almost as many receptionists. The joint was jumping. Receptionists and patients worked and waited. Jo approached a receptionist who spoke.

'Good morning. Can I help you?'

'Would it be possible to see Dr Carr?'

'Do you have an appointment?'

Jo hated this part of her job. She didn't like flashing her ID and using a sentence like, "This is a police matter". It was fine if she was about to collar a crim. But this witness was, as far as she knew, an upstanding citizen who had nothing to do with the crime being investigated, and she was in his work place. She discreetly revealed her ID and spoke softly.

'I'm Detective Senior Constable Best, and I'm investigating the disappcarancc of onc of Dr Carr's paticnts.'

'Little Candy?' gasped the receptionist. If people nearby had not heard Jo's intro, they certainly heard the receptionist's response. They looked and listened. Jo nodded. 'Please tell me you've found her safe and well.'

Jo grimaced. 'I'm afraid not as yet.' The receptionist put her hand to her mouth. Jo persisted. 'Is Dr Carr available?'

'I'll see.' The receptionist looked at her monitor. Her colleague called the receptionist's name and pointed because Dr Carr walked in.

'Dr Carr,' called Jo's receptionist. He headed towards them.

'Good morning, ladies.' He smiled and Jo felt better.

The GP was somewhere between 30 and going gray, tallish and wore the smartest of casual clothes which snuggled into his trim body.

'This lady's from the police enquiring about little Candy.'

Immediately the doctor turned serious. 'You have news?'

'Sadly no, sir. Just some questions if you'd be so kind.'

He seemed sad. 'Of course. One moment, please officer.'

He went to an elderly couple, spoke to them then came back and indicated a direction.

'We can chat in my room.' In the consulting room he indicated a chair. 'Please.' Jo sat and he approached with his hand extended. 'I'm Jack.'

They shook and Jo was momentarily flustered. 'Jo.'

He looked sad. 'Damn, I was hoping you'd be Jill.'

He grinned and sat. Jo got the attempt at humour and liked him.

Any man who can make me laugh gets my vote.

'So, how can I help?'

He made smiling easy and Jo had to concentrate to do your job.

'There's a new Detective Inspector in charge of the search, and we're checking with those who made a statement to see if there's anything they could add.'

Carr thought about things. 'Don't think so. Only Candy and Donna are my patients. The father I've met only once.'

'Why was that? Oh I'm sorry. I understand patient confidentiality and don't want you to break any rules.'

'That's fine. Candy fell I think—anyway she injured her leg and Dad brought her in.'

'Not her mother?'

'I think Donna was away. I do remember Dad being worried he'd be in trouble for not looking after their daughter.'

'Do you think the parents are in a happy marriage?'

He pursed his lips. 'Hmmm, that sounds like a leading question, officer.' He smiled and Jo took the reprimand in good humour. 'I really can't say,' he said.

Can't or won't?

'I shouldn't be telling you this, Doctor, but ...'

'Jack, please.'

Jo half smiled. 'Jack, we are up against it with this case. A straw to grasp would be wonderful.'

'I'm sorry. The Candy I know is a happy and healthy little girl.'

'I like your use of the present tense.'

He smiled and waxed lyrical. 'Hope smiles from the threshold of the year to come, whispering "it will be happier"'. Jo enjoyed being speechless. 'Big Al,' said Jack. He was talking double Dutch. 'Alfred Tennyson is one of my favourites. "Tis better to have loved and lost, than never to have loved at all." Sometimes Jo, I reckon poetry is just as good as medicine.'

Jo found herself tongue-tied.

He stood, meaning their meeting was over, and he had patients to see. Jo was reluctant to stand.

'Poetry and medicine,' she said, rising. 'I like that.'

He opened the door and stood back to let her exit.

'Good luck in your search, Jo. In the corridor, she turned. They shook hands.

'Thank you, Doctor Carr.' He frowned. 'Thank you, Jack.'

He walked with her to Reception.

'I think I'm going to have to call you Jill. Do you mind?'

You can call me whatever you like, Doctor Carr.

'No, I don't mind at all.'

'Goodbye and good luck.'

She walked out desperately wanting to look back while lacking the courage to do so.

In the street she took out her phone and was about to call the DI when a car tooted. Goddard had parked across the road. Jo hopped in and the questions came thick and fast.

'Anything?'

'Sorry, ma'am. Lovely man with nothing to add to his interview.'

'Nothing about the marriage or the wife or child being abused?'

'That's mandatory reporting, ma'am, and being a family man, I'm sure he would have spoken out if that were the case.'

'Did he tell you he was a family man?'

'He wears a wedding ring, and there's a photo of him and a woman and two kids on his desk.'

Goddard sniffed. 'I heard you were good at photos.' Jo smiled. 'I too got nowhere. They said the child was happy, well adjusted, and good socially which, translated means, "might be easily led, and would go willingly with a friendly adult".'

'Especially if the adult was someone she knew.'

Goddard slapped the steering wheel in frustration. 'Don't let it be an unknown paedophile who struck on a whim.'

Back in the Incident Room, Goddard called the officers to order.

'What do we know about people known to the parents? We were given the names Kylie and Lawrence.'

Gregory explained. 'Who gave you those names, ma'am?'

'He did. She gave us nothing.'

'Kylie Wren is the mother's girlfriend. We know she and the father were once an item before the parents met.'

'And?'

'That's all we know, ma'am.'

Goddard flared. Her audience (and underlings) confirmed another rumour about their new boss—she has a short fuse.

'That's not good enough. We need far more detail. Who ended the Gavin and Kylie relationship? When? Was there, *is* there any enmity between them? How close are the two women who've shared the same man? Come on, people. Try harder.' She settled a little. 'Next?'

Jo reminded the DI. 'Lawrence, ma'am.'

'Yes, Lawrence, who's he?'

Gregory explained. 'Lawrence Blair is a former neighbour who had a fling with Donna while she was married to Gavin.'

Gregson stopped because he had no more information.

'Don't tell me that's it.'

Gregson stood up to his boss. 'He's like Kylie, and a number of persons of interest, ma'am, they all have a rock-solid alibi. Once we discovered they were nowhere near the playground on the day, we ruled them out.'

'And have you double checked all their alibis?'

'Yes, ma'am.'

'And were the people who did the checking not involved with the suspect the first time around?'

'Yes, ma'am.'

'And have you ruled them out as possible conspirators?'

Gregson froze then spoke softly. 'No, ma'am.'

Goddard sucked in a big breath. She wanted colleagues who thought as she did. She wanted them to unearth details and facts.

'Come on people, learn from the experts. "To a great mind, nothing is little," said that chap from Baker Street.'

Team members looked at one another on the sly.

Is she nuts as well?

Goddard reckoned they needed instruction but training could wait.

'Right, I went to introduce myself to the staff at the child's crèche. Bad news in that they confirmed the victim was happy and mixed well with people, which increases the chances of her going willingly, certainly with someone she knew, and possibly even a stranger.' She looked at Jo. 'Senior Constable Best met the family GP.'

Jo got the message.

'Nothing new. Dr Carr met the father once and got the impression Gavin was more worried about being told off by his wife than the injury to his daughter. I reckon the GP's the type who wouldn't hesitate to report any abuse.'

Jo looked at Goddard who took over.

'So, ladies and gentlemen, what has your research uncovered?' Silence. 'Oh come on. New eyes. You must have found something.'

'Sorry, ma'am,' said Gregory. 'We've not finished but so far, nothing new.'

'Nothing?'

Gregory shook his head. Goddard grew tense. She had a record of solving cases. When offered this missing child case, she thought long and hard. It had risks. If the child was found weeks after going missing, Goddard's reputation would soar. Promotion would come sooner. But as with many things in life, you're only as good as your last case. If the child remained missing, Goddard might go missing.

'Right, we crack on with the double checking. Sergeant, put Senior Constable Best to work. And people, please concentrate.'

She left and Jo began work with a fellow senior constable, Connie Bryant. They waded through witness statements, making notes to compare later. Half an hour later, they took a break.

'So what's she really like?' asked Connie.

Jo wasn't sure. 'The DI?'

'Word is she gets results but burns people along the way.'

Jo shrugged. 'I only met her today but, yes, she does work hard.'

'And what's it like in Homicide?'

Oh, they know. Again, Jo was unsure how to reply. 'Fine.' She paused and looked at Connie. 'Truth is I clashed with the boss, and as my sergeant and DI Goddard are mates, this is a kind of overseas posting till the cyclone runs out of steam.'

Connie smiled. 'And how did your find the gorgeous GP? Did you get the poetic treatment?'

This time Jo grinned. 'I did - and he's ... rather sweet.'

'Rather sweet?' Connie was less romantic. 'He can give me an intimate examination anytime.'

A raised eyebrow from Jo then more work, then more nothing.

Jo finished her first day in Major Crime. It wasn't exactly action-packed but more in the "interesting" category. She went home thinking about Trish Goddard, Dr Jack Carr and the 4-year-old Candy White.

4

JO'S PHONE RANG. It was nearly 7 pm on her first day working at Major Crime. She enjoyed her healthy pre-packaged heat 'n eat meal, famous for its so-called lack of calories. Despite her good BMI, Jo was in a watch-my-weight phase. She ran most days, and stuck to her ultra-healthy diet—mostly. She answered her phone.

'Hello?'

'Hello Auntie Jo. This is Timothy speaking.'

'Hello Timothy speaking. How is my favourite nephew?'

'Good.'

'And school? How is school?'

'Good.'

'Tell me, are you married yet?'

Giggling sounds from a young boy before he spoke off mic.

'Auntie Jo asked me if I was married yet.'

The boy's mother is heard in the background. 'She's teasing you.'

Timothy returned to his phone call. 'Mummy said you're teasing me.'

'Never. Hey, a little bird told me someone's having a birthday soon.'

Tim was super excited. 'That's me. *I'm* having a birthday.'

'Are you? Really? Okay, let me guess. You're going to be ... 100.'

More squeals down the line as Timothy went off mic. 'Auntie Jo said I'm going to be 100.'

His mother grew impatient. 'What are you going to ask her?'

Jo heard that, and wasn't thrilled. She loved her niece and nephew to bits but didn't enjoy the company of her sister and brother-in-law. Timothy returned to his phone call.

'Auntie Jo?'

'Yeeees?'

'Will you please come to my birthday party?'

'Oh, Timmy, I'd love to come.'

'It's going to be at Puffing Billy.'

'Shit,' said Jo to herself. Normally such an outing to the hills would be a great day but Jo had recent memories of that tourist train in the Dandenongs just out of Melbourne. One of her first homicide cases took place on that very train. Yes, she made multiple arrests but no, she made some powerful enemies, so powerful she got the sack from Homicide, and even now was on a sort of punishment sabbatical.

'That sounds wonderful, young man. Thank you for asking me.'

'I have to go to bed now.'

'Okay. Bye.'

'Auntie Jo?'

'Yes?'

'Did a little bird really tell you it was my birthday?'

It was Jo's turn to laugh. Her big sister Caitlyn came on the line.

'Thanks for that. He's got you at the top of his guest list.'

'Good for him.'

'How are you?'

'Fine. Yourself?' Caitlyn noticed that her sister never enquired about her brother-in-law.

'We're all good. Have you heard from Dad?'

'Not since his run-in with the law.'

'And Mum?'

'I think she's got a boyfriend.'

'She has and he's rich and old.'

'Good for her.' Jo's doorbell sounded. 'Gotta go, that's my front door. I'll talk to you later.'

Jo was glad to end the call. Caitlyn wondered if her sister rang the doorbell herself just to end the call. Jo wouldn't describe her family as dysfunctional but ... no, wait, maybe she would.

Who's at my front door?

She opened it and smiled. 'Hello stranger,' said Jo.

'Hello you,' replied the visitor.

They embraced and the former school friends settled on the sofa.

'How long has it been?' asked Jo.

'Two years, no three.'

'So how did you find me?'

'I went to your old family home and there was your Mum.'

'Of course. Good sleuthing. And how are you? Married I heard.'

'Married and a mum.'

'No. Congratulations. Girl or boy?'

'It's a boy called Daniel. And he's wonderful. Keeps me going but we're all very happy.'

'I don't even know your husband's name.'

'Matthew, Matthew Glover.'

'You're good with the biblical names—Ruth, Matthew and Daniel.'

'Yes but no Ezekiel or Habakkuk.' They smiled.

Ruth got serious. 'I was surprised to meet your stepfather.'

My stepfather?

'Oh?' Jo tried not to sound worried.

'I met him at your family home.'

The penny dropped. 'Yes, my mother is always on the go. Out with the old and in with the older. So, cuppa?'

'Yes, please.'

Jo went from her sitting room to her kitchen, a journey that on a good day, took about 1.9 seconds. She got the kettle going and searched for some half-decent biscuits. She called.

'So what brings you here? I'm sorry I've not been in touch.'

Ruth appeared in the doorway. 'Me too. Your Mum told me you're still with the police.'

'I am, and I never like it when people say that. Problem?'

Ruth took out her phone. 'Do you remember my sister, Elisabeth?'

'The beautiful blonde with the longest legs in the world.'

'She's got herself a problem and I'm hoping you might be able to give us some advice.'

'Sure, what's up?'

Ruth hesitated then turned on her phone and handed it to Jo.

She mimed "Wow". 'Is that Elisabeth?'

Ruth nodded. 'There's a text message below.'

Jo read it then handed back the phone. 'I'm so sorry. Your family must be devastated.'

'They don't know. Elisabeth is staying with me and you're the only person we've told.'

Jo made the tea and they drank it in the kitchen as Jo heard the sad saga of Elisabeth and Darren.

'But why go out with him let alone move in?' Ruth couldn't reply. The lump in her throat got bigger. 'I'm sorry,' said Jo. 'Let's go inside.' They sat on the sofa. 'There are laws dealing with revenge porn. I can get you more details. But tell me if I'm wrong. You want two things—the image removed, and the ex-boyfriend punished. True?'

'Definitely the first but we're not sure about the second.'

'Is that because of the publicity?'

Ruth nodded. 'It's unfair he did this and unfair if he gets away with it, but Elisabeth would rather die than go to court.'

'I think it's a bit more than unfair. Look, Ruth, leave it with me. I'll talk to a few people and get back to you. What's your number?' Jo punched it into her phone. 'And what's the address of that web site?' Sadly, Ruth had no trouble remembering.

At the front door, Ruth hugged Jo and wouldn't let go. She cried as she spoke. 'When this is over, you must come and meet my boys.'

'I'd love to.'

Ruth waved from her car with Jo watching. She had an idea.

'Michael Chan speaking.'

'Good evening. My name's Ponzi. Can I interest you in a scam?'

'Not funny, madam, although I am smiling a little bit.'

'How are you, Michael? Are you receiving at this late hour?'

'Yes and no.'

'I'm sorry?'

'You're welcome to visit but I'm not available for your schemes.'

Jo laughed. 'I'll see you soon.'

She had happy memories of her time with Michael Chan. Mind you there were scary memories too—very scary. The two had pulled off a couple of spectacular scams and would always be friends.

Michael opened his front door. Jo stood there with a big grin, and a packet of treats for the real owner of the property, the resident cat Alan, named after computer genius, Alan Turing.

After catching up on their respective news, mainly concerning their parents, Michael cut to the chase.

'So what's your latest project? And don't say a scam.'

She laughed then told him the Elisabeth Thorne revenge porn tale.

'That's horrible. The poor girl. What can the police do?'

'Unless she reports it, nothing.'

Michael nodded. 'And she can't or won't do that because the last thing she wants is publicity.'

'Which is why I've come to you. Please will you think about what could be done to get some justice for the young woman, while at the same time, giving that bastard a very tasty slap.'

'So now you want me to arrange an assault or are you going the whole hog and planning a hit?'

'No,' protested Jo. She looked offended but inside was grinning.

'Oh I get it. You have me kill someone allowing you to step in and solve the case.'

'I couldn't do that. I'd have to arrest you and then who would carry out my criminal activities?'

They were joking and knew it. But he knew she was serious in wanting some response to the creep of a boyfriend. Michael mused.

'Sometimes I think you really have a death wish. If you keep on breaking the law, one day it's going to come back and bite you. Even if your cause is just, a crime is a crime is a crime.'

Jo spoke in a quiet voice. 'Michael, you must know I know that.'

'If you keep helping people like this, word will spread. "See Jo Best. She helps the downtrodden and victims of crime". Your kindness will kill you. You're on a slippery slope, Detective.'

He was serious and she knew he spoke the truth. Both paused until she looked at him with a pleading look.

'But will you give it some thought?'

He paused then nodded. 'You know I will.'

She moved to him and kissed his cheek.

'Thanks, hero.' She gave him a slip of paper with the URL of the revenge porn site.

He exclaimed. 'Oh that's one of my favourites.'

She slapped his arm. 'Stop it. This is serious.'

He knew that. 'Leave it with me. Now, coffee?' She didn't speak. He groaned. 'There's something else.'

She gave him her best smile. 'Can you help me find a missing child?'

'What, now?'

5

NEXT MORNING, IN THE INCIDENT ROOM, Trish had a problem. She wanted to read the Riot Act but at the same time, wanted to encourage her team to go that extra mile. They settled.

'I'm worried, ladies and gentlemen. To me the odds are shortening on this being a random abduction, a lucky—for the abductor—impulse kidnap from a paedophile with no connection to the child or her family, and that is our worst possible scenario. Where do we start to find the unknown, invisible abductor? If the people we've interviewed are not involved, either directly or indirectly, then we are up the proverbial creek with not even a toothpick for a paddle.' She paused. Nobody spoke. 'Okay, I've got a plan, but first I want to give everyone a chance to suggest how we might proceed. Don't be shy. There's no right or wrong answer. So, who's first?'

She moved to one side removing her schoolteacher status. DS Gregory began.

'I know we didn't follow up on certain people because once we checked their alibi, we eliminated them as a suspect.'

'Good,' said Goddard. 'What's wrong with that?'

DS Peter Grimes, known as Ben, (as in Benjamin Britten, composer of the opera *Peter Grimes*) and the oldest member of the team, spoke with his soft Scottish burr. 'They could still be involved even though they weren't at the playground.'

'Which means what?' asked Goddard.

'It's a conspiracy,' said Senior Constable Connie Bryant.

'Excellent,' bubbled Goddard. 'Now you're cooking. Yes, it could be a random abduction but let's exhaust all possibilities. Conspiracies usually involve multiple players. So let's look again at people we know who have an alibi and consider if they hate one or both of the parents?

Do they feel cheated in life? Have they been mightily pissed off by someone or something? Are they mentally ill? And yes, I know we're not trick cyclists but everything needs to be considered. Keep asking; are they part of a conspiracy?'

Cathy Drew had a question. 'Are you suggesting, ma'am, that Kate Langdon, the woman Donna was speaking to in the playground, is part of this conspiracy?'

'I'm not suggesting anything ...'

'Senior Constable Cathy Drew, ma'am.'

'Thanks Cathy. I'm not suggesting, I'm ordering all of you; do not rule out anything. Someone with a cast-iron alibi is not ruled out, instead, you consider them as part of a possible conspiracy.'

She looked at her team. No further comments were on offer. She turned back to the board to discuss the suspects when Jo spoke.

'Ma'am, have we considered the local police who were first on the scene?'

Some thought this a silly suggestion. Goddard didn't.

'Explain.'

'Have we interviewed them to get their impressions? Being fresh to the case and first on the scene, they may have spotted or heard something, however small, which may help us.'

'Been done, ma'am,' said Gregory.

'Send someone else to do it again. Someone new. You, Jo.'

'Ma'am.'

'Right,' said Goddard pointing to the board and four photos. 'The woman in the park, the stepfather, the former girlfriend, and the former lover—these four need further investigation. Any others?'

'Gavin's son, Alex,' said Gregory gaining in confidence.

'Why,' asked Goddard.

'He hates his father, and I mean hates. If he could hurt his old man, he would.'

Senior Constable Bruce Harcourt dropped a bombshell. 'This could get very broad.' Goddard looked at him. He gave his name and rank.

'Thank you, Bruce. Please explain.'

'If we follow the conspiracy theory then surely there are others to investigate. Other family members, angry neighbours, work colleagues and the parents themselves. Where does it stop?'

Goddard pursed her lips. Jo and the whole room were hooked.

'I'll tell you where it stops, Bruce. It stops when we find the missing child. With a plan, using a system, we look everywhere and at everyone, and we stop only when we find the child or when the powers that be close us down. Is that clear?'

'As crystal, ma'am,' said Harcourt who wondered if he would be the first to be "reassigned".

'Trust me, folks, you do not want to be the officer who overlooks the one tiny detail that could solve this case or far, far worse, could have saved the life of this little girl. Comprende?'

They understood.

And so it began. Suspects, leads, or persons of interest were listed and given a rating or priority. Officers were assigned to these people, and regular team meetings heard reports of information gained. Every morning reports were given and new tasks created. Team members asked questions and made suggestions. But from all this activity, not one definite suspect was found; lots of possibles but no one definite.

One of Jo's tasks was to re-interview the uniforms who were first to arrive at the park on the morning of the abduction. It produced nothing new.

Goddard's blood pressure rose. With every passing day and with no progress made in finding Candy White, Trish and her stress levels got serious. The top brass asked for an update. She had nothing to report. She sat in Assistant Commissioner John Crowley's office.

'What, not even one suspect?'

'Plenty of those, sir, but all seem to have an alibi of sorts.'

'Should we pass this to Homicide?'

'Definitely not, sir. Despite what seems like slow progress, I believe my team are smart enough and keen enough to find this child. Besides, she may still be alive.'

'Well, if you believe that, Inspector, you're in a very small group. Another week and then we consider calling in Homicide.'

'Sir.'

Trish returned to Major Crime in a foul mood. She wanted the child found for obvious reasons, but also because her career prospects could take off or tumble depending on the result.

She called her team together for yet another review, and tried to hide her frustration. She failed. Her attitude had a huge influence on the attitude of the other detectives. Everyone was miserable and resigned to failure. Then it happened.

An admin staffer knocked and entered, handing Goddard a piece of paper. The staffer got out in record time not wanting to be the messenger who got shot.

'What!' screamed Goddard. She had everyone's rapt attention.

'Problem ma'am?' asked Gregory.

'Records have discovered a paedophile on the sex offenders' register we were not told about.' Many murmured. 'Ricardo Smythe, now Leo Smythe, is alive and well, and living in Abbotsford.'

'That's next to Richmond,' said Gregory.

'What was he charged with?' asked Grimes.

Goddard read. 'Charged and convicted with the abduction and sexual assault of a minor.'

The murmurs turned nasty.

Gregory went to a wall map. 'What's the address?'

Goddard joined him. '24 Albion Street.'

Everyone gathered around. Gregory searched then pointed.

'There. It's about ... a K from the playground.'

'That's two blocks from the White house,' added Bryant. 'The child lived five minutes from the paedo.'

'Why weren't we told?' asked Harcourt.

Goddard studied the document and shook her head. 'He changed his name at Christmas, and his address last month. Clerical cock-up.'

'We need him here now,' said Gregory stating the bleeding obvious.

'Thank you, Sergeant. This needs a softly softly approach. If the child is there, and alive, a raid may spook them all. I want everyone in on this but no gung-ho tactics. Understood?' Her team agreed. 'Right, Colin, we need a detailed road map—lanes, drains, the works. Ben, we need forensics. And Bruce, you're the postman.' People got busy.

Jo piped up. 'Ambulance, ma'am?'

'Good thinking, Jo.' She looked at her watch. 'Have them there in 20 minutes and no sirens. Tell them to wait out of sight.'

Jo got ringing.

'A couple of uniforms might help, ma'am,' suggested Drew.

'Thanks, Cathy, do that and stress no action, no sirens and stay out of sight.' Goddard raised her voice. 'We meet in the car park in ten minutes, no, make that five.'

They travelled in three cars and all parked in the adjoining street. The house in question backed onto a lane, once used by the night cart man, the last of whom married a woman with constant sinus problems.

Bruce Harcourt arrived in an unmarked van, double-parked, and carried a parcel into number 22. An elderly woman answered the door.

'Good morning, madam. I have a parcel for Mr Smythe.'

'There's no Mr Smythe here.'

A voice called from inside the house. 'Who is it, Ma?'

'A parcel for Mr Smythe.'

The middle-aged daughter appeared.

'Good morning,' said the Senior Constable dressed in his most ordinary of street clothes. 'This is 22 Albion Street?'

'Right house, wrong name,' said the daughter.

'Do you know a ...' Harcourt pretended to read the label. '... a Mr Leo Smythe?'

Both women shook their heads.

The daughter remembered. 'I think I heard one of them next door call the other guy Leo, although it might have been Theo.'

'Next door,' asked Harcourt pointing to number 20.

'No, that side, number 24.'

'And is he at work, do you know?'

'No, I think they're both on Centrelink.'

'Great, I'll try there. Sorry to have bothered you.'

He went to the van and called DI Goddard.

'Neighbour says there's a Leo in 24 and both male residents are on the dole.'

'Nice work, Bruce. Shift the van, and come and join us.'

The police moved into place. An ambulance arrived and parked at the end of the street. Two uniformed officers from Richmond joined the party. Goddard had allocated locations and tasks.

Grimes, Bryant and Drew went to the lane at the rear of the property. Goddard, Gregory, Harcourt and Jo would enter via the

34

front. The sergeant carried a battering ram, nicknamed Rambo. It weighed 15 kg and had an impact force of about 3 tonnes.

The DI looked at her colleagues. This was a first for Jo. She'd knocked on plenty of doors before but never searching for an abducted child. 'Ready?'

Gregory, Harcourt and Jo nodded. There was no doorbell, not even a knocker. The glass in the door was frosted and looked tired. Goddard aimed for the wooden frame. She knocked. Her knuckles yelled. No response.

'Try the glass,' said Gregory.

'I heard something,' said Jo.

The police waited, straining to hear. Footsteps sounded but not heading to the door.

'Glass, ma'am, and yell,' said Gregory preparing to give Rambo his outing for the day.

Goddard rapped on the glass. 'Police, open the door now or we break it in. Police!'

More footsteps, then muffled voices were heard.

'Stand back,' cried Gregory, and lined up Rambo and the door lock.

Just as he prepared to swing, Jo put out her hand. 'Someone's coming.'

Gregory froze, the police paused, and then the outline of a person appeared through the frosted glass. The door was unlocked and opened, resting on a chain. Worried eyes looked at the cops.

Goddard wanted in and didn't mince words. 'Police. We need to search these premises. Open the door now or we'll break it in. Now!'

The chain was removed and the door opened. Goddard didn't wait. She was in. Gregory, Harcourt and Jo followed. The uniformed police entered the small front yard. One minded the door while the other minded Rambo. The house occupants were bundled down the hallway.

Goddard went on a whirlwind tour. Her colleagues took their time each checking a room more thoroughly. Goddard opened the back door and entered the back yard.

'You there?' she called.

'Ma'am,' called Ben Grimes.

'Anything?'

'Nothing.'

'One of you stay, the others get talking to neighbours.'

Goddard went back into the house. Its two occupants and her three colleagues stood in the kitchen. It was small and untidy.

The DI knew the man on the Register of Sex Offenders from his file photo. 'Are you Ricardo Smythe, now Leo Smythe?'

'So what?'

'Where were on the morning of March 24.'

'Why?'

'Leo Smythe, I'm arresting you on suspicion of the abduction of a child. You do not have to say anything ...'

Leo exploded. All four officers grabbed him with Gregory applying the cuffs. The other man, rather than join the protest, burst into tears.

With the furious Smythe restrained, Goddard turned to the teary housemate. 'What's your name?'

'Say nothing,' spat Leo, 'nothing.'

The housemate couldn't handle the situation. He'd do anything to make his fear and distress disappear.

'Jake Freeman,' he blubbered. Leo's hatred of the police filled the entire house.

'Jake Freeman, I'm arresting you on suspicion of the abduction of a child.' Goddard read him his rights during which time he sobbed and his housemate swore, blaming the police for everything.

The cops and their prisoners moved to the front of the house where the uniformed cops assisted. The occupants departed as three forensic officers arrived.

'Ah, gentlemen, welcome,' said Goddard. One of the officers pulled down her mask revealing a mouth with well-decorated red lips. 'My, apologies, madam.' Goddard led them inside and introduced herself. 'This is the residence of a convicted paedophile. Almost a month ago, a young girl went missing from a playground in Richmond. To date, we have no idea who took her, where she went or where she is today. Any evidence of a child having been here will bring possible joy to her parents, and massive relief to my ulcer.' She looked at them. 'Happy hunting.'

She left and returned to HQ, crossing her fingers, toes and anything else she could find.

The prisoners were interviewed separately with Goddard and Gregson interviewing Leo, and Grimes and Jo Best going first with the crybaby. The DI wanted a lead, a clue, a scrap of info, anything from the weaker man before she went after the known paedophile.

Grimes was old school. He was surprised the DI assigned the newcomer to sit in with him. He politely told Jo he would lead. Jake Freeman remained distressed. He'd never been arrested before, and something had clearly upset him. Jo was keen to see how another senior officer ran an interview.

Was anyone as good as Billy Hughes?

'Mr Freeman,' began Grimes, 'you've been cautioned and I want to confirm you have declined to have a solicitor present. Is that correct?'

Freeman nodded.

'Speak aloud for the tape, please.'

'Yes,' from the squeaky voice.

'We are investigating the disappearance of a child from a playground in Richmond a month ago. Do you know anything about that case?'

'No.'

'Have you heard about it on the news?'

'Yes.'

'What do you know?'

'Just what was on TV.'

'What is your relationship with Leo Smythe?'

'Friend.'

'What sort of friend? Is he your boyfriend?'

'No.'

'How did you meet?'

'We were friends years ago.'

'What, school friends?'

'We lived in the same street.'

'What was his name?'

'Ricky ... Ricardo Smythe.'

'How long have you been living together?'

'A few months.'

'Why are you living together?'

'I came from the country and didn't have anywhere to live.'

'How did you find him?'

'My mother rang his mother and I went to his flat.'

'Where was that?'

'I don't know. Kensington, I think.'

Ben looked at Jo who made a note.

'Did you know Ricardo or Leo has been in prison?'

'Yes.'

'Do you know why?'

'He said he had some child pornography on his computer.'

'He was convicted of the abduction and sexual assault of a minor.'

'He said it's not true. He said he never touched her.'

That last answer came out stronger and faster than those before. Grimes used the silence to build pressure. He looked at Jake then at his notes. He took a deep breath.

'Did Leo take the little girl?'

Jake turned on the water works. He wailed. 'I don't know.'

Ben threw in another pause, and waited for the crying to settle.

'Why are you crying, Jake? What did Leo say about the little girl?'

'He said the police would come and find him and say he took her and it would all be a lie. He said his record would kill him.'

Grimes looked at the sobbing Jake. If this was all an act, he was bloody good at it.

'Where were you on the weekend when the child went missing?'

'I was at home with my family in Colac.'

The interview ended and, unlike Billy Hughes, DS Peter Grimes didn't consider giving Jo the opportunity to ask a question.

6

LEO THE HOUSEMATE GAVE THEM NOTHING. Jake was a family friend, well, acquaintance from years ago. He was weak, easily led, and if Leo had abducted the child, Jake might have cracked. He cracked all right but said nothing about the abduction. In fact, his alibi about being in Colac at the time of the abduction was true. But now it was Leo's turn and Goddard and Gregory removed their gloves.

Leo had a Legal Aid solicitor and Goddard led the charge.

'Tell me, Mr Smythe, why did you change your name?'

'There's no law against it. Anyone can change their name.'

'Do your neighbours know you're on the Register of Sex Offenders?'

'You can't scare me. If you release that, you'll lose your fucking job.'

'Where were you last Saturday morning?'

'At home.'

'And the Saturday morning before that?'

'At home, I'm always at home because if I go out you bastards arrest me.'

'Tell me about your friend, Jake.'

'Leave him alone. He's done nothin'.'

'Whereas you have?'

That caused a momentary pause. Leo was smart but knew his anger and hatred of police might cause him to say something they could use against him. He sniffed.

'No comment.'

Goddard paused. She hid her desperation. She wanted to solve this case. She needed to find out if this man was involved.

'What do you know about the disappearance of a little girl from Citizens' Park in Richmond last month?'

'Nothing.'

'What, you don't watch TV, read newspapers, or go online?'

'I saw something on the news and that's all I know.'

'Does your parole officer know you've changed your name and moved to a new address?'

'Ask him.'

'Breaking the terms of your parole means you could go back inside.'

'It won't work.'

'What won't work?'

'You, trying to stitch me up for this abducted kid.'

'I didn't say she was abducted. I said she disappeared.'

Leo had to think about that. 'Whatever,' he said. 'Listen, bitch.' His solicitor placed a hand on Leo's arm. It was ignored. Leo moved into second gear. ''You think because I've got a record, I'm guilty of every fucking crime in town. Well prove it. I'm sayin' nothin' more. You've got nothin' otherwise you would have charged me so cop this, copper— put up or shut up.'

He glared at her and, in her stomach she sensed a sinking feeling. He was right. She had zip.

Someone tapped on the door. Connie Bryant entered and handed Goddard a folded piece of paper. She read it showing no emotion. She passed it to DS Gregory. He read it showing no emotion.

Goddard looked at Leo. He glared back with even a touch of a grin.

'Mr Smythe, since early this morning, officers from Forensic Services have been examining your home in Abbotsford.'

'Here we go.'

Goddard used police speak in its formal sense. Leo didn't seem worried. 'The officers found something of interest.'

'It's a plant,' snapped Leo. 'You're stitching me up.'

'The forensic officers found traces of blood splatter in the bathroom and signs of an attempt to remove it.'

He glared at her. 'That proves nothing.'

'So you accept the blood is there?'

Leo lost it and smashed his fist on the table then pointed at Goddard. Gregory stood, the solicitor placed a hand on Leo's arm, and the constable on duty moved forward. Goddard didn't move. Leo swore and made specific accusations about being framed. The DI lost that sinking feeling in her stomach. She waited for him to lose some anger and switched to the personal.

'Leo, someone tried to remove that blood splatter with bleach. They left a bit. We will test that blood and any bleach in your home. DNA doesn't lie, Leo. So I'll ask you again. Do you know anything about the missing girl?'

He shook his head. Was this an admission of guilt, despair that he hadn't cleaned the place properly, or muted rage that he'd been stitched up by the police?

'Leo, if the blood matches the DNA of the little girl, it takes your offending to a new level. Child pornography and sexual assault of a minor is one thing. Abduction and murder is throw away the key time.' She paused. Leo seethed. She spoke softly, so softly that Leo could barely hear her. 'Where is she, Leo?'

He looked at her. The police desperately wanted to know the whereabouts of little Candice White.

If Goddard didn't know better, she would have thought Leo was taunting her. He knew what the police bitch said about DNA was true. He knew that the evidence they found plus his record could put him away forever. His face shouted anger and fear but his mind started to laugh. He roared making a sort of primeval sound, and the sound echoed and lingered. Then he said nowt.

And that was that. Goddard ended the interview. Leo was cell bound, and the wait began. What would the DNA say?

The Incident Room buzzed. Everyone rabbited on about the arrests, interviews, forensics, and Leo and Jake's behaviour. They had something; not sure what but something. Goddard brought the team up to date. Like her, they were pleased with what looked like a breakthrough but the question remained—where is Candy? When would they hear back on the DNA and what would it reveal?

Jo decided to make an offer.

'Ma'am, I know a couple of the scientists at Forensic Services, and could try and ask a favour.'

'Good thinking, Detective. Do you need anyone?'

'No thanks, I'll be fine.'

'Right, give them a call.'

'Ah, I think a face to face might get a better result.' Goddard waved her away. 'No promises, ma'am,' said Jo grabbing her bag and leaving.

She had one person in mind, the pushing 40 and never been kissed Alastair Dean, dressed by his mother, and awash with DNA knowledge.

Today he wore his standard outfit of white coat over beige slacks, white shirt with a button-down collar, brown cardigan, and a grey tie. Mr Primary Colours he wasn't. He looked up when the detective knocked and entered.

'Hello,' he said pushing his glasses up his nose and remembering the perfume she wore on her last visit.

'Hello, Alastair, remember me, Senior Constable Jo Best.'

'From Homicide. Of course, how are you?'

Jo let the "from Homicide" slide. 'I'm well. And you? Still busy?'

Alastair's tongue tripped over itself. 'Yes ... I am.'

'I've got a serious problem, Alastair, and I thought, who is the one person in the world who can solve it? Straightaway I knew the answer—Alastair Dean, the wonderful scientist from Forensic Services.'

He didn't know whether to smile or blush. She didn't know if her baloney was over the top. It was but Alastair purred.

'How can I help?' was all he could muster. But it was said with sincerity to burn.

Jo explained the case of little Candy and the urgency of the DNA found in Leo's house, and that samples of Candy's DNA had already been collected and were held here on site.

Excitement consumed Alastair who went looking for the material. 'Yes, I think it's just come in,' he said searching with zeal. 'Here it is,' he boasted when bringing the material back to his desk. 'I'll get on to it immediately.'

'Could you? Oh thank you, that would be brilliant.'

'Of course. Anything to help find that little girl and her killer.'

Jo felt bad. With fluttering eyes and honeyed lips, she teased the poor man. He rarely—make that never—had a woman pay him such attention. And when said woman looked lovely in her standard police clobber, he kept imagining what she'd look like in a party dress. His mother would have said "frock".

Mind you, Mother would never approve of this 'pushy' woman, this Jezebel. *Bugger Mother*, thought Alastair. *What she doesn't know ...*

Jo placed her card on his desk and underlined her phone number.

'I'll be forever grateful, Alastair, if you could ring me as soon as you get a result.'

She left it at that and simply looked at him. He looked at the card then at her. His mind had a problem.

This lovely woman with the perfume from Paris has given me her phone number. What do I do now? DNA was a doddle. Chatting up birds? Way, way too hard.

Back at Major Crime, everyone waited on the DNA results. But they knew real life and TV cop shows were light years apart. This wasn't a 41-minute edition of *CSI*. It could take days even weeks for the DNA news to arrive, although perhaps not that long thanks to the femme fatale, Jo Best. She returned and downplayed her meeting with Alastair. Goddard was grateful.

'Well done, Jo. With a bit of luck, we'll get the result this year instead of next. Now, you and I are off to see the family.'

In the car, Jo decided to ask questions. 'Is this a cold call, ma'am?'

'They're almost always cold calls, Detective. Remember the element of surprise.'

'Even for a grieving victim?'

'Especially so; we're not social workers.' Jo considered that. 'I rang Gavin at work, and he's gone home feeling unwell. So we may strike both of them.'

'And how much do we tell them?'

'*We* tell them nothing. I do the talking and will be careful with the facts. It's tricky. If we tell them we've got nothing, they may continue to shrivel up inside and die. If we tell them we've got a hot suspect and possible smoking gun evidence, we raise their hopes which, if the DNA doesn't match, will shatter their dream.'

Jo thought about the latest events.

'Do you reckon Leo took the girl?'

'Remember we call the girl Candy in front of the parents.'

'I thought you didn't want me to speak, ma'am?'

Goddard looked at Jo. 'Careful, Senior. Clever good, smart-arse bad.' They drove to the White house in silence.

Gavin opened the door. He looked miserable but when Donna came into the room she looked terrible. She thought an unannounced visit meant the worst possible news and couldn't wait to ask.

'Have you found her?'

Goddard shook her head. 'I'm afraid not. We wanted to keep you up to date with what's been happening, and to see how you both are.'

'What do you think?' Gavin was feeling the strain and reckoned the police had failed in their duty.

When all four settled, Goddard began. 'There's been a development. We're talking to two men who are helping us with our enquiries.'

Gavin was straight in. 'That's police talk for arrest.'

'We're hoping they may know something we don't.'

'I'm confused,' said Donna.

Me too, thought Jo, wondering about the DI's approach. *So much for being careful with the facts.*

Goddard was quick. 'As soon as we get something definite, we'll tell you. But we want you to know the search is still very much active, and we will keep on looking until we know what's happened to Candy.'

Gavin sniffed. 'You mean until you find her body?'

Donna gasped. Goddard didn't respond. She changed tack.

'We've been going over the statements from people who were in or near the playground. One line of enquiry we're following is that more than one person was involved in taking Candy.'

'Wow,' added Gavin with sarcasm, 'who would have thought it? The police do the bleeding obvious.'

Goddard was tempted to fire back but restrained herself. She had an even more powerful rocket up her sleeve.

'We're looking into the possibility that someone you may know was involved.'

That was the rocket and, for a moment it worked.

'I don't understand,' said Donna.

I do now, thought Jo. *In case the DNA is not from Candy, we need to look elsewhere.*

Gavin let fly using his topped up supply of sarcasm. 'Oh I get it. The cops have failed monumentally in finding our daughter so now they use the old smoke and mirror routine by blaming us and our friends.'

He had a point.

'No,' gasped Donna.

Goddard stood her ground. 'There are a number of people who were nowhere near the playground when Candy disappeared but who may have helped the abductor. Can you think of anyone who may have a grudge against you?'

'This is the pits,' snapped Gavin, who stood and glared. 'You come into our home, increase our misery to tell us our friends and family have conspired to abduct and murder our baby. Is that the best you can do. Is it?' He pointed. 'Get out. Get out before I throw you out.'

Goddard returned fire but with restraint. 'You were the one who told us about them, Gavin.'

Boy, did that shut him up. Donna reeled. 'What? Gavin?'

Goddard kept punching. 'You suggested the names.'

'What names?' asked Donna who was getting close to losing it.

Gavin fell back on the denial defence. 'I never said that. You're making this up to cover your own arse. You've failed so now start making wild accusations to save your own skin. I bet your bosses have told you to make an arrest or you'll get replaced.'

Ah, Gavin, how prescient thou art.

'We were in your carpet store, Gavin, when you asked us about two people who are or were known to you. Do you remember?'

Goddard kept herself in check—a cool professional. But her intention was clear. No more tippy-toe treatment for Gavin. Let's be having you, my son. Stop lying, and repeat what you said but this time in front of the missus.

Gavin wasn't sure how to respond. His anger rose as he clenched his fists. He hated his wife for allowing their daughter to go missing. He hated the idea that someone he knew might be involved. And if an unknown pervert took Candy, Gavin felt impotent being unable to rescue his daughter and hurt the evil abductor. His stress level was stratospheric. He clenched his fists and looked ready to explode.

Goddard went harder. 'Do you want me to remind you of the names you mentioned, Gavin?'

'Yes, who were they?' demanded Donna.

'Shut up,' ordered Gavin.

He treated his wife with contempt. He clung to the moral high ground with a tenuous grip. Of the two names he mentioned, one was his former partner who was now his wife's best friend. The other was an adulterer who had it off with Gavin's wife. He gave in.

'All right,' he snapped. I told them about Kylie and Lawrence.'

'What?' screamed Donna.

'Kylie hates me because I dumped her, and she only pretends to be your friend.'

'Liar!'

'And Lawrence hates you because you wouldn't run away with him.'

Jo was quick out of the blocks and needed to be. Donna was up and en route to scratch, slap, slash or spit on her husband. Jo's dive prevented the assault. In grabbing Donna, both women took a tumble. Gavin laughed and strolled out of the room.

Goddard helped the females to their feet. 'Sit, Donna.' She did. 'Take it easy, deep breaths.' The recovery took a while.

'They're lies, what he said, they're all lies. I hate him.'

Goddard moved and sat beside the distraught woman. She even put a hand on her arm. Jo observed.

Detective Inspector Mother Hen.

'Gavin's gone, Donna. Now this is just between the three of us.'

Donna sniffed. 'What else did he say?'

'Nothing. He asked if you mentioned Kylie and Lawrence.' Pause. 'Why did he do that?'

She thought about her answer. 'Because he hates rejection. Kylie dumped him before he took up with me, and I rejected him when I had an affair with Lawrence. Gavin's a typical male. When you hurt their ego, they lose it big time.'

Tell me about it, thought Goddard with Jo thinking about one or two former boyfriends. Goddard changed tack.

'Donna, we have some news about the case.' That got her attention.

Her face crumpled. 'No!'

Her plaintive cry was so loud it brought Gavin back sharpish. He glared at Goddard who explained.

'About those two men I mentioned. Both deny any involvement with Candy's abduction and they may be telling the truth. We searched their home and found no trace of Candy. But we want you to know that we are doing everything possible to find your little girl.'

'Yes but why did you arrest these men? How did you find them?'

'You know we can't tell you that,' replied Goddard.

'Are they perverts?' asked a desperate Donna.

'Look I'm sorry. I only mentioned the two men to show that we're working non-stop to find Candy. If these men are charged, you'll be the first to know. But they may be innocent and if so, they'll be released.'

'And you searched their home?' asked Donna.

'We did.'

'Where is it? What's the address?' Gavin wanted details.

Goddard looked at him without answering

Donna piped up. 'Can you tell us anything about these men?'

'Sorry, no.'

'Just tell me one thing. Have they got criminal records?'

Silence joined the discussion. Goddard decided it was time to leave.

'We'll let you get on. But please understand that you and Candy are constantly in our thoughts. We have a dedicated team of officers working fulltime to find your little girl. As soon as we know more on this latest lead, or any other news, we'll let you know.' She looked at Jo who was ready to leave. Donna followed them to the front door.

'Why has it taken so long to find these two men?'

'Many reasons, Donna, and if anything changes, we'll let you know. We'll check and re-check to find Candy. Thanks for being so patient.'

Donna wasn't finished and turned to Jo.

'I'm sorry, I've forgotten your name.'

'I'm Jo.'

'What do you think, Jo? Is my daughter still alive?'

Jo took a deep breath. 'I'm a glass half full person, Donna. I believe we'll find Candy and bring her home to you safe and well.'

Donna couldn't stop the tears, and suddenly embraced Jo. It was normal and natural. It was a long embrace. Donna stepped back.

'Thank you,' she said and watched the detectives walk away.

She closed the door and turned to face her husband.

'They're lying,' he said. 'Those cops are lying.'

7

BACK AT MAJOR CRIME, Jo received a text message. She read it. Goddard was addressing the troops when Jo interrupted.

'Ma'am, text message.'

'Show me.' Jo walked to the DI and handed her the phone. Goddard read the text and swore. The team waited. Goddard read the text aloud.

Detective Best
The sample of the blood from the house in Abbotsford
is animal blood and thus not a match for the abducted
girl. I'm so sorry.
Alastair Dean

More swearing came from different sources. Jo walked to the back of the room, rang Alastair and thanked him profusely. He wanted to ask her for a drink but lacked the courage and wimped out. Goddard led the discussion.

'Right, was the blood a simple mistake or a deliberate tactic?'

'Deliberate?' asked Harcourt. 'What's the point of throwing animal's blood on the bathroom floor and then trying to remove it?'

Goddard looked at the team. 'Anyone?'

'Someone playing funny buggers,' said Ben Grimes, 'someone who hates police and wants to waste our time.'

'And no prize for guessing who,' added Goddard.

The entire team spoke as one. 'Leo Smythe.'

'What did you tell the parents, ma'am?' asked Gregory.

'Nothing about the blood, thank God. I told them we were talking to a couple of new witnesses and would keep the Whites in the loop if anything came of it.'

Jo found it interesting that Goddard gave a redacted version of what happened. The DI wanted to move on.

'All right. Let's have another crack at both the Abbotsford lads, first thing tomorrow. Jake's the weak link. Put him under pressure. In the meantime, we push on checking and crosschecking. I want total silence on the two arrests. The press get nothing—no pillow talk, loose lips and ships, and all that jazz. Yes?'

'But you've told the parents, ma'am,' said Gregory, enjoying being able to get a punch in at his boss.

'They won't say anything. I told them to keep schtum.'

Another lie, thought Jo.

'So not a word,' called Goddard. The others agreed. 'Louder,' demanded Goddard.

A louder response filled the room. 'Yes.'

'Yes, ma'am,' she cried, and they echoed her words and delivery.

The atmosphere changed. The breakthrough they hoped for came to nothing. They may well have found the person or persons who abducted little Candy but without any evidence let alone powerful evidence such as DNA, few shared Jo's message of hope. 'I'm a glass half full person, Donna. I believe we'll find Candy and bring her home to you safe and well.'

Even Jo began to have doubts.

At home that night her phone pinged. The text was from Michael Chan. She felt bad having not contacted him for some time. All his text said was *Monte Christo*. She smiled. That was their original code for getting in touch. She rang him.

'Michael Chan speaking.'

'Joanna Best speaking. I got your not so cryptic message.'

'I thought you'd emigrated. You set me a task then disappear.'

'Michael, I would never emigrate without telling you first.'

'I thought you were going to say without my permission.'

She laughed. 'Have you got something to show me?'

'I have.'

'Is the kettle on?'

'Is the Pope a Catholic?'

'I'm on my way.'

As Jo drove to Northcote, Ruth Graham nee Thorne drove her sister Elisabeth to their parents' home in Chatham. They'd been told their younger daughter had ended her relationship with the dreadful Darren what's-his-name. Now, days later, Elisabeth was to visit her parents and everyone was nervous.

Mummy opened the door. Elisabeth and her mother fell into one another's arms. Ruth closed the door and kissed her father. They stood and watched the other family members. The embrace lingered and tears mingled. Daddy got involved. Then Ruth kissed her mother and all four retired to the lounge room.

To avoid discussing the elephant in the room, Ruth spoke about the only grandchild with the son-in-law getting a modest mention.

Then it was time. Elisabeth said sorry and repeated her apology ad infinitum. Her father took control.

'Darling girl, listen to me. Your mother and I are over the moon you are here and looking so well. But we do have one small favour to ask. Please do not apologise—ever again. You've done nothing wrong. We have always loved you; we still love you, and will always love you. Do you understand?'

Elisabeth did, and found the energy to cry again. She went to her father. He stood and embraced his daughter, and soon the other two females made it a group hug.

'Right, that's enough of all this nonsense,' said Dad, and a few smiles finally appeared. They enjoyed supper, and Elisabeth made her parents almost excited when she accepted their offer to move back into the family home.

'But not forever, Elisabeth,' admonished her father. 'I'm getting used to having only two females in the house.' Rosie, the Labrador barked on cue and everyone laughed.

Jo stood beneath Michael's atmospheric *film noir* light. He opened the door. 'Hello, stranger,' he said with his miniature smile.

They hugged platonically and settled in his warehouse. Alan sidled up to Jo and accepted pats and whisker rubbing.

'No news on the missing girl?'

'No but there's been a breakthrough on a possible abductor.'

'Forgive my ignorance but why is Homicide investigating when a body hasn't been found?'

'Ah,' said a slightly guilty Jo. 'I've moved. I'm working in Major Crime and they're investigating the missing girl.'

Michael was shocked. 'They sacked you again?'

'Not sacked, transferred—temporarily.'

He looked at her and, being well brought up, didn't make further enquiries. He changed the subject.

'I've been thinking about that poor young woman, the victim of revenge porn.' Jo brightened. 'I've produced a web site.' He turned on his monitor and Jo watched in eager anticipation. She nearly died.

It was a stunning web design with the title *Abusive Bastards*.

'Wow!' she said.

'Too much?'

'Not necessarily. Show me more, please.'

He did. The site didn't identify the so-called transgressor but anyone who knew him knew who it was. To date, Darren was the first and only "star" of the site.

There was a photo of him with face pixilated. He wore a tee shirt with the slogan, *Cowards Abuse Women*. It was a photo-shopped image thanks to Mr Chan. There was a description of what he'd done without any photos—naturally, with not even a hint of the woman he'd destroyed.

'Where did you get the photo?'

'Where do you think? Facebook owns the world.'

'But,' said Jo, struggling to know what to say, 'is this legal?'

'Me? Do something illegal? Never.'

'Can you be traced?'

He looked at her as if she'd asked a silly question.

'It's on the Dark Web, like that Dee-Fat site I created. The aim is to tell the lovely Darren he's been pinged. Give him the URL and let the moron suffer. Like the Crimm brothers, Darren won't know it's on the Dark Web.' Jo looked worried. 'You do want him to suffer?'

'I do. But what happens after he sees himself on the big screen?'

'Who knows? Maybe he'll remove the revenge porn pic. But at least your friend will have the satisfaction of knowing Darren's been exposed, not like her, but arguably worse. Victims so often feel helpless. Here's a chance for the victim to feel empowered. Darren won't know only a handful of people are looking at it. He'll think the world is laughing at him. Prick a prick's ego and the suffering can be horrendous.'

'And you think he'll remove the revenge porn pic?'

Michael shrugged. 'Jo, I don't know the guy. He's a coward, so who knows? The alternative is to get the Crimm brothers to pay him a visit.'

Jo knew he was joking. The Crimm brothers were brutal gangsters Jo and Michael outsmarted not long ago.

'So a text arrives on Darren's phone with this web address?'

'That's it.'

She took out her phone and found Darren's mobile number.

'But if I send it, he'll be able to trace me.'

'Probably. But I could send it via an overseas connection. Does he know anyone in Russia?'

'Russia?'

'What's his number?'

She showed him.

'Are we playing with fire, here, Michael?'

'You mean as opposed to what we did with romance scammers and gangsters?'

She nodded. Fair point. He set to and sent Darren a text via Moscow. If the slimy ratfink did try and trace the text, getting angry with Russian gangsters would be a bad idea.

Sitting at home, smoking a joint, Darren Sandilands heard his phone announce a text had arrived. He clicked on the link in the text.

Casually he checked his phone. The words "eyeballs" and "organ stops" could well be used to describe the reaction of this shit of a plumber.

He fumed. He produced steam. He studied the site on his phone in more detail. He knew it was him. The world would know it was him. He grabbed his iPad and typed in the URL. On a bigger screen, there he was in living HD colour. He finally got to make use of his degree, his Bachelor of Swearing.

Who did this?

He rang mate, Jordan who knew nothing. Darren sent the URL. Jordan shared his mate's amazement.

'Wow, that's unbelievable man.'

'Can you take it down?' demanded Darren.

'It's not my site.'

'Not the site, the picture,'

'Dunno. I told you, it's not my site.'

'Try,' screamed Darren. 'And can you trace the people who made it?'

'I might but why?'

'Why?' Darren was going hoarse. 'Because I want to fucking kill them, that's why.'

'Mate, you don't know who they are.'

'Just find their name and address. Do it.' He went to end the call but stopped. 'And listen, Jordan, if you tell anyone about this web site, I'll fucking kill you too.' Jordan believed him.

Then he ended the call.

Elisabeth and her sister and parents knew nothing of this Dark Web site but all would have felt a tremor of happiness had they seen the misery currently dominating poor Darren.

Suff-er.

8

NEXT MORNING WAS CRUNCH TIME. Bring on the second separate interviews with Leo and Jake. But with nothing in the way of serious evidence, unless one of them cracked—Jake seemed the more likely— both men would have to be released without charge.

DI Goddard used the same people. She and Gregson would tackle Leo, while Grimes and Jo would take Jake. The other senior constables wondered why Jo Best got the gig head of them. One rumour was that she had something over the DI giving her whatever job she fancied. Another rumour reckoned she first best friends with the Assistant Commissioner (Crime), John Crowley.

Goddard felt her pulse get busy. She wanted this case solved. Of course she wanted the kid to be found alive and well but after a month, few seriously believed that would be the case.

Grimes and Jo entered the interview room. Immediately things were different. Jake didn't look so terrified. Beside him sat a seasoned and smart solicitor. Ben knew the brief from way back.

How could a kid on the dole afford Jonathan Limb?

Once the preliminaries were completed, the solicitor started.

'Before we begin, my client wishes to submit a written statement, and he instructs me to say that he will answer no further questions.'

'I haven't asked one, yet,' said a peeved Grimes.

Limb submitted the statement, and Grimes and Jo read it. They looked at one another. Before they could speak, the solicitor got in first—again. Did he have a pressing engagement?

'On behalf of my client, I will be making a claim for an immediate release.'

Jo played it well. 'Have we charged Mr Freeman yet, Sergeant?'

He liked her question and decided to return the solicitor's fire.

'Now Jake, you seem like a fine young man.'

'Say nothing,' said his brief.

'But things have changed since we last had a chat. Before you wander off, let me tell you a little of what's happened. Forensic officers have examined your home in Abbotsford and found a splatter of blood which someone has tried to remove with bleach.'

'Say nothing,' said the solicitor.

Jo worried. Yes, a blood splatter was found but the lovely Alastair dismissed it out of hand.

'Jake, we know you were not in Melbourne on the weekend when little Candice was abducted but you did return on the Monday.'

'Tuesday,' blurted Jake.

'We'd like you to tell us what your friend Leo told you about the missing child.'

'Say nothing,' said the solicitor.

'Jake, we have a little girl missing for weeks and her family and friends, in fact the whole of Melbourne is desperate to find her. Surely you'd like to help ... please.'

The solicitor whispered in Jake's ear. He looked brave. 'No comment.'

Watching in the next room, Goddard felt her energy draining. No evidence and a clever solicitor meant no reason to hold Jake let alone charge him.

Grimes kept trying. 'So, Jake, have you anything to say?'

'Say nothing,' said Limb.

'Nothing,' said Jake without a scintilla of irony.

Grimes continued. 'You are perfectly at liberty to say nothing, Jake but you have told us that you know the man you're living with has a record as a sex offender, that you know he went to jail for a crime involving children. He may be charged with abduction and more.'

'This is irrelevant nonsense,' said the solicitor. Jake still worried.

Watching in another room, Goddard got involved. 'Go for him Ben,' she said, and Ben did just that.

'When you returned to the house, you may have seen something, heard something, or suspected something about Leo and the child, and now, if you say nothing, you could be charged as an accessory and, if found guilty, go to prison for a long time. And if that little girl has been murdered, your time in prison could be mighty long. Do you understand, Jake?'

'Have you finished?' asked Limb.

'This is your chance, Jake, to tell us everything you know about what happened to the little girl.' Grimes paused. 'Last chance, Jake.'

The solicitor had had enough. He stood, demanding the interview end but froze when his client ignored Limb's advice and spoke.

'He said he never done it.'

Limb seethed. 'Be quiet.'

'Mr Limb can only advise you, Jake,' continued Grimes. 'If you want to speak, you speak.'

Limb sat and fumed. Jake wasn't brave enough to look at the well-heeled solicitor. He wasn't brave enough to look at anyone. But he was brave enough or desperate enough to have his say.

'When I came back to Melbourne, Leo showed me the newspaper story about the kid. He was angry and said they'll come after him. They'll plant evidence, he said. I asked if he knew who did it and he went quiet. Maybe it was because he did know and didn't want to grass them up or because he did it and didn't want to say.' Finally, Jake looked at Grimes. 'That's all I know. That's all I'm going to say.'

Ben looked at Jo. He mimed, 'Anything?' She gave a small nod and looked at Jake.

'Jake, hi. I'm Detective Senior Constable Jo Best. Can you tell me who does the cleaning in your house?'

He shook his head. He didn't know or the answer was no one.

'Well who does the washing, changes the loo paper, and puts out the rubbish bins?'

Jake thought these were strange questions. 'I put the bins out. Leo doesn't like to go out in the street.'

'And the washing?'

Again Jake thought. 'We both do although sometimes I take stuff home and my Mum does it for me.'

'Do you know the name of the little girl who disappeared?'

Jake had to think. 'Cindy?'

Jo smiled at Jake. 'Thanks, Jake.' She looked at Grimes.

Goddard watched all this on CCTV and swore as the interview ended. If she thought Jake would crumble and turn on his housemate, she was disappointed—bitterly so. She would have to make Leo sing.

The former criminal, the man who changed his name from Ricardo to Leo, couldn't afford a high-flying solicitor. He had another Legal Aid rep who urged the Marcel Marceau response—say nothing.

Goddard felt the butterflies playing Chasey in her abdomen. Jake had emerged scot-free. He had not grassed up Leo.

The DI began with innocuous questions, which Leo dismissed with ease. His confidence grew. They had nothing. He even grinned.

Why? Goddard felt ill. *The prick is even smiling.*

Leo wanted to repeat his histrionics at his first interview with the accusations of being framed, of police corruption, and how again they were blaming the guy with the record. He wanted to tell them the evidence was planted. But strangely he remained calm. The police were expecting fireworks and got balloons. He looked at his solicitor who leant in and whispered in his ear. Leo nodded. That in itself was strange. No frown, no swearing, no anger. Was it time to confess?

Goddard tried the good cop approach.

'Leo, you know how the system works. If you co-operate, things become easier. We don't press for so severe a sentence. We tell the judge you've been a good guy. And then, when you help the poor suffering parents, you get another gold star. This is do-yourself-a-favour time, Leo. Tell us what happened to little Candy and where she is, and life for you will immediately get better.'

She sat back. She looked at Leo. He would make a brilliant poker player. His face gave away nothing.

Leo stalled. Everyone awaited his response. Confession, contrition, explanation. Even one of those would be great. Goddard began to dream of victory. Her butterflies disappeared. But not for long.

Leo leant forward, calmly put his clenched fists on the table, and spoke directly at the detective. 'Fuck you.'

Later in the Incident Room, the team despaired. Goddard asked for comments. Almost everyone had a say.

'We have to let him go.'

'He's got form, no alibi, and lives close to the crime scene.'

'Circumstantial evidence is all we've got.'

'He's on the Register of Sex Offenders.'

'I bet he planted that animal blood.' That comment from Grimes stopped the commentary. 'He hates the police. He knew we'd find him eventually. He's playing games, playing us for mugs.'

The team divided. Goddard stewed. If they released Leo and it later turned out he was involved in Candy's abduction, even her death, the repercussions didn't bear thinking about.

Gregory made a suggestion. 'Why don't we charge him with failure to notify a change of name and address and hope any bail application fails. Being on the Sex Register should make life difficult for him.'

'And we add wasting police time,' added Grimes. 'We claim he deliberately put the animal blood in the bathroom and made a deliberate effort to almost clean it to frustrate our enquiries.'

'Which he did. He was laughing at us.'

Goddard was not convinced. 'It's hardly crime of the century.'

'But it means we can hold him while we work our backsides off to find some evidence,' added Grimes.

Goddard thought it was better than releasing Leo. 'Okay, we charge him and hope like hell we find something new.'

Leo was charged with parole violations and wasting police time and returned to remand. Jake was released. He returned to Abbotsford hoping his mate would soon join him.

Goddard reported to the AC Crime, John Crowley.

'We thought we had strong DNA evidence, sir, and believe the man arrested, remains a strong possibility.'

'But you're no nearer to finding the little girl?'

Goddard grimaced. 'Not yet, sir, but we have other lines of enquiry.'

'Did I hear that Senior Constable Joanna Best is on your team?'

Goddard hid her surprise. 'She is, sir, and a fine detective.'

'Give her my kind regards. Oh, and the clock is ticking, Inspector.'

Goddard stood. 'Yes sir.' She headed back to Major Crime thinking about Jo Best, and about Homicide taking her case.

9

SEX FIEND DARREN SANDILANDS had never heard of the word *incandescent*. Pity because it described him to a tee. The morning after discovering himself on a web page as a coward, a piss weak moron, and the butt of a joke, several jokes, he was, well, incandescent with rage. His mate, Jordan, had failed to discover who had created the web site. No wonder, as it lay buried on the Dark Web. To try and appease his mate, Jordan removed Elisabeth Thorne's graphic photo from the revenge porn web site where he'd placed it. But it didn't shift Darren. His fame and shame were alive and well online.

Darren craved revenge. It was payback time. Jordan was useless so Detective Darren got cracking. He told his boss he had urgent business and would be late for work. He knew where Elisabeth worked. He parked near a T intersection, two blocks from the kindergarten in a narrow, one-way street.

He sat there waiting, tapping his steering wheel to the beat of some mindless so-called song with lyrics created by a vending machine. He looked in his side mirror and saw her car. Elisabeth Thorne passed him, not noticing him, and slowed for the stop sign. She stopped and then it happened.

Crash!

Her car jolted forward being rammed from behind. His 4WD bull bar suffered a minor scratch. Her small hatch copped a major dent. She screamed in fright at the collision and then terror kicked in because she thought she'd be pushed onto the busy road with cars rushing by in front of her.

Before she could gather her wits, Darren yanked open her door. Always lock your door, Elisabeth. He reached in and removed the ignition key. The engine died and so did Elisabeth.

'You bitch,' were his opening words.

She reached for her phone but he got there first. He leant across and snatched her bag. A car pulled up behind Darren's and tooted. He threatened his petrified ex.

'Who made that web site?'

Together with naked fear and horrific memories of what this man had done to her, Elisabeth found his question confusing.

What web site? Did he mean the one on which she was exposed, literally, for the world to see? And if so, why was he angry? He put the picture there. He must know who created it.

The car behind Darren's tooted again. He ignored it.

'Tell me or I'll slash your fucking face.' He produced a Stanley knife with sharpened razor eager to slice some flesh.

Elisabeth was trapped. No car key, her seatbelt locked tight, and an enraged bully in her face. She couldn't cry, couldn't move and couldn't speak.

His anger exploded. 'Who did you tell about that photo?'

Elisabeth fought for her life. Finally she muttered. 'Only my sister.'

'Only your sister?'

'Yes.'

'Does she know about computers? Did she put up that web site?'

Elisabeth's confusion got serious. *What web site?* The car behind tooted with feeling.

'No.'

'Well who else did you tell?'

'No one. Only my sister.'

'And who did *she* tell?'

Elisabeth lost it. Fear consumed her body and mind. 'I think her friend.'

'What friend? What's his name?'

'Jo Best.'

Darren heard Joe Best. 'Where's your sister live? Tell me.'

She muttered the address. Then the driver of the tooting car arrived demanding they move. Darren turned and saw a well-built man sans fat, but replete with attitude. Darren spat in Elisabeth's face, then threw her keys and phone on the floor of her car.

'You tell Joe Best to remove that web site or I'll fucking kill him.' He screamed. 'Do you hear?' He glared at the indignant motorist, got in his vehicle, and drove off squeezing past Elisabeth's car and ignoring the stop sign.

Elisabeth never made it to work. She pulled over and cried. Just when she thought her life was on the mend, the monster, aka Darren Sandilands, the nightmare from her past, came roaring back, threatening her and promising even more harm.

She rang the kindergarten and apologised. She rang her sister and sobbed.

'Can you drive home?' asked Ruth.

'I'll try.'

She made it and told her sister everything.

'I think it's time we called the police,' said Ruth.

That only added to Elisabeth's woe. 'No, not the police. If this becomes public, everyone will see that photo.'

'It's gone.'

'What?'

'I just looked and it's not there.'

Elisabeth had trouble believing her sister. 'Gone?' Ruth nodded and fetched her laptop. 'Completely gone?'

They looked at the revenge porn web site. There were so many smiling females, semi-naked or not even semi. Ruth scrolled through the site. No sign of Elisabeth's photo anywhere. Her mind spun out of control.

'But Darren attacked me because of the web site.'

'Maybe he was angry because your photo's gone.'

'But he asked me who made that web site?'

'This web site?' Elisabeth couldn't explain. Ruth joined the confusion club. She picked up her phone.

Jo was at work checking witness statements for the umpteenth time. There were so many people in Citizens' Park when Candy disappeared. Her mobile phone rang.

'Jo Best.'

'Jo, it's Ruth.'

Those three words contained fear.

61

'Hi Ruth, is everything okay?'

'No. Elisabeth's just been assaulted by that monster.'

'Is she okay? Where is she?'

'She's here at my place. But Jo, we looked on the revenge porn site, and couldn't find her photo. And Darren kept demanding Elisabeth tell him about some web site. Do you know what's going on?'

'Yes. Perhaps I'd better come and see you.'

'That'd be great. Oh and I'm sorry but Elisabeth was so scared she told Darren your name.'

'Okay,' said Jo wondering if this meant bad news or really bad news. 'What's your address?' Ruth told her. 'I'll see you soon.'

Jo asked Goddard if she could visit a friend who'd just been assaulted—the truth but not the whole truth—and was waved away without hesitation.

Jo headed off not knowing Goddard's thinking. It was simple.

Any friend of the Assistant Commissioner (Crime) is okay by me. Jo Best might be able to help me move up the ladder.

Darren eventually made it to work but kept spewing about the *Cowards Abuse Women* web site. At least he now knew the person behind it. Joe Best. Who is he, where is he and when can I break his legs? His intention was not so much to have the web site removed, which obviously he wanted, but mainly to inflict serious punishment on its creator. For Darren, Joe Best was a dead man walking.

The real Jo Best arrived at Ruth's place. She got Elisabeth's story and then decided to spill the beans.

'I'm pretty sure Darren took down your photo, Elisabeth, because *his* photo is now online.' She let that sink in. Both sisters were in shock.

Elisabeth gasped. 'Darren took down my photo?'

Jo shrugged. 'Darren or someone instructed by Darren.'

Ruth wanted more. 'Did you say there's a photo of Darren online?'

'He's all over Facebook,' said Elisabeth.

'I don't mean that sort of photo,' said Jo. She indicated the laptop. 'May I?'

Jo pulled up the Dark Web site starring the lovely but pixilated Darren, and showed it to the sisters.

They mimicked Darren with their eyes keen to pop out of their heads.

After the gasps expired and the questions were answered—some not truthfully—Jo asked for instructions.

'Do you want this site removed?'

The sisters looked at one another.

'I think we should,' said Ruth.

'I think we should leave it there forever,' said Elisabeth.

'But, Jo,' said Ruth, 'Elisabeth gave Darren your name.'

'I'm so sorry,' cried Elisabeth.

'Forget it.' Jo was not worried about possible threats from a bully. She worried about stuffing up her police career—again—and never getting back into Homicide.

'The thing, ladies, is that Darren's web catastrophe is on a hidden part of the Internet. He thinks the world is looking at it but they're not. Only a few people know the site exists, and three of them are in this room. I bet he's not been bragging to his mates about it.'

Silence took over. Ruth summed up matters. 'The main thing is Elisabeth's photo's gone. If Darren's photo goes too, maybe he'll forget about revenge. So can you please remove his site?'

'No problem,' said Jo. 'I can't but I know someone who can.'

She didn't mention two facts. Elisabeth's photo may have been snapped up by other porn sites, and might even now be online elsewhere. The former ballerina was hot, and going viral was a real possibility. And Darren was a male with a massive ego. When such a person is slighted, even if the slight has been removed, they become an elephant—they never forget. Darren may never rest until he finds Joe Best.

Jo left, and was heading back to work when Goddard rang.'

'Yes ma'am?'

'Are you anywhere near the White house?'

'I am, about ten minutes.'

'Get there now. Leo's arrest for parole violations and time wasting has made the news. We have to tell them before the press do. And I want to know their reaction.'

'Will they both be there?'

'No idea. Just get there, tell them as little as possible, and observe.'

'Yes ma'am.'

'And how's your friend?'

'Fine. Well, not fine but she's okay.'

'Good. I want the White reaction. Ciao.'

Jo knocked and Donna appeared. She looked terrible. She didn't have to ask about Candy, her face screamed the question.

'No news, Donna, but may I come in? There's something you should see on the telly.'

They sat and turned on the TV. 'What's happening?' asked Donna.

'I'm not sure myself but I think there's been an arrest.'

Donna called loudly, 'Gavin.'

Jo was surprised when the husband walked in.

'What is it this time?' he asked. 'Come to tell us you've still not found her?'

'I thought you'd be at work, Gavin.'

'What work? They've sent me home.' He mocked his boss. 'We're sorry for your loss, Gavin, but you're upsetting the customers.'

'I'm sorry.' Jo had an eye on the screen. 'This is it. Turn it up.'

Jo remembered her instructions. She had a parent on either side so couldn't observe both at the same time. The Candy arrest item lead the bulletin. The missing child had been news for more than a month.

A picture of Candy appeared on screen. Donna cried aloud. 'No!'

'Shut up,' said Gavin. 'Listen.'

The information was basic. A man was arrested and charged over bail violations and wasting police time in the disappearance of Candy White. There was no mention of the man's name, a photograph, or mention of the whereabouts of the child. DI Goddard appeared on screen as part of an impromptu press conference.

'The man arrested has not been charged with Candy's abduction. We believe he may be able to help us with our enquiries.'

A reporter called. 'Is Candy still alive, Inspector?'

She looked straight at the camera and thus straight at the Whites.

'We're treating Candy as missing, and will continue do so until we have further information.'

More questions followed but the Whites had stopped listening. Jo kept observing.

'She has to say that,' said Gavin. 'She's been told to say that.'

'How did you find him?' asked Donna.

'Persistence. We kept checking statements and interviewing people and he turned up.'

'Bullshit.' Gavin didn't buy Jo's explanation.

Donna wanted information. 'Has the man you've arrested got a police record?'

Jo hesitated. 'I can't talk about it, I'm sorry. It's more than my job's worth. But I can tell you we are finding new evidence all the time.'

'For what,' barked Gavin, 'abduction or murder?'

Donna gasped but she too wanted more. 'Does this man know what happened to Candy?' She begged. Jo felt terrible. It seemed like she was telling the parents their little girl was dead. She stood.

'I'm sorry, Donna. All I can tell you is what's on the news. We wanted you to be told before the press made it public.'

The atmosphere was awful. Donna was desolate, Gavin abusive and angry, and Jo helpless.

'I'll see myself out. She stopped in the doorway. 'Is there anything I can do for you?'

'Yeah,' snapped Gavin. 'Find my daughter.' Most fathers would have said *our* daughter.

Jo left as Donna sobbed and Gavin cursed.

10

SATURDAY WAS TIMOTHY'S BIRTHDAY. Jo awoke and checked her clothes, camera and present. It was her 6 year-old nephew's day in the Dandenongs. Timmy and his big sister Millie were great fun. But their parents, plus Jo's father (Malcolm X) and his trophy wife (Jo's stepmother) and their two kids would be there too. Not so great. Her father's second marriage had produced two children—Rupert and Emily—meaning Jo and her sister Caitlyn had stepsiblings who were about 20 years younger. Sheesh.

The plan was for Jo to drive to Caitlyn's house and travel with them. The weather was good for train trips in the Dandenongs.

'Hello, Auntie Jo,' yelled Tim and Millie as she approached the front porch. The porch was about half the size of Jo's apartment.

'Happy birthday, young man,' said Jo, handing the lad a wrapped present. He beamed.

'What do you say?' demanded his mother.

'Thank you very much, Auntie Jo,' beamed the youngster. He unwrapped his new set of building blocks. Millie gave her favourite aunt a power hug.

Then came the obligatory kiss from her brother-in-law, investment banker, Jeremy. Jo had never taken to him only because he was selfish, snobbish and self-opinionated. Jo had perfected fake sincerity in dealing with her sister and brother-in-law.

'You're coming with us,' said Millie, taking Jo's hand. 'You can sit in the back next to me.'

'No, next to me,' demanded Timothy. 'It's my birthday.'

'Why don't I sit in the middle?' asked Jo. That settled the dispute and into the BMW 4WD touring machine they clambered, and off to the hills they went.

They'd only just got going when Caitlyn piped up from the front. 'Dad and Natalie and the kids aren't coming. Emily's got a cold and Dad has three really important auctions.'

Jo was delighted. She had the same opinion of her stepmother as she did of her brother-in-law. 'Well that won't stop us having the best time ever, hey kids?' They screamed their approval to which their egotistical father responded.

'Thank you, children. We behave at all times and especially in the car.' While some men have a trophy wife, Jeremy and Caitlyn had trophy children.

Jo made a face with her eyes and mouth open and the kids loved it. Being cheeky behind their father's back was seriously cool.

Caitlyn supported her husband. 'Now don't forget Auntie Jo's a police officer, and she might have to lock you up if you're naughty.'

Oh boy, that sounded less like a punishment and more like the best adventure ever.

'Have you got a gun, Auntie Jo?' asked the birthday boy.

'Not with me. Not even my handcuffs. So that means I'll have to find another way to lock you up.' She tickled him and he squealed. His father spun around and the poor kid went suddenly quiet. Another face from Jo put Tim right off the old man with his Auntie moving ever higher in the favourite grown-ups' hit parade chart.

'Auntie Jo?' asked Millie.

'Yeees?' replied Jo.

'Can girls be in the police?'

'No,' said Caitlyn and Jeremy as one. Let's kill that idea now.

'Well I'm a girl and I'm in the police,' said Jo, 'so I guess the answer has to be yes.' The back seat smiled, the front seat glowered. This was going to be a long day.

Caitlyn changed the subject. 'Tell Auntie Jo about your piano lessons, Timmy, and Millie, you can tell her about your ballet lessons.'

Jo listened with genuine interest. The kids told all but really wanted to know about the life of a cop.

'Have you ever catched any robbers?'

"Caught" came from the grammar police in the front.

Timmy started again. 'Have you ever caught any bad people, Auntie Jo?'

'Sometimes.'

'Does your car have a flashing light and go very fast?'

'Sometimes.'

Millie got in on the act. 'Do you wear special clothes?'

'Sometimes.'

The siblings looked at their aunt. She grinned and wiggled her eyebrows. They grinned back.

'Auntie Jo?' asked Timmy.

'Yeeees?'

'I'm going to call you Auntie Sometimes.'

That brought the house down and the drive improved with the natural and genuine wit of the young birthday boy.

There were hordes of people at Gembrook waiting for a ride on Puffing Billy. Photos with the Fat Controller, face painting, souvenirs, a jumping castle and an animal farm were all in full swing. Jo had a child in either hand and off they went exploring.

They went from attraction to attraction. Jeremy and Caitlyn regretted the whole venture. It would take hours whereas a swish soiree at home—fully catered of course—would have been done and dusted in 90 minutes. But here they were mixing with the hoi polloi, in the dirt and dust of the bush, for what seemed like, and was, ages.

Jo and the kids stood on the platform watching Puffing Billy coming back from its latest trip when a terrible scream exploded. More screams followed. A small child had run along the platform, tripped, and fallen onto the tracks. No train there yet but diving head first onto the metal rails and ballast of the line could mean any sort of serious injury or worse.

'Go and wait over there,' said Jo, pointing to a bench on the platform. The children did so as Jo darted towards the accident.

Parents were trying to comfort the stricken toddler but had no first aid training. Jo politely pushed through.

'Let me help,' she said and bent to examine the child. Her confident manner gave assurance to the family. She knew not to move the victim in case of causing further injury. The worry was the child was quiet. Screaming in pain would have been preferable.

Jo couldn't see any blood but the little boy was having trouble breathing. She knew CPR and how to staunch bleeding but worried her training was insufficient. She heard a voice.

'Can I help? I'm a doctor.'

Jo felt enormous relief as people parted, and a man knelt and examined the boy. The doctor made a decision, and looked up to get some help. Jo looked into the eyes of Dr Jack Carr.

They both took a second to recover. 'Doctor Carr,' she said.

'Detective Best,' he replied. Then it was action time. The GP examined the child then together, he and Jo lifted the boy onto the platform where the medical man cleared the blood from a bruised nose. The child had understandably panicked, and his panic attack combined with his restricted breathing made his parents panic. Nose cleared, the boy yelped, started bawling, which was good, and breathing normally.

He suffered from fussing family members. Dr Carr produced some cotton wads from his backpack and plugged one side of the boy's nose.

'He'll have a headache pretty soon but should be okay to travel.'

'I think we'll take him home,' said his father.

Jack knelt beside the boy. 'Would you like to ride on Puffing Billy?'

The bruised and plugged young man tried to smile and nodded. Jack looked up at the father.

'No bones broken but he'll have a shiner tonight. Maybe doing something exciting will take his mind off the accident.'

'Okay,' said the father, 'we'll go for a ride. Thank you, Doctor.'

'You're welcome.'

Family members buzzed, and the parents again thanked Dr Carr while an aging grandmother planted a huge smacker on his cheek. He looked embarrassed.

'So that's how you get paid,' said the smiling detective.

The party broke up. Jack and Jo were alone on the platform although both looked around and beckoned.

Instantly, two sets of children ran to them. The adults looked at one another and laughed.

'Snap,' said Jack, and Jo kept smiling.

It was train ride time. Jo and her tribe joined Jack and his in the same carriage. Caitlyn and Jeremy found the journey and Jo's new friends underwhelming. The delight enjoyed by their children did little to warm the cockles of Timmy and Millie's parents' ... no, that's impossible. Without a heart, there were no cockles to warm.

After the trip, and back on the Gembrook platform, Caitlyn, without any prompting from her husband, announced they were off home. Their children were unhappy. Why did this great day have to end?

Caitlyn got her sister aside and issued a warning. 'Be careful there, sister. Single father, his turn for the kids this weekend, Mr Kisses without commitment, steer clear, kiddo.'

Jo looked at her sister. 'Very kind,' she said, 'thanks for the advice.'

Caitlyn didn't do irony and genuinely thought (a) she was right and (b) was doing her baby sister a favour.

Jack's kids, Grace and Harry, had hit it off with Jo and her kids and all four youngsters were keen to kick on. Jack announced.

'We're going strawberry picking. Why don't you all come?'

Tim and Millie were definitely up for it. Caitlyn immediately thought of her Jimmy Choo boots and expensive manicure. Dirt? Mud? Yuk. Jeremy would prefer root canal surgery without anaesthetic.

'Sorry,' said the merchant banker, who was a perfect example of the rhyming slang, 'we have to get going.' He held out a hand to Jack. 'Nice meeting you.' Jeremy had forgotten Jack's name. No, he'd never bothered to remember it.

Jack turned to Jo. 'What about you, Detective? Fancy a strawberry hunt?'

There was a dramatic pause. Jo was being asked on a date. She felt terrible leaving her nephew and niece. Caitlyn's eyes flashed alarm bells. Jo fancied the excursion but felt an obligation to her nephew and niece. Jack sensed her dilemma.

'Bring the kids. I'll get you all home safely. We've got an 7 seater so there's plenty of room.'

Tim and Millie were busting to go. Strawberry hunting with their favourite aunt was slightly better than sensational. They begged their father. Jeremy weakened.

'Okay.' The kids jumped for joy. Brother-in-law stared at Jo. 'You can be a bad cop if you like.' He and Caitlyn hugged their kids for show then left—gladly.

It would be unfair to report their conversation going home.

'Right,' said Jack, rubbing his hands, 'let's go pick some strawberries, which, we can eat tonight with ...'

His kids chorused as one. 'Ice-cream.'

The strawberry picking was a hit. The kids had a ball and the adults had a different kind of enjoyment.

Topping up his container, Jack turned to Jo. 'I forgot to ask if you even like strawberries.'

Jo looked at him then popped the biggest piece of fruit she had straight in her mouth, just managing to smile despite chewing.

Complete with enough strawberries to last a fortnight, the sextet piled into Jack's people mover and headed back to Melbourne. The seating arrangements sorted themselves. The adults were up front, the girls behind them, and the gossiping gents settled in the peanut gallery.

The kids were chatting non-stop but the grown-ups were not so garrulous. Why? Jack concentrated on driving but opened the batting.

'So, do you come here often?'

Jo smiled. She wasn't sure why but she found it easy to relax. An expensive car included comfortable seating but there was more to it than that.

'So where's your car?' he asked.

'It's at my sister's place in Canterbury. If you can drop us there it will be fantastic. And thanks for this last adventure. The kids absolutely loved it.'

'But not you?'

She looked at him. He took his eyes off the road for a second and looked at her.

'It was great.'

They drove on. He broke the ice, again. 'I know we're in the post #Me Too age so I hope this doesn't sound too movie producer-ish.' She was fascinated. 'When I first saw you with Tim and Millie, I couldn't believe someone so young could have two kids that age.'

'Oh I've left the babies at home.'

For a moment his heartrate kicked hard then he twigged and laughed. 'Touché.'

Another pause before Jo dived in the deep end. 'My sister described you as "the single Dad who has the kids every second weekend".'

He looked at her. 'Would you be fishing, Detective?' She was and felt guilty. She felt much worse when he replied. 'I'm a widower. I lost my wife almost two years ago.'

Jo felt terrible. She had used her sister's crassness to discover the good doctor's marital status.

The best she could offer was, 'I'm sorry for being so insensitive.'

'Not a problem. So where are you dining tonight?'

She laughed. 'In my flat, in front of the telly, with a calorie-counted microwaveable dinner.'

'We're having pizza. Come and join us.'

Jo felt a kind of pressure, not bad, just different.

'That's very kind but ...'

'The kids'd love you to be there; we've never had a real police officer before.'

She looked at him, and again he took his eyes off the road for a second, and their eyes locked.

She nodded. 'Thanks, that'd be lovely.'

Jo and her two children alighted and waved goodbye to Jack and his two. Tim and Millie were exhausted but happy. What a day. They marched to their front door balancing two overflowing punnets of strawberries. Jo stood with them as their mother appeared and Jo gave a singsong greeting.

'We're ba-ck.'

'Just a minute,' barked the matriarch. 'They stay outside.'

The children placed their punnets and shoes on the porch and entered meekly.

'Say goodbye to Auntie Jo.' That was code for "we're not inviting you in for a meal or anything". Jo would've declined anyway. She had a better offer with the single Dad who has the kids every second weekend.

The kids gave their aunt a giant hug with lots of thanks. They departed.

'They'll sleep well,' said Jo.

'How was the weekend Dad? Try anything did he?'

Jo didn't know anything about the death of Jack's wife but chose to be a bit of a bitch. 'He's a widower; lost his wife to a terrible cancer. Bye.'

Jo turned and left, leaving her sister, for once, lost for words.

Using her GPS, Jo parked in the quiet Mont Albert street. The Carr residence was modestly magnificent with a glorious garden. Lights blazed both inside and out. She rang the doorbell and was surprised when a middle-aged woman opened the door.

'Oh,' said the detective, thinking she had the wrong house.

'You must be Jo. Come in.' She did. 'They've gone to get the pizzas. Can I take your jacket?' Jo handed it over. 'I'm Margaret, Jack's mother, but everyone calls me Peg.'

'Hello,' replied Jo admiring the furnishings, the décor and the smile from Grannie Carr.

'Come through. What can I get you to drink?' She stopped. 'Jack said you're a police officer. Do you have special rules or anything?'

'Not quite. Some of the world's best drinkers are cops but thanks, I'll settle for something soft, please.'

Jo heard a flapping sound and a lively labradoodle appeared.

'Hello,' said Jo. 'What's your name?'

'Rags,' said Peg who fussed. 'They weren't sure when they'd be home so I'm here to feed the dog and the cat. And you had a great day I believe?'

'We did, exhausting but the kids really enjoyed it.'

Jo accepted her drink as they heard a car arrive. Soon the kids raced in, greeted their grandmother then swooped on Jo.

'We've got three pizzas,' said Grace, 'so you're sure to like one of them.'

'Thank you, Grace, I'm sure I will.'

Harry was so excited to have a police officer in his own home. 'Have you got a real gun, Jo?'

'Harry,' reprimanded his sister. 'Dad said you weren't to be rude.'

Jack arrived with the grub. 'Who's being rude?'

'No one,' said Jo, 'just inquisitive.'

Peg removed warm plates from the oven. Jack placed the pizza boxes on the large kitchen table.

'Hand washing, please,' he said and his children departed.

'That should be me too,' said Jo.

'Through here, Jo,' said Peg, and showed her the downstairs cloakroom. When Jo returned, Peg was ready to leave. 'I'm off, Jo. It was lovely to meet you, and enjoy the pizzas.'

The kids called their goodbyes. Jo waved and smiled.

'Right,' said Jack. 'Take a seat, Detective Best, anywhere you like, and please, help yourself.'

She did and had a ball. She ate too much but still found room for the strawberries they picked, topped off with expensive ice cream. It beat the pants off a frozen TV dinner on your lonesome.

Jack took the kids off to bed. Jo did the washing up. The kids returned in their pyjamas to say goodnight. Jo put down the tea towel to shake hands. Grace, 7, was perfectly polite. Harry, 5, started the handshake then morphed that into a hug. Jo was touched. The kids ran off calling 'Goodnight'.

'Coffee?' asked Jack.

'Please.'

'Just flick that switch. I'll see the kids are okay. And thanks for doing the dishes.'

'It's the least I could do.'

He followed his kids, and Jo got the coffee started. It was ready when Jack returned.

'Come through.'

They sat in the lounge on a sofa Jo wanted to take home.

'Well,' said the doctor, 'it's funny the people you run into.'

'I think it's called serendipitous.'

'I'm not sure I can even spell that.'

The atmosphere was quiet with an undercurrent of uncertainty. Neither knew what the other was thinking.

'I think you've done a brilliant job with your kids, Jack. They're a real credit to you.'

'Thanks. And I couldn't have done it without my folks. Yours were delightful too.'

'Despite their appalling parents.'

He looked at her to be sure he understood. He did and they laughed.

He changed the subject. 'I see you've made an arrest with Candy.'

'We have although still no sign of the little girl.'

'I wish I could help.'

She left that hanging. 'I've spent some time with Donna and Gavin. They're not going so well.'

'Who would? It must be unbearable not knowing if she's still alive.'

Jo looked at him. 'What do you think?'

He paused then shook his head. He had no answer. They chatted about the case in broad terms then Jo made the move, and stood.

'Jack, I must be going. Thanks for a lovely day, and a superb meal.'

'My pleasure.' He followed her to the hallway, and helped with her jacket. He opened the door and walked out to her car.

He broke the silence. 'I pride myself on being a pretty good judge of character but I've learnt to rely on my kids.' Jo wasn't sure where this was going. 'Jack thinks you're wonderful but Grace is much more reserved. When I tucked her in she said, "Dad, I like Jo. She's a very nice lady".'

'Oh, that's sweet.'

He opened her car door. 'And for the record, I agree with my kids.'

She didn't know what to say so slid inside.

'Safe home,' he said, and closed her door. He stepped back and raised a hand as she drove away.

11

IT WAS AN EARLY START and Goddard rallied the troops. 'Right, summary. Leo's locked away but any half-decent lawyer should have him out sooner rather than later. Jake's home free and charged with nothing. Comments?' The troops were reluctant. 'Come on, you know the drill, there's no right or wrong answer. Talk to me.'

'We'll never get anything out of Leo,' said Gregory. 'Even if he took the kid and murdered her, he'll never confess. Apart from wanting to save his own neck, he hates all cops with a vengeance, and will never give us the satisfaction of discovering the truth.'

The DI looked around the room. 'C'mon, anyone else?'

'The weakness is Jake,' said Grimes. 'He may not have been there on that weekend but there's no way he didn't see or hear or feel something when he got back.'

'I agree,' added Bryant.

'Okay,' said Goddard. 'Assuming both those points are true, what next?'

'Work on Jake,' said Harcourt. 'Find a way to make him talk. And if you give me 5 minutes alone with him, he'll sing his head off.'

The others ignored the Neanderthal.

'Come on,' urged the boss, 'sensible suggestions please. How can we discover what Jake knows?'

'He needs a new housemate,' said Cathy Drew. 'Can we get an undercover cop in there?'

'What about Jake's family or friends back in Colac?' asked Jo. 'Maybe he said something to them.'

Goddard shrugged. 'Both possible, and certainly worth a try. Draw up a plan, both of you.'

'There's money there somewhere,' threw in Grimes. 'They hired Jonathan Limb, and if he's still involved, we'll never get Jake to talk.'

'Word is Jake's uncle's an estate agent,' said Gregory.

The team sensed Goddard's frustration. 'Doing nothing means we admit the child is dead. We have to be proactive. Ideas, people, come on. Assume the child is alive. Where is she? How can we discover that one vital piece of evidence?'

'What about asking some crims?' Gregory was serious. Murmurs from some but Gregory persevered. 'We offer money for information or shake down some crims who might have heard something.'

'Thanks, Colin,' said the DI. 'Draw up a plan to hit the underworld.'

'Ma'am.'

'My gut feeling is Jake's the key. I want a tail on him 24/7 for at least a week. Where does he go? Who does he see? Does anyone come to the house? Get authority for a phone tap. Hunt down his contacts. If he won't talk, his family or mates or enemies might. All of you show me a plan to get inside Jake's head. And I want a roster of who will watch Jake for the next week on my desk by noon—that's today. Connie, draw that up, please.'

'Ma'am.'

'Jo, you know the parents. Look again at anyone who might be involved in a conspiracy against either or both parents. Include everything we know, and try and find anything or anyone new.'

'Ma'am.'

'Right, everyone get cracking. I want that little girl found.' She whispered. 'Dead or alive.'

Jo's first shift was that night. She and Connie Bryant scored the jackpot, the graveyard shift. They sat in an unmarked car in Foley Street, Abbotsford and shivered. They had a view of Jake and Leo's house without being parked outside the front gate.

'What if he slips out the back?' asked Connie.

'You want to stand in that lane for eight hours?'

They chatted away discussing their careers, boyfriends, ex-boyfriends and fellow officers. There were times when they ran out of things to talk about and drifted into a sort of sleep. Jo was dozing when she copped a whack.

'Oi,' snapped Connie. 'Action on the waterfront.'

Jo was wide-awake. Someone came out of number 24 wearing a hooded jacket. It was dark and they couldn't ID the person.

'That's Jake,' said Jo. 'That's his body shape and gait.'

Cathy reached for the ignition. 'Wait,' said Jo.

'We've got to follow him.'

'He's on foot. I'll follow him on foot. Be ready to follow in the car. I'll call you if he's getting away.'

'Yes, ma'am,' said Connie not sure why Jo was giving the orders.

Jo set off on the other side of the road to the suspect. She made as little noise as possible. He reached the end of the road, turned left, and headed towards Smith Street.

Not public transport, thought Jo.

The person kept up a steady pace. Jo kept following but on the opposite of the road. The bright lights of Smith Street beckoned.

Once there he would be harder to follow. Night revellers occupied the footpaths and Jo would be well lit. If the suspect jumped in a cab or on a tram, she might lose him. She crossed the road to his side. Suddenly he stopped. Jo stepped into a shop doorway, paused, and then peered around the corner. She lost him.

Shit!

She hurried forward grabbing her phone. She hit Connie's number when loud cries grabbed her attention. She ran. In a car park outside a convenience store, two males were attacking her suspect. She ran harder yelling as she ran as well as shouting at Connie.

The attackers looked at the strange sounding woman racing towards them. They fled. Jo knelt beside the victim. It was Jake and he was terrified. Jo called an ambulance and did her best to pacify Jake.

Connie arrived as did the ambulance. The cops decided that one should go with the ambulance. Jo won the short straw. She sent a text to the DI thinking she might not see it till morning. In the ambulance, Jo's phone pinged and there was a text from Goddard.

Which hospital?

They went to St Vincent's and Jo escorted the gurney inside. She waited outside the curtained area where all emergencies are initially treated. Time ticked by. She didn't think he could escape. Connie arrived and two minutes later, the DI herself.

Jo related the story.

'And you didn't recognise the attackers?'

'No ma'am.'

'What was he doing?'

'Late night shopping I guess. He was outside a convenience store.'

'This could work to our advantage.' The senior constables looked at her. 'If we can convince Jake he's in danger, he may confide in us.'

'It might have been a simple mugging, ma'am,' said Jo.

'So what? We need to make him trust us.' She looked at Jo. 'Whose side are you on, Detective?'

Jo went to find coffee.

Half an hour later and the police were allowed in. The DI tried her "you're in serious danger and only the police can help" line. Jake didn't buy it.

'I want to go home,' he insisted, refusing to answer any questions. Goddard persisted. Jake retaliated. 'You can't do this,' said Jake and called, 'Nurse, nurse.' He sounded desperate and two nurses burst in. They thought he was in pain. 'These officers are harassing me.'

The nurses looked at the police. What could they say?

'Jake,' said the DI in one final attempt, at least let us give you a lift home.'

'No, go away. Leave me alone.'

The nurses stared at the police. They had no option and left, gathering outside.

'If it was a mugging, we've got nothing. If was intimidation from Leo's mates, we've still got nothing but at least a line of enquiry.'

'You want us to maintain the surveillance, ma'am?' asked Connie.

Goddard shook her head. 'Nah, call it a night. I don't think Jakey boy will be going out again tonight.'

Next morning, Cathy and Jo were late. They had little sleep. Goddard, who could function on very little sleep, had explained the Jake incident to the rest of the team.

'Speak of the devil,' said the boss as the two senior constables arrived. They apologised. Goddard continued.

'Despite being rebuffed by Jake, we may be onto something. If he's being targeted, we have his attackers to add to our list. And I reckon Jake can't handle pressure, so we offer him protection.'

A phone rang and Gregory answered it. Goddard kept talking but she stopped and everyone turned to Gregory when he said one word.

'Oh shit.'

Okay, he said two words, but the sentiment was the same. He looked stressed. Everyone stared, demanding an explanation.

'Incident at 24 Foley Street, ma'am.'

'What?'

'Homicide.'

This time it definitely was only one word and spoken by the DI.

'Fuck.'

Jo sat in the back with Bryant and Grimes. Gregory was driving with the DI beside him.

'We don't know if it's Jake, ma'am,' said Gregory.

'Oh, we have the cock-eyed optimist with us. Got your letter to Santa ready, have you Detective Sergeant?'

He didn't reply. Nobody replied. Goddard was doubly furious because she it was who stood down her surveillance team giving the murderer free reign. She couldn't let go of the thought that, had she kept the surveillance going, whoever was dead in that house might still be alive. The thought started eating into her.

'I don't want anyone speaking to Homicide except me. Is that clear?' Murmurs of assent. Happiness and joy were in short supply.

They parked and walked as a group. Police cars, police tape and police surrounded the property. Jo felt sick. She'd been banished, hopefully temporarily, from Homicide, and here she was walking into the middle of their investigation. She hung back.

Billy Hughes was talking to an officer from Forensic Services when she spotted the Major Crime team led by her pal, Trish Goddard.

The two women nodded.

'The bad news, Billy, if you please,' said Goddard.

'Single male, Jake Freeman, bashed and trashed.' Goddard groaned. 'Looks like revenge with *child killer* graffiti over the walls.'

'Great. He was our one genuine lead to find the girl.'

'I can't let you in, Trish. Steele's here and ...'

'Say no more.'

There was bad blood between the two DIs. They were both ambitious and saw each other as rivals only because they were. In addition, they hated each other's guts.

Suddenly a minor commotion erupted with a loud protestor trying to gain access to the house. Uniformed officers became security guards and blocked the way. Jo stifled a laugh.

'Oh get out of the way you silly boys, I'm the pathetic pathologist.'

She was indeed and Jo stepped forward. Dr Strange's face lit up like a Christmas tree on full power.

'She's okay,' said Jo. Then the fireworks kicked off.

'It's the deranged detective,' she exclaimed and embraced Jo.

'Good morning, Doctor.'

'Good morning, my arse. Where have you been darling girl? I heard they've sacked you again. I'll fix it. They'll listen to me.'

Jo understood about airing one's dirty linen in public. Gabrielle was the world's best friend with the world's loudest and biggest mouth.

Billy Hughes saved the day. 'This way, Doctor, your body awaits.'

The medico left but called to Jo. 'I want a word with you, Missy.'

Goddard stood behind Jo. 'Who don't you know, Detective?' Jo turned. 'The AC Crime, the police pathologist, and don't tell me you're first best friends with the Pope.' Jo looked at her. 'Okay, not him.'

Then the fan and the proverbial made contact as DI Grant Steele came out of the house. He saw DI Goddard, Satan, and beside her, Detective Senior Constable Best, Satanette. He made for them both.

'This is a homicide—my patch, my body, my case.'

'Understood,' replied Goddard. 'But we have the deceased involved in a major crime of abduction and possible homicide.'

'Well he can't tell you much now. And the obvious question is, Inspector, if he was so important a witness, why didn't you place him under surveillance?' Goddard couldn't decide between abject depression or assaulting a fellow officer. He pushed her towards the assault. 'If we need your input, we'll ask. Now my officers need the area cleared.' He indicated the rest of Abbotsford.

Goddard turned and led her team away. Jo froze when her former DI spoke.

'Senior Constable Best, a word.' He could have added "if you please" but didn't. Even more public humiliation for Jo who stepped forward.

'Sir?'

'You're no longer a part of Homicide. Steer well clear of this investigation. Understood?'

'Sir.'

'And a word of advice. DI Goddard has a reputation for hanging her officers out to dry.'

Just like you.

'Dismissed.'

'Sir.'

Jo headed off only to be stopped again.

'Mademoiselle, s'il vous plaît.' This time she didn't mind being stopped and observed by all and sundry.

'Good morning, sir,' she said to DI Richelieu who took her hand and kissed it. This too was embarrassing but for all the right reasons.

'We 'ave missed you, sorely, Mademoiselle. *I* 'ave missed you sorely. But why are you 'ere?' She explained about Jake and her case. 'But surely you should be involved in this 'omicide. You already know the victim.'

'No, sir. DI Steele has made it clear I am persona non grata.'

He mused. 'I think you should be, 'ow you say, kept in the picture, n'est-ce pas?'

Jo shrugged. 'It does make sense, sir.'

'I will keep you informed. Let me be, 'ow the British say, your pig.'

'My pig, sir?'

'Sorry, I mean snout.' They laughed. How could Jo refuse? 'Tonight I will explain all over dinner. Please be my guest and I will introduce you to some wonderful cuisine in preparation for your trip to Paris.'

Whoa, hold your horses, Monsieur.

'Text me your address. I will send a carriage for you at 1930 'ours.' He kissed her hand again. 'Au revoir.'

He turned and went back into the murder house. Jo was finding it hard to think straight.

From no social life, I've had pizza with a dashing doctor, and soon dinner with a delicious detective. What the hell is going on?

12

BACK AT MAJOR CRIME, things became hectic. Goddard fumed that Jake was murdered and fumed even more at being shut out of the murder investigation. She didn't know Jo Best had been offered inside info from a high-ranking member of the murder squad. But Goddard's anger vanished in an instant. A bombshell moment arrived. Goddard went from depressed to delighted.

'Listen people,' (she couldn't bring herself to say "Listen up"). We've just received footage of the playground on the day of the abduction.' Gregory fussed with the equipment. Questions fizzed.

'Who shot it?'

'Why has it only just surfaced?'

'What does it show?'

Goddard waved down their queries. 'Chinese grandparents, here to see their only grandchild, filmed the toddler then took off, literally, with camera and footage, and flew back to Beijing. Last week they sent a copy of the footage to their daughter here in Melbourne. It took her a week to put 2 and 2 together and she's only just contacted the police.'

'Ready, ma'am,' said Gregory.

She joined the team looking at the screen. The video rolled. The picture quality was excellent. They looked at the crime scene on abduction day. It was much better than CCTV. They recognised people who'd given a statement. It was exciting. The case was about to be solved before their eyes. Then Cathy Drew shouted.

'There she is.'

'Freeze it, Colin,' called the DI.

The picture froze.

'Bottom left,' said Cathy. 'Donna and Kate are talking while the child gets pinched.'

'Donna's not even looking at the kids, never mind her own,' said Harcourt.

'We need that body language bloke. Connie?'

'Yes, ma'am,' said Bryant heading for her phone.

'And as soon as. Okay, roll it.'

The film clip continued with every officer straining to see little Candy. They knew what she was wearing—how could they forget?—but saw no toddler who looked like her.

As the Chinese Australian grandchild moved to the swings, the camera panned across the playground. Then Grimes shouted.

'That's her!'

Gregory didn't need to be told to freeze the footage. Grimes moved to the screen, and pointed. The child in the bottom right corner of the screen was only partly visible and had her back to the camera.

Grimes was certain. 'That's the hat, that's the outfit, that's Candy.'

Others moved in and were convinced. Goddard became nervous.

'I don't think she's struggling. She looks like she's going willingly. She knows her abductor. Roll it.'

The footage rolled, and an audible groan erupted. Other children blocked their view. Candy and her accomplice disappeared. In filming, Grandpa followed his offspring and obviously not Candy. Of the person beside Candy, all the police could see was long blonde hair.

'That has to be a woman's hair,' said Bryant.

'Did any witness mention a woman with long blonde hair?' Heads shook and mutterings in the negative followed.

'Could be another child,' offered Gregory.

'No, that's Candy,' said Grimes.

The screen went black.

'That's it, ma'am, end of the tape,' said Gregory.

Disappointment surged. Goddard swore for everyone then ordered copies and stills of the times when Candy was in shot.

'Ma'am,' said Jo, 'the adult beside Candy might have been bending down.'

'Explain.'

'The person beside Candy was obscured by children but if the adult had been standing tall, we would have seen their upper body.'

Jo was right. Cathy Drew was an IT fan.

'What about that software where you can turn a picture around and get a view from the other side? I saw it on a show once.'

'Too much CSI, Cathy,' said her boss. 'But check with IT or Forensics.'

'Ma'am.'

Jo took on board Drew's suggestion about a reverse picture. If it existed, she knew an IT expert who would know about that software.

Goddard gave orders. 'Okay, priority now is to find the person with Candy. And we need the body-language expert to tell us about Donna and her girlfriend. Go.'

As the team at Major Crime discovered a new sense of energy to find Candy White, someone else set off on a mission. Darren Sandilands had nicked off from his work site in Malvern and driven to Camberwell, to the address of Elisabeth's sister, Ruth. He wanted a name and address.

He parked and walked on the opposite side of the road. He checked the house and made a plan. Once inside, he needed an easy escape route. His car faced away from Ruth and her husband's maisonette.

He chose a plan. He would knock on the door, flash a knife, get in, and get the name of the prick who created the *Cowards Abuse Women* web site and get out.

Suddenly he dumped that plan. Ruth came out of her front door pushing a pram containing her pride and joy, little Daniel.

'Brilliant,' murmured Darren. He looked around. No one was in the street. He crossed the road and walked behind Ruth on the nature strip. He kept as quiet as possible.

He passed her then stopped, turned and showed his knife. 'Scream bitch, and I'll cut you.'

She knew who he was. The voice, the description, the news about his exposure, and now these threats announced him as her sister's tormentor.

'Your fucking sister told me you know who made that web site. I want a name.' She hesitated. He moved closer to the pram. 'Tell me now or I'll cut your kid.'

Ruth was terrified. She couldn't scream or move.

'No,' she pleaded, 'don't touch my baby.'

'Then give me the name—now!'

'Jo, Jo Best,' blurted Ruth.

'Where's he live?' She hesitated because she struggled to remember the address. Darren flashed the knife and grabbed the pram.

Ruth spoke quickly. 'Flat 2, 24 Stanley Street.'

'Stanley Street where?'

'Clifton Hill.'

She found it hard to breathe. Her heart rate sprinted.

He snarled at her. 'Tell anyone, and especially Joe Best, and I'll come back and make you wish you never was born. D'ja hear me?'

'Yes,' sobbed Ruth. She dropped her head and tasted bile. When she looked up, Darren was gone. She turned and saw him climb into his wagon. She looked at her baby. He knew nothing of the terror his mother endured, and gurgled with happiness.

Jo went to see Goddard. 'I know someone, ma'am, who may know about manipulation of a video. He's an IT expert.'

'Is he the whiz who helps you run your scams?'

Jo froze.

Right. Does the whole world know about my criminal past?

'Don't answer that. Just get him to solve our problem. Go.'

Jo nodded. 'Ma'am,' she said and departed in haste.

She rang Michael, having abandoned his request for limited or at least secure communication. *If my new DI knows about him and our nefarious schemes, why bother with secrecy?*

He was home—he was always at home—and she drove to Northcote. He greeted her with a slither of suspicion.

'Do I assume because you are leaving phone records of our dealings that you have abandoned your life of crime and no longer fear being arrested?'

'Hello, Michael, it's lovely to see you.

He smiled that almost-a-smile grin. 'Just curious, that's all.'

'Michael, the last scam we ran had an Assistant Commissioner in on the plan. I think it's fair to assume that secrecy has left the station.'

'You're a showoff, Senior Constable.'

'And before I left to come here, my DI asked if you were the expert who helped me with my scams.'

'Our scams, surely?'

'The point being, sir, the whole damn world knows what I've done so trying to hide our relationship would seem a tad unnecessary.'

'Copy that. But something tells me you're not here for the coffee and cat chat.'

On cue, Alan sidled up to Jo expecting a treat. She had only an ear rub to spare.

'Sorry old chap, next time.' Jo handed Michael a USB stick. 'Would you care to look at this?'

Michael placed the device in one of his supersonic computers.

'Family snaps or gruesome murder?' he asked.

'It's the missing toddler. We've been given playground footage from the day she disappeared.' The footage appeared. 'She doesn't appear until the end and we can't see who she's with. One of the squad talked about looking at the footage from another angle.'

'You mean, standing on your head?'

'She told me she saw a movie where they reversed the POV.'

'So she likes science fiction, none of us is perfect.'

'So it can't be done?'

'Why don't you go and stand behind the monitor?'

That comment and his expression answered her question. Then the footage with Candy appeared.

'There she is,' pointed Jo.

Michael stopped the film and Jo explained the situation. He studied the footage. 'May I copy the clip?'

'Of course.' He did so and returned her stick. 'Michael, if you can help us find the abductor, you'll be feted by everyone at Major Crime.'

'But not Homicide?'

She went quiet. 'We're hoping Homicide won't be required.'

Again, his look spoke volumes. He headed to the kitchen to make coffee. They reminisced.

Michael was curious. 'Any word on our old friend, Ponzi?'

'Poor George, he'll not be troubling us for a while. His deal with the police flopped and that was his ticket to the slammer. Do not pass Go.'

'And your mother, how's she going?'

'She's landed on her feet—found a sugar daddy.' Michael laughed in a way Jo had not heard before. 'She's met some older bloke who has more money than sense and they're off on a world cruise next month.'

'Good luck to her.'

'And your folks, have they recovered?'

'They have and are now even more respected within the Chinese community having sent the Brothers Crimm to prison.'

Jo's phone pinged. 'Excuse me,' she said and read the text.

Mademoiselle, please send your address so the limousine can collect you for our dinner date. 1930 hours. Pierre.

He signed off with a heart emoji.

Michael looked at her puzzled expression. 'Bad news?'

'I don't know. A senior officer has invited me on a date.'

'Not my field of expertise, Detective. I'm with Sherlock on that one.' She looked puzzled so he quoted the great detective. 'Now, Watson, the fair sex is your department.'

'Interesting. So are you Dr Watson or Mr Holmes?'

'Drink your coffee.'

Jo thanked Michael and hoped his IT genius would help him find something new in the film clip. She drove home thinking only about her date. Several questions pinged inside her brain.

Does the gorgeous DI really fancy me?
Is he after info from Major Crime to help solve the murder?
Does anyone in Homicide know about this date?
What the hell will I wear?

She settled for her black leather pants. They were so tight she needed a coat hanger to put them on. It was either that or spray paint. Was she using them as a defence mechanism? She wore her favourite black pumps, a classy long white shirt and a gorgeous red scarf with a floral vine trim.

On the dot of 7.30 she heard a car horn. Knowing her street was usually quiet, she wandered out, and there was the DI leaning against his Alfa Romeo.

Okay, so he's handsome, charming and seriously loaded.

He was away from his vehicle in a flash and greeted his date. He kissed her hand—naturellement—opened the door and guided her into the vehicle. Her pants and the car seat were second cousins.

The meal was a raging success. People in the chic restaurant kept looking at the attractive couple never knowing their occupations.

Jo was continually wondering why she was here and with the DI? As the evening progressed, she stopped wondering and got on with enjoying herself while having the occasional thought.

How will this end?

She worried when Richelieu declined coffee but, as charming and as gracious as ever, allowed his partner to partake. She declined and immediately wondered if this was a tactic.

When they arrived at her abode, would she feel obliged to invite him in? She did and he accepted.

He parked and they walked to her apartment. It was more a flat but when you're trying to impress a senior officer who has the looks and wealth to die for, inflating your abode status just has to happen.

Jo's flat was usually clean and tidy, and tonight she'd made it sparkle in case what might happen happened.

She made the coffee and joined him on the sofa. She thought about Gabrielle Strange and Billy Hughes. What would they suggest I do?

Bugger them, I'm here and they're not.

Richelieu chatted about work. 'I would be delighted to share any intelligence about the Foley Street murder, Jo. Please contact me if you 'ave any questions about the case.'

'And you would like me to return the favour?'

He shrugged. 'You scratch my back, Mademoiselle, and I will very gently scratch yours.'

Jo thought she could see the sexual tension.

'I 'ave enjoyed our little rendezvous, Mon'Amie. Perhaps we could do it again sometime?'

Are you kidding? How about tomorrow?

'That would be lovely, Pierre.'

She still couldn't get used to calling him by his first name. She called him Sir a couple of times and still found it easy to do so.

They chatted away until, without warning, the French Australian stood and prepared to depart. 'I must depart, Jo. I 'ave a meeting with the top brass first thing in the morning.'

'Well if it's an interview for promotion, I would love to give you a reference.'

She smiled to reinforce her offer, and the sexual tension began doing star jumps. He smiled then walked to the door. She leant past him to open it and their bodies brushed with the softest of touches.

Before she could speak or move, he bent and kissed her mouth without force. It was over in a second, okay two. Jo's pulse burst into song. He smiled and spoke with a velvet lining. 'Au revoir, Mon'Amie.'

Peggy Lee started to sing. "Is that all there is?"

Jo watched him disappear past the hedge then closed her door and sighed. It was a sigh you could enter in *The Guinness Book of Records*.

She tried to find the strength to wash the coffee cups.

Outside, Richelieu thought the same thoughts as Jo. He wasn't concentrating as he approached his car and didn't see a man who stepped from the shadows.

'Oi, Joe Best.'

Richelieu turned as a wrench, the type used by a plumber, headed for his head. The detective instinctively jerked to one side but still copped a glancing blow. He fell but twisted onto his back looking up at his attacker. Darren Sandilands breathed fire.

'You made a web site to make me look like a prick—now you pay.'

He raised the wrench to smash it into the kneecap of the man on the ground.

Richelieu spread his legs as the wrench smashed into the road. The Inspector drove his shoe into Darren's groin. The thug bent in pain and as Darren hesitated, Richelieu scrambled to his feet. Big brave Darren realised his opponent was no pushover. He swung his wrench and, to avoid the blow, Richelieu stepped back. The weight of his swipe pushed Darren off balance. It was a good time to scarper.

Darren spat. 'This is not over, Joe Best. You are dead meat.'

In true coward's form, Darren turned and fled. From his vehicle, he saw Joe Best go back to the apartment. Darren waited. He would follow this prick.

Richelieu, his quality shirt and jacket stained with his blood, needed help and staggered towards the flat, no, apartment of the real Jo Best.

Her doorbell rang. Her heart couldn't make up its mind.

Oh God, he's gone all randy and wants to make love on the first date after all. Confusion reigned. How could she politely repel his advances? Did she want to?

Taking a deep breath, she opened the door and her date fell into her arms. It should have been the other way around but he was bleeding.

'Sir,' she gasped easily slipping into the recognition of rank. She helped him inside and guided him towards the sofa. He held a white, now red and white handkerchief to the side of his head.

'The bathroom,' he commanded and she changed direction.

What a gentleman. He's thinking of my carpet and furniture.

'I'll call an ambulance,' she said handing him a towel.

He sat on a stool. 'No, please, I am okay.'

'No you're not. What happened?'

'I was attacked by a madman who is extremely short-sighted.'

Jo looked puzzled.

'He thought I was Jo Best.'

She instantly knew the attacker. 'What did he say?'

'Something about a web site making 'im look like a prick.'

'Oh Pierre, it's all my fault. He thought Jo stood for Joseph when he wanted Joanna.' She looked at him. 'I'll take you to hospital.'

'No, please, I don't wish to make a fuss.'

Why does he want to avoid an ambulance and hospital?

'It is, 'ow you say, a glancing blow.'

Jo tried another line. 'Will you see a private doctor?'

'Is he discreet?' Now she was seriously curious about his behaviour.

'No, and he's a she, and the most indiscreet person I know.'

He twigged. 'Not Doctor Strange?'

'It's either her or the hospital.'

He took a deep breath. 'Okay. Merci, and I am so sorry to put you through all this.'

'Come on, we're going.'

'Okay, you win, Jo, but we must take my car.'

She gasped. 'You want me to drive your car?'

91

'Please.'

She knew why. If blood was to be spilt, it would not be in the lady's vehicle. Darren would never think like that. He waited and watched.

She helped him into the street and his car. There was a lot of physical contact, which neither had envisaged. It wasn't romantic. They set off, and en route she called Gabrielle who was wide awake.

'Good evening, Doctor. It's the deranged detective speaking. I have a friend who needs some medical attention.'

'Call an ambulance.'

'We'll be at your surgery in five minutes.'

'How dare you,' she flared. Then in a spooky voice she said, 'I hope it's an amputation.'

The line went dead and Richelieu looked at his driver who grinned.

'She's the best, sir.'

'I don't need an autopsy.' He looked at her and they laughed—a bit tricky in the circumstances.

'I think you bring me bad luck, Mademoiselle. With you, I am shot in Port Melbourne and now bashed in Clifton Hill.'

'I bring you good luck,' she replied. 'Both times you survived.'

When Gabrielle Strange saw the patient, the look on her face was priceless. He looked a mess and she immediately had him seated, then worked on his wound. She cleaned and bandaged it with no stitches required.

'You'll live,' she said. 'But this'll teach you to take liberties with this fine young detective, who, I might add is looking decidedly ravishing.' Silence. 'What? So now I am to be denied the gossip I so desperately crave.'

Jo tried to explain. 'Monsieur Richelieu was attacked by a man who thought he was Joe Best.'

Strange looked strange. 'I'm sorry I asked.'

'My attacker thought I was Joseph Best, not Joanna Best.'

'I'm still sorry I asked.'

She packed up her equipment. 'Now I prescribe a brandy, Detective Inspector, perhaps two.' She left the room.

He called after her. 'Ah, no thank you, Madame. I 'ave partaken of some wine tonight and cannot drive with any more alcohol.' He whispered. 'You 'ave to 'elp me, Joanna, please.'

The next moment, Gabrielle entered with a tray on which were glasses and a bottle of brandy.

'Not a problem, Monsieur. You can kip here tonight with me.'

While Gabrielle fussed with the brandies, Jo looked at Richelieu. His eyes screamed for mercy, his lips mouthed, 'elp'.

Dr Strange toasted her colleagues and was into her first brandy before the others had raised their glasses.

'Dr Strange,' said Jo. 'I have Pierre's car outside. I can drive him home.'

'Oh, Pierre is it,' said Strange in an exaggerated camp way. 'Back to his place is it?'

Richelieu interrupted. 'Please, Madame, this is unnecessary. Joanna and I, we are just good friends.'

'Oh God, how original.' She mocked him. 'We are just good friends.' She snorted and finished her brandy. 'All right then, bugger off. The pair of you.'

Jo and Richelieu made their way out of the house. Strange called.

'And don't forget to tuck him in. And I said "tuck" him in.'

Jo drove her colleague home. She wasn't sure what might happen. Should she stay and see he was all right? Should she stay in his bed? She didn't observe the car which followed them.

Richelieu lived in an apartment in East Melbourne that set Jo's mind spinning. It was worth millions. How could a cop afford a place like this? She drove into his secure carpark.

'Now I will not offer you a brandy, Mademoiselle. But I will order you a cab and place you inside myself.'

And so ended the night of romance and repairs. As Jo went home by cab, she thought about the gorgeous Frenchman, his car, his apartment and his intentions. She thought about her latest fling with crime, the phony web site, and the man who was looking for Joe Best. That man sat in his car in East Melbourne having observed the event.

13

THE POPE WANTED RESULTS. This latest homicide in Abbotsford had him hopping mad. The victim was part of the Major Crime investigation into the abducted child. No way was DI Goddard getting the chance to solve this murder. It belonged to Homicide.

Richelieu had called in sick. This was unusual. He rarely missed work, and Steele laid down the law.

'DS Hughes is acting OIC and I want all reports to go through her.'

'What's wrong with the DI, sir?' asked Baldwin.

'I was told he slipped in the shower and whacked his head.'

That produced a few murmurs. The team missed the man with the French accent and his sentences ending in s'il vous plaît.

'Right, Sergeant,' said Steele, 'get on with it.'

Billy Hughes stood in front of the display board and pointed.

'The victim, Jake Freeman, 24, shared a house with Leo Smythe, who is currently inside charged with parole violations and wasting police time as a suspect in the abduction of a little girl in Richmond last month.'

'So Leo's got an alibi,' said DS Fleming.

'Getting Leo to talk looks hopeless as he won't talk to Major Crime.'

Baldwin had a suggestion. 'Will he talk to us if we offer him help with the abduction?'

Hughes was frustrated. 'He hasn't been charged with abduction.'

Steele was furious. 'Forget the bloody abduction. We'll be given it anyway as Major Crime has got bugger all.'

Everyone could see Steele was in his protect-my-empire mood. He didn't want anyone encroaching on his patch. Hughes continued.

'Leo couldn't have done it so who did? Was he worried his housemate would grass him up or do a deal and, if so, did he order the hit? There's plenty of motive to silence Jake.'

'That's assuming he had something to say,' added Baldwin.

Hughes nodded. 'With the paedo graffiti inside, you'd reckon an irate parent, friend of the family or vigilante killed Jake believing he abducted the child.'

'How would they know where Jake lived?' asked Baldwin.

'Or who he was?' added Hughes. 'He was never charged.'

Nobody spoke. Senior Constable Stephen Payne joined the fray.

'What did the PM say?'

Hughes picked up Dr Strange's report. 'Definite signs of torture with cause of death manual strangulation.' She looked at them. 'What does that suggest?'

'This wasn't a hit,' said Fleming. 'When someone is strangled with bare hands, whoever did it, had it in for the victim. Skin to skin makes it personal.'

Baldwin asked about DNA.

'We're still waiting to hear from Forensics. Apparently the place got a serious workout when Major Crime made the initial arrests.'

Steele fumed. 'So what's the plan, Sergeant?' It was more of a demand.

'I think we need to liaise with Major Crime, sir.' Steele bit his tongue. 'They knew the victim and his mate. They'll have interview records which might point us to the murderer.'

Steele knew this was logical and appropriate. His desire to solve the case clouded his judgement. Then when Baldwin made a suggestion, everyone thought Steele would have a stroke.

'The ideal person to work with, sir, would be Jo Best. She knows our methods and knew the victim.'

Steele decided that to say anything or to rule out the suggestion would make him look churlish even stupid. He knew Jo had an admirer in Assistant Commissioner Crowley.

'You decide, Sergeant,' he said to Hughes and left.

Murmurs bubbled.

'All right, settle down,' said Billy. 'Justin, you and Stephen have a chat to Dr Strange and get a detailed explanation of her PM.' Payne groaned. He hated the pathologist. 'And then have Forensics detail all they discovered at the house after the arrests by Major Crime.'

Yes boss,' said Fleming in a mock deferential way.

'Charlie, we're off to see your erstwhile friend, Ms Joanna Best.'

'Can hardly wait.' She looked at him. He became respectful. 'Sarge.'

Hughes and Baldwin arrived at Major Crime. Trish was expecting them and greeted her pal. She shook hands with Baldwin. There was a tap on the open door and the ex-Homicide detective appeared. Jo greeted her former colleagues.

'I'm acting OIC,' said Billy, 'because DI Richelieu is off sick.'

'Nothing serious I hope,' said Goddard.

'Whacked his head in the shower is the latest.'

Jo sat there with lips sealed, permanently. There was no way she would say anything about her date being assaulted outside her flat, and then being treated in private by the forensic pathologist. Charlie Baldwin winked at her.

Jo worried. *He can't know, surely not.*

'We have to work together on this,' said Goddard. 'I know DI Steele wants to leave murders to Homicide but the abduction and Jake's death are possibly linked. It's crazy not to share evidence.'

'Agreed,' replied Billy. 'The DI wants that to happen.'

'Really?' Trish was surprised. Jo was more than surprised.

Billy began. 'So we have a PM report suggesting Jake was tortured before being manually strangled.'

'Ouch,' winced Goddard.

'This suggests the killer hated, even loathed the victim. Now, did Jake know about or was he involved in the abduction? If so, was he killed by Leo's mates to keep him quiet or, as an act of revenge by the parents, their friends, or some "keep the streets safe" vigilante?'

The discussion went back and forth with only Goddard and Hughes speaking. They both stopped when Jo spoke.

'Is it possible the killing and abduction are not related?'

Silence. All three officers had experience with Jo Best before. All three knew she had good ideas, often great ideas, and what she said needed careful consideration.

'Go on,' urged Goddard.

'We only found Leo because of a clerical error. Because we had nothing else in the way of suspects, and as Leo's on the sex register, and lives near the park, we assumed he was a real possibility.'

'He is,' said Goddard.

'But if Leo had nothing to do with the abduction, then Jake's killer has got it all wrong. Maybe Leo and Jake had nothing to do with Candy's capture.'

'And your point is?' queried Hughes.

'Is it possible that Jake is not a paedophile, and Leo had nothing to do with the abduction?'

'Of course it's possible,' added Goddard.

'Then if true, we won't find the missing child by charging Leo with abduction or conspiracy to murder his housemate.'

More silence and Hughes looked at the unspoken Baldwin.

'Charlie? What do you reckon?'

Baldwin worried because he knew he wasn't as smart as Jo and didn't want to advertise the fact.

'I agree with Jo. Leo's the obvious abduction suspect but perhaps too obvious.'

Billy kept at him. 'And Jake? Who murdered him and why?'

'Well if Jo's right, the murder of Jake is to throw us off the real abductor and make Leo the suspect who killed Jake and the child.'

'And if that's true we're nowhere,' said Hughes.

The two senior officers blew air. Goddard walked to a window. She spoke with her back to the others.

'I'll come clean. The AC reckons the abduction investigation has stalled, taken too long and he reckons the missing child is likely dead. I've got until the end of the week to find the child or the case moves to Homicide.'

Goddard turned and looked at the others. What could they say?

The Homicide duo left, and Jo and Goddard felt flat. Jo wanted to know the truth.

'Is what you said about handing the case to Homicide true, ma'am?'

'You think I made it up, Detective?'

'Of course not, ma'am.'

'I was told by your friend the Assistant Commissioner himself.' Silence. 'Perhaps you could have a word with him and get him to give us more time.' A strong whiff of sarcasm hung in the air.

More silence. Goddard was angry. Jo didn't know if her anger was directed at the failure to find Candy, Homicide taking over the case or Jo being friendly with the Assistant Commissioner. Or all three.

Gregory popped his head in to tell them Professor Marcus Priest, the psychologist and expert in body language was waiting in the Incident Room.

With the team around him, he watched the video taken in the park on the day of the abduction. The subjects studied were Donna, Kate, Candy and the person in the blonde wig.

'The mother and her friend appear normal and natural. I can't see their eyes and facial expressions up close but their body movements, and hands show no stress.'

Goddard was keen to glean anything. 'Can you tell if the woman, Kate, is genuine and not part of any proposed abduction?'

'She doesn't appear worried or distracted, if that's what you mean.'

The team caught the DI's frustration. This break of finding the video was so far yielding little.

'What about the child?'

'Again it's difficult as she has her back to the camera and we can't see her whole body but she doesn't seem to be under any stress.'

'Not being forced or taken against her will?'

Professor Priest shook his head. 'On the contrary, she appears relaxed and happy to be going where she's going.'

This time the disappointment from the team was audible.

'And the person in the blonde wig?' asked Goddard.

'Because we can see so little, it's almost impossible to say. If you have stills as well as a copy of this footage, I'll show it to some colleagues and see if they can suggest something.'

What a letdown. Another hope dashed. They thanked the psychologist, he took copies of the footage and left.

Goddard faced her team. 'I have news.' This sounded ominous. 'I know I'm new. I know you've been working all hours to find this little girl. However, the top brass has made a decision. Either we find Candy White this week or the case goes to Homicide.'

A powerful string of objections exploded. These officers had given blood, sweat and tears to find the missing child. They'd taken the job home, worried non-stop, and even dreamt about it. No team could have worked harder—perhaps a tad smarter—or with such dedication as had this group. Now they were facing the sack. When the complaints and anger subsided, Goddard spoke.

'I want us to give this thing the smartest effort yet for the days remaining. There are six people I want re-interviewed—Gavin and Donna, Gavin's son and Gavin's stepfather, and Kylie and Lawrence.'

Gregory was confused. 'Is Leo no longer a suspect?'

'He is but we can't get at him. Homicide reckons one of his mates murdered Jake to stop him rolling over. I say let Homicide do their best with Leo, while we attack everyone else.'

Connie Bryant felt angry. 'Who says Homicide will do any better than us?'

'We're ruled by results, Connie. They make the world go round. Right then, the only people relatively new to this investigation are Jo and me. Ben, you partner Jo, and Colin, you're with me. Two teams and six interviewees. I'll take the parents and the stepfather. Ben and Jo, you've got Gavin's son Alex, plus Kylie and Lawrence.'

'And what about us, ma'am?' Cathy Drew spoke for herself, Bryant and Harcourt.

Goddard had them checking and collating. They weren't happy but understood the need for their roles.

'This is D-Day, folks,' said Goddard. 'Find something, anything, or we're all working elsewhere next week. Not sure about you, but I don't want to fail.'

Nobody spoke. They were still shocked about facing the sack, being told to ignore the main suspect Leo, and returning to old interviews.

The four interviewers planned their attacks. Goddard's rule of "never announce your arrival" was in vogue. They would start tonight.

Ben Grimes and Jo arrived at Alex's home. He lived with his mother, Peta, Gavin's first wife. She answered the door.

'We'd like a word with Alex, please,' said Grimes in his softest burr.

Peta was meek but even she protested. 'What for? You interviewed him weeks ago. He knows nothing about his stepsister.'

Alex called. 'Who is it, Mum?'

'The police.'

Alex came to the door.

Grimes introduced Jo and asked for a chat. Alex agreed, much to his mother's annoyance. All four sat inside and Grimes began.

'We're talking again to everyone connected to Candy, Alex. We know you're not directly involved but sometimes people tell us things which help point us in a new direction. Okay?' Alex nodded. 'So can you tell us some more about your relationship with your Dad?'

'Why?'

'Please, the sooner we can have this chat, the sooner we can leave you alone.'

'She's dead, isn't she?' This came from Peta.

Ben looked at Gavin's ex-wife and grimaced.

Alex spoke. 'I hate him. He was a shithouse father, he cheated on me Mum, and he gave her nothing to live on after he left. I hope he gets cancer and dies.'

'Alex,' protested his mother.

'It's true. He treated us like dirt and still does.'

Grimes paused. 'What do you think happened to Candy?'

'No idea. But it wouldn't surprise me if he was involved. That's the sort of thing the bastard would do. You know he hit me Mum?'

Peta's despair took off and the police were shocked at the venom pouring from young Alex's mouth. Grimes looked at Jo. She gave a short shake of her head.

Grimes asked a few more general questions before they left. Driving to interview Kylie, Ben asked Jo for her thoughts.

'That's one mixed up young man but I can't see him wanting to hurt his stepsister,' she said.

'Agreed. But what about his mother? Could that have been her in the blonde wig? Remember both are giving the other an alibi.'

'Sorry, Sarge, but while they both have motive aplenty to hurt Gavin, doing so by kidnapping an innocent toddler doesn't fly with me. Abduction? Hardly. Murder? No way.'

Grimes agreed without saying so. 'Now, let me tell you about Kylie.' He did and Jo was shocked. Gavin abandoned Peta and young Alex, took up with Kylie then, when that ended, hooked up with Donna and fathered Candy with Donna.'

'Interesting.'

'Interesting? Give me the feminine POV, Detective. You've got a boyfriend, and your girlfriend, your bestie, seduces him. He leaves you for your girlfriend so what would you think of her?'

'Is that what happened?'

'Depends who you believe.'

'Well if I wanted to dump my boyfriend, I'd be quietly delighted.'

Grimes sneaked a look at Jo. 'Are you winding me up?'

Jo smiled. 'No, Sarge, but you're thinking only of the obvious.'

'Which is?'

'Kylie would hate Donna and never speak to her again.'

'Exactly. So how come they're still bosom buddies?'

Jo thought about it. 'Maybe my first theory's correct.'

That silenced Grimes. He reckoned Kylie should hate Donna.

They arrived, again unannounced, at Kylie's ground floor flat. It reminded Jo of her own abode in Clifton Hill.

'Hello, Kylie, remember me, DS Grimes? And this is Detective Senior Constable Jo Best.' Kylie looked nervous. 'May we come in?'

'Okay,' she said opening the door.

They sat in her modest living room and Grimes gave her the usual spiel about doing another check on things. She answered calmly and repeated all she'd said before at previous interviews. Grimes did as before and gave a nod to Jo. So far, Kylie had been polite if nervous but when Jo spoke, wow, the storm clouds arrived.

'How is your mother? Brenda isn't it?'

Kylie exploded. 'You leave her alone. She's not well.'

Jo remained calm and turned on the sympathy. 'I'm sorry to hear that. Nothing serious I hope?'

'The doctor said she needed complete rest. She's gone to Grandma's farm in the country.'

'That's nice.' Jo pointed to a photo on the wall 'Are they your grandparents?'

Kylie looked and went defensive. 'You leave them alone.'

'It's just that I've spent a lot of time in Ballarat and that looks ...'

'They don't live in Ballarat. And I'm telling you, they're not to be disturbed.'

'Of course, I understand.' She paused. 'Kylie, we've been told that Gavin has been violent in the past.'

'Who told you that?'

Jo grimaced. 'Different people.'

'Well he was never violent to me, never.'

'Was he ever violent to Donna?'

'This is ridiculous. You can't find Candy so you start blaming people because you've failed.'

'I agree,' said Jo with what sounded like sincerity.

That flattened Kylie's anger and surprised Grimes.

'What do you mean?' asked a quieter Kylie.

'You're right. We've looked really hard but found nothing, and now we're going back over old interviews trying to find a new clue.'

Jo paused. She remembered how Billy Hughes used silence to ramp up pressure. Kylie wanted to break the silence.

'What about the men you arrested?'

'What about them?'

'Did they take Candy?'

'Possibly. What have you heard?'

She was back to being angry. 'I don't know. How would I know?'

Jo half smiled. This interview was going nowhere.

'Thanks Kylie. And I hope your Mum is feeling better.'

Jo's sincerity took the anger out the visit, and the police left. Driving to their third interview, Grimes repeated his request.

'So, what did you learn, Detective?'

'I would have liked to search her flat.'

'Oh?'

'And I reckon that body language professor would have had a field day with encoding.'

'Encoding?'

'It's the study of someone's body language. You discover their hidden emotions from non-verbal signs like hand movements, posture, eye contact, etc. Alas I only know the basics.'

'You've studied body language?'

'The dangerous way.'

Grimes took a peek at his partner. 'Dangerous?'

'I used Dr Google.'

He smiled then told Jo about Lawrence. 'Our lucky last customer is Lawrence Blair, a former neighbour of the Whites, who had an affair with Donna and when it ended he moved.'

'How long did it last?'

'He says six months, she says six weeks.'

'Interesting. So why is he a suspect?'

'He reckons he loved Donna—still does. He wanted her to leave Gavin and run away with him.'

'And Candy?'

'Most definitely. He reckons he loves Candy as much as Donna.'

'You keep using the present tense.'

'Because *he* does. That's his story, and here's his current address.'

They pulled up outside a new build, a new house on the site of a demolished one, the way today's graceful suburbs are re-invented.

Lawrence opened the door. He knew Grimes and met Jo. They sat in his sitting room with its polished boards.

Grimes went through the preliminaries then tipped Jo the wink.

'I've forgotten, Lawrence but when is Candy's birthday?'

'July 19. She'll be five.'

'And what did you give Candy for her last birthday?'

Her question came with a ticking time bomb. Grimes still wasn't used to her tactics and he'd been in the game for donkey's years.

Lawrence let it all hang out. 'She loves playing pretend games so I got her a toy kitchen.'

Jo ran with his enthusiasm, his unrequited love. 'I bet she loved it.'

His eyes seemed to sparkle and his voice brimmed with pride.

'She did. She set it up herself and could do everything. She even made me my favourite breakfast.'

'Which is?'

'Full English. I taught her the ingredients including mushrooms. She knows it all.'

Jo was thinking. *He certainly is a present tense man.*

The officers sat and observed. Jo fed Lawrence more leading questions and off he went. He sounded like Candy's proud father.

During Jo's quizzing, Grimes thought he could try profiling and encoding. He failed—totally. Jo had seen and heard enough. They left and Grimes drove her home.

'Your thoughts, Senior?' he asked.

'If he abducted Candy, it wasn't to punish Donna but to show her how much he cared.'

'Or to persuade her to leave Gavin and start again with him,' said Grimes.

'Well if that's true, why hasn't Lawrence been in touch with Donna?' Grimes didn't answer. 'Is he the one with no alibi?'

'He's the one. But being so tall, we would have spotted him in that park footage if he'd been there.'

'He could've been the getaway driver.'

'But I don't think he's the leader of the pack, he's more the playful puppy. If Lawrence is involved, he's the gopher.'

Jo was driven home, thanked her colleague, went inside and checked her phone. She had it on silent because of the interviews and didn't want distractions.

There were three text messages. Three male persons all wanted her mind and/or body. Michael Chan, Jack Carr and Pierre Richelieu had joined the admirers of Joanna Best club.

'Right,' she said, 'who's first?'

14

IT WAS JUST AFTER 9 pm when she contacted the first on her list.

'Good evening, Turing's master, this is Turing's best friend.'

Michael smiled and it showed in his voice. 'I hope you appreciate, Ms Best, that I actually sent you a text via your public number.'

'I did, Mr Chan, and I'm delighted. Do you have some news? Sorry, I apologise. I know you always have news. Please tell me about it.'

He smiled gain. 'I've blown up the wig image and had a mate who runs a wig business take a look.'

'You have a friend who's a wigmaker?'

'We went to Melbourne High. I chose IT, he chose wigs and he makes in a month what I make in a year.'

'I'm shocked. Michael Chan has a mercenary bone in his body.'

He ignored that. 'And his response is you can buy that wig in any respectable $2 shop.'

'What?'

'It's an el cheapo made from synthetic garbage. Does that help?'

'Sure, I'm looking for a child abductor with little money or no taste.'

'Or who's clever knowing that wig is sold in shops all over town and will be almost impossible to trace.'

'I still reckon you should join the police, Michael.'

'But you need me here to set up your criminal enterprises.'

This time it was she who laughed and out loud.

'As ever, thanks heaps, Michael. I've got to go but I'll call you soon.'

'Turing misses you. Bye.'

He ended the call. She wondered if, for Turing, read Michael.

Next text off the rank was that smiling GP, Dr Jack Carr. His text was simple.

Hi Jo, I know you're busy but please call when you're free. No rush.
Jack.

Now that's intriguing, thought Jo. *Has he got some info on Candy and her parents? Is he getting personal?* She saw it was 2112 but hey, he called me.

'Jack Carr.'

'Good evening, Doctor.'

'Hello Detective Senior Constable Best. Thanks for returning my call, and how are you?'

'That's a long opening statement, Doctor. Should I be reading you your rights?'

He laughed and Jo felt a warm glow at the sound of his voice and infectious laugh.

'Look Jo, this might be nothing but about little Candy being missing —no news I suppose?'

'Sadly no.

'I've remembered the second last time I saw Candy. She and Donna had their consultation. I'd left a letter in my car and when I was in the carpark, Donna and Candy were just leaving. I waved to them and then a few seconds later, a car started and drove out of the carpark at a scary speed.'

'Did you see the driver?'

'No, sorry.'

'What can you remember about the car?'

'Not much. Light-coloured sedan is the best I can do, I'm afraid. It's probably nothing.'

'No, no it's definitely worth noting. Every little bit counts. And thanks for taking the trouble.'

'If I remember anything else, I'll let you know.

'Thank you, kindly. And how are those lovely kids of yours?'

'They're well. Still talking about a certain policewoman but that's all your fault.'

She laughed. 'Say hi to them.'

'I will. Goodnight.'

'Goodnight,' said Jo. She pondered. *Where is this heading?* 'Two down, Joanna, one to go.' She rang DI Richelieu.

'Bonsoir, Mademoiselle, 'ow are you?'

'I'm fine. But more to the point, how are you?'

'Fantastiquie now I 'ave 'eard your dulcet tones.'

Wow. I've got three wealthy, handsome and single males coo-cooing in my earhole. Well via a smart phone.

'DI Goddard and I went to Homicide today for a joint approach to the abduction and murder.'

'So I 'eard.'

'You heard?'

'Oui, I 'ear everything.'

'Your name was mentioned with your absence being down to a slip in the shower.'

'Well I could 'ardly say I was beaten up outside Senior Constable's Best's abode, and was then repaired by the very Strange pathologist.'

'You're not ashamed of me, I hope, sir?'

'Ashamed? Au contraire, Mon'Amie, I am extremely proud. And to prove it, 'ow about we meet for a light supper to exchange information, s'il vous plaît?'

'Now, sir?'

'Of course, why not? The night is young. Do you know *Il Duca* in East Melbourne?'

'I do.'

'It is my local.'

'I thought you were French.'

'I can be whatever you desire, Mon'Amie. Shall we say in twenty minutes?'

'Ah, okay, maybe twenty-five.'

He spoke in a broad Italian accent. 'Ciao baby.'

Richelieu lived close to the restaurant. He checked his appearance—his war wound was healing—and set off to walk along Powlett Street. He didn't see two men sitting in a parked car. Darren nudged Jordan who was dozing.

'What?'

'There he is, that's Joe Best. He's walking, no fancy fucking car.'

They hopped out of Jordan's Ford Falcon and quietly closed the doors. Both were carrying.

'Shit.' Jo rushed around trying to look presentable, wondering if this was a wise move. Could sharing information help find the missing child? Would it increase her chances of returning to Homicide? Did she want an intimate relationship with a senior officer, an older man? It worked for her father. Did she fancy a holiday in Paris?

She found a park in East Melbourne and walked to the restaurant. A smiling waiter opened the door, and she spied the smiling Pierre Richelieu.

He performed the standard charming Frenchman role and kissed her hand. 'Bonsoir, Mademoiselle.' The waiter attended to her chair. The other diners observed her arrival and had a private, some were less private, ogle at the dashing couple wondering who they were. They would never have guessed.

Richelieu ordered coffee and cake then got down to business speaking intimately which Jo found strangely exciting. She wasn't sure if she was a frustrated spy or the whole thing was sexually arousing. Perhaps it was both. He whispered.

'I can tell you, that DI Steele believes 'e knows who killed your suspect Jake Freemen.'

Jo was shocked. 'He knows or thinks he knows?'

Richelieu shrugged. 'You know the Inspector. 'e does not like to be wrong, and wants to outsmart your new boss.'

'Tell me about it. But how strong is your case?'

'I 'ave not been there to know for sure but I think pretty strong.'

'I don't like this.'

'You know something?'

'No, but I think the abduction and murder are linked.'

'And you 'ave evidence?'

Jo shook her head. She wanted to share her thoughts with someone but wondered if Richelieu, as charming as he was, would report back to Steele.

Richelieu the spy? Surely not.

She changed the subject and talked about his injury from last night.

The coffee and cake arrived. Jo could get used to this—superb food and a somewhat superb dinner guest. Between enjoying her slice of *Cassata alla Siciliana*, Jo revealed her big news.

'The big brass decided we have until the end of the week to find the abducted girl or the case is handed to Homicide.'

'So I 'eard.' He wasn't bragging just stating a fact.

She looked miffed. 'Pierre, what is the point of sharing information if you know everything I know?'

He shrugged. 'Not everything. For instance, I do not know if you like the cake.'

She relaxed. 'I do, it's delicious.'

'And I do not know if you 'ave thought about an 'oliday in Paree.'

She stopped eating. He didn't but looked into her eyes and that alone, plus the coffee, made her feel relaxed and tense at the same time. Spooky.

'Pierre,' she began. She stopped when he put a finger to his lips.

'I do 'ave some more news, which is not related to either case, but I will perhaps tell you on our next rendezvous.

Jo wanted to say, "What the hell does that mean"? but didn't. More chat ensued about Goddard versus Steele before they left and wandered back towards Jo's car.

'Can I offer you a nightcap, Detective?' he purred. 'Do you remember my apartment is in the next block?'

She was sorely tempted. 'Only if you tell me something I don't already know.'

'Ah, the clever detective. You drive an 'ard bargain, Mademoiselle.'

They wandered towards his apartment. Across the road, the thugs crouched behind a parked car.

'That's the bird he met last night,' growled Darren.

'What?' Jordan was the blunt knife in the drawer.

'He came out of her flat in Clifton Hill. That other bitch gave me the wrong address. He lives here and she's his bitch.'

'Do we fix 'em both?'

'We wait. I wanna get the bastard alone.'

Jordan reckoned Darren was only brave when he couldn't lose but would never say that mainly because he, Jordan, was cut from the same cloth.

They stayed out of sight on the opposite side of the road. This was easy because Powlett Street was wide with cars parked on both sides and had a plantation down its middle. From a distance, they followed the police officers, Joe Best and Jo Best.

The cops reached Pierre's "hideaway", his sumptuous apartment, one of several in a former church. He ushered Jo inside. If he was trying to impress his colleague or date (Jo wasn't sure which), he succeeded.

'Welcome to my pied-à-terre, Mademoiselle.'

Pied-à-terre? There was nothing small about this gaff.

'Please take a seat, s'il vous plaît.

She sat, or rather luxuriated in an armchair made by an artisan, and wondered why this man with his obvious wealth was a plodding police officer. Well, perhaps not plodding. He mixed a cocktail.

To Jo he appeared Mr Perfect. He had everything—wealth, looks, charm, impeccable manners—and the ability to make a delicious cocktail. What's not to like?

But do I want to sleep with him? Of course I do. But will it be a smart move? Come in, jury—give me your verdict.

'Now DI Richelieu, I believe we have an arrangement, n'est-ce pas?'

He nodded. 'Ah, the woman who is the negotiator.' She paused. He promised news and she wanted to hear it. 'This is crazy but DI Steele 'as put pressure on Forensics to 'ave all results sent only to 'im.'

'Crazy is right. We could and should be helping one another.'

'DI Steele figures 'omicide takes preference and besides, 'e will be running the abduction case from next week.'

'And?'

'The blood splatter in the bathroom is from an animal—a bull I think. And it was washed or scrubbed with bleach.'

Jo almost spluttered. 'Is that it? Pierre, we knew that ages ago. Your information is ancient history.'

He looked crestfallen. 'Ancient 'istory?'

'The supper was superb, your apartment is stunning but if we are to help one another, you're going to have to lift your game, Monsieur.'

He understood. 'I should 'ave known a brilliant detective would always be ahead of the game. I promise to do better next time.' He raised his glass and toasted his guest. 'Merci, Mademoiselle. You are too kind.'

She found it difficult to be angry with such a gentle and kind man. They sat and sipped, he on the sofa and she on her armchair. If he was applying pressure, it was definitely subtle. He looked at her and patted the empty space beside him. She endured turmoil. One part of her wanted to skip, even run to the sofa and into his arms. Another part featured a red warning light flashing and ringing. The red light won— this time.

She placed her glass on the side table and stood.

'Merci Monsieur, but I really must be going.'

Being a gentleman, he didn't push the matter. He wanted to but knew if he forced the situation, there was a good chance it would end badly for both of them.

'Of course,' he said and escorted her out of the apartment. 'Where is your 'orseless carriage, Mademoiselle?'

She laughed. His language was fascinating anyway but when he included an alternative expression for her car, it tickled her funny bone. He tickled some other parts of her anatomy as well.

They wandered along Powlett Street to Jo's horseless carriage. Richelieu offered his arm and Jo didn't hesitate to oblige. The touch of his arm felt strong and inviting. They were lost in one another's thoughts and didn't notice the two yobs crouching behind a car.

'There he is,' whispered Darren.

'About fuckin' time. I'm freezin',' complained Jordan.

'We wait till Best is alone. He's gotta come back this way.'

'Well I hope it's bloody soon.'

'Shut up,' growled Darren. He planned to enjoy this.

Richelieu and Jo reached her car. She hit the remote and went to open the door but his hand landed on hers. They were close, touching close. She looked at him. He took his hand off hers and placed it under her chin. He didn't need strength to tilt her head upwards. They both wanted something to happen and it did.

Their kiss was gentle but active. She turned to face him and their bodies connected. Their hands and arms joined the party. Just as the pash in the passion got interesting, a car turned the corner and headlights lit the couple. Richelieu didn't care. But the powerful headlights from an upmarket European car illuminated the lovers and Jo withdrew. She preferred her romantic activity away from the public gaze. They looked at one another with neither willing to speak.

Jo leant in and kissed him quickly and softly, and whispered, 'Merci, mon cher,' opened her door and slipped in. She had the engine running in record time. He blew her a kiss as she drove away.

It started to rain. Richelieu cursed and started trotting. He turned into Powlett Street and the rain increased.

He swore softly and broke into a run. He was about fifty metres from Hotham and home when he saw two maniacs racing across the road aiming, he realised, to cut him off at the pass.

Not again, thought Richelieu. This time there were two. Should he try and outrun them or stand and fight? There was no time for think music.

Then Buster Keaton joined the movie as first Jordan tripped on the curb of the centre plantation and dived face first into the grass moments before Darren, who slipped and found his arse on the grass. Richelieu took the outrun option and flew home.

The hapless hoodlums limped back to their chariot.

'Forget the prick,' said Darren. 'We'll get Joe Best through his chick.'

'What's her name,' asked Jordan checking his jaw.

'No idea but I know where the bitch lives. We'll give the bastard a real thrill when he finds out we've both had his babe.'

Jordan liked that idea.

15

JAKE FREEMAN'S FUNERAL was like many funerals today. Mourners under 50 wore clothes better suited to the beach or a barbecue. Floral tributes were garish and the coffin the same.

Goddard, Gregory and Best stood well away from the masses. The cops were the best dressed there. Jo nudged her boss.

'Nine o'clock, ma'am,' she said.

Goddard and Gregory shifted only their eyes and saw Steele, Hughes and Payne from Homicide. If anything, their clobber was even better than that worn by the Major Crime trio. Had Richelieu been present, Homicide haute couture would have won by a mile.

'Bastards,' said Goddard. 'They know the abduction will become a homicide next week. They're here to rub it in.'

'Are we going inside, ma'am?' asked Gregory.

'Too bloody right we are. We'll make them stand.'

She took off and her colleagues followed. Steele observed and smiled. He would have the last laugh. He had ordered all forensic material to come directly to him and only him. Murder took priority and besides, next week Homicide would have both cases, the murder of Jake and the abduction, assumed homicide of Candy.

What Steele didn't know was that Richelieu, currently on sick leave, had been wooing Steele's hated foe, one Detective Senior Constable Jo Best, and feeding her titbits from her former boss and squad. Oops. God help everyone if Steele ever twigged.

Goddard and co sat at the back and observed. If they were hoping Candy's abductor would appear and give him or herself away, they were sadly disappointed. Nothing at the funeral suggested Jake was involved with the missing child, and none of the mourners made any impression on the detectives. The Homicide crew was in the same boat. Goddard and her colleagues left, returned to base and reviewed the situation.

Jo said nothing about her deal with Richelieu. Here, she was playing with fire. She could recover from a broken heart but there was no cure for a broken career. She worried about remaining silent.

'Right,' said Goddard, 'reports on interviews. Sergeant Grimes.'

As Ben began, Jo's phone pinged. She moved to the back of the room and read the text.

She froze. She wanted to scream but settled for interrupting Grimes. 'Sorry to interrupt, Sarge but something's just come up.'

The team turned and looked at Jo. 'What's happened?' asked Goddard as Jo moved to her holding out the phone. The DI was so shocked she said nothing. The team stared in wonder. 'Read it,' said Goddard. Jo did.

> *Detective Best*
> *The hair sample found in the Foley Street address*
> *is a match for the missing girl. Please tell your boss*
> *DI Steele and feel free to call me if you require*
> *more details.*
> *Kind regards*
> *Alastair Dean*

It was hard to comprehend. Silence dominated before the torrent of comments and questions exploded with officers speaking over the top of one another with 'What hair sample?' being the popular refrain.

Goddard called for order and put Jo under the spotlight. She explained who Alastair was and how he'd given her a heads up before. Jo had not told him she left Homicide.

It took some time for people to settle.

'How do you want to play this, ma'am?' asked Gregory.

'I wish I knew. Why did Forensics not find the hair after we arrested Leo and Jake?'

'And how do we charge a dead guy with abduction?' asked Grimes.

'We should tell DI Steele, ma'am,' added Gregory.

Goddard pondered. 'Jo, call this guy now. Find out everything. Who found it, when, where and why was it missed before? Go.'

Jo walked out of the room and called the lovely Alastair.

Goddard seemed unsure and Grimes said what he thought. 'This helps Homicide more than it helps us. If Jake had a role in Candy's abduction, we're cactus.'

'I still think we should tell Homicide, ma'am,' added Gregory.

'Yes, all right, as soon as we hear from Jo. But until then we carry on. Ben, let's hear your interview reports.'

Grimes paused. The silence was loud. He began and spoke on behalf of Jo. 'Gavin's son, Alex, hates his old man with a vengeance but getting back at his dad by kidnapping his little step-sister just doesn't fly. Kylie is unusual. Her best mate, Donna, pinches her boyfriend, Gavin, and yet the two women remain best friends.'

'Meaning?' asked Goddard.

'Dunno, ma'am. I only can only speak as a mere male, but if my mate had a go at my missus, he wouldn't be me mate for long.'

Goddard wanted more. 'And?'

'Kylie has an alibi and she's Donna's friend.'

'Okay, who else?'

'Lawrence, a former neighbor and former lover of Donna while she was married to Gavin.'

'And?'

'No alibi but he's more of a lovesick puppy. He thought he found true love whereas all Donna found was a willing stud. Lawrence couldn't organize a piss-up in a brewery, let alone a successful child abduction.'

Goddard's mood grew darker. 'Thanks, Ben. Oh, what happened about that reverse angle of the video?'

'That was Jo, ma'am.'

'And?'

Cathy Drew took over. 'I got that wrong, ma'am. Jo said her IT expert referred her to Jules Verne.'

'Who?'

'It's science fiction, ma'am.'

'Great. Right, push on. Colin, our interviews please.'

Gregory spoke about the interviews with the parents, and with Gavin's stepfather, Gordon.

'The lecherous stepfather has no interest in children, and if either Donna or Gavin are involved, their acting as concerned parents is brilliant.'

Goddard agreed and continued.

'So, come Monday and failing some bloody miracle, we lose the case to Homicide.' Jo came back into the room. Everyone turned to her. 'Unless Detective Joanna Best has some stunning news.'

Jo explained. 'Forensics searched the house after Jake's murder. There was a plastic bag of laundry and they found the hair on a jumper in that bag.'

'So it wasn't there when we arrested them,' said Goddard.

'Jake said he took stuff home to Colac and his Mum did his washing,' added Grimes.

Cathy Bryant knew the timeline. 'We know Jake went to Colac the day before the abduction and didn't return until two days after Candy disappeared.'

'So how did the hair get in Jake's laundry?' asked Cathy Drew. 'Was she taken to Colac?'

'Or did Jake travel somewhere wearing that jumper and help in the murder of the kiddie?' asked Grimes.

Silence. The news raised more questions and what made the mood even darker was that Jake would never be able to help them.

'There's another possibility, ma'am,' said Jo. 'Jake had nothing to do with the abduction and someone planted that hair in his laundry.'

Goddard ran with that thought. 'Just like Leo put the animal's blood and bleach in the bathroom.'

'Well Leo didn't plant the hair,' said Gregory, 'because he was inside.' He paused. 'I'm sorry to repeat myself, ma'am, but I reckon we have to report the hair discovery to Homicide.'

Goddard nodded. 'Agreed. I'll notify DI Steele. But if the blood and the hair were planted, what does that tell us?'

'Criminals are dumb,' said the voice of experience, Ben Grimes.

'What else?' asked Goddard.

Jo replied. 'It adds weight to someone other than the residents coming into the house.'

'And if so that rules out Leo and Jake,' added Gregory.

Goddard summed up what the others were thinking. 'So if the fake blood and Candy's hair were planted, that means Candy White was never in that house.'

Silence took over. Their one strong lead, Leo Smythe, convicted paedophile, and on remand for bail offences and wasting police time, was probably innocent of child abduction. And the other possible suspect or at least someone who may have been able to convict Leo, Jake Freeman, got himself buried today.

This is the way the world ends, not with a banged-up villain, but with a whimper.

The word *failure* loomed large. The team fell silent until Jo spoke. 'Ma'am, I only spoke to the uniforms from Richmond who backed up our raid at Foley Street. I never spoke to the ones who attended the homicide. Should I do that?'

'Might as well,' said Goddard. 'Anyone else?'

More silence. Then Gregory made a speech. It was farewell time.

'I reckon you've done a brilliant job, ma'am in very difficult circumstances and in such a short time.' Others agreed.

'Thanks, Colin but an honourable defeat doesn't solve the case. As far as the parents are concerned, we failed. Even finding the body would be preferable to nothing.'

Sadness descended.

Grimes had a question. 'Do you reckon Leo and Jake were ever involved, ma'am?'

She pondered the situation. 'I don't know what to think. But let's keep working and we'll start the wake on Monday.'

Things were far different in the Homicide Squad incident room. Billy Hughes was talking about a possible suspect for the murder of Jake Freeman. She pointed to a photo.

'This is George Little. He's a convicted paedophile and served time with Leo Smythe.' She pointed to Leo's pic. 'Major Crime has charged Leo with parole violations and wasting police time. Apparently he put animal blood in his bathroom intending to frustrate the investigation of the missing child, Candy White.' She pointed to Candy's photo. 'Still no sign of the little girl and rumour has it, we take over the investigation as a murder from next week.'

'It's not a rumour,' said the Pope without raising his voice. 'And I've just heard that a hair from the abducted child was found in the Foley Street house on clothing owned by the victim, Jake Freemen.'

A buzz of chatter began.

'Should we pass that on to Major Crime, sir?' asked Hughes.

'They told me.'

Before Billy could continue, someone knocked on the open door.

'Excusez-moi,' said DI Richelieu entering with an XXL size smile.

Team members greeted him. 'Good to see you back, sir,' said DS Hughes. 'How are you?'

'I think the Aussie saying is, 'as fit as a Mallee bull.'

That provoked laughter and the meeting lost its purpose.

'Okay, party's over. Let's solve this murder.' Steele spoke, the man who once moonlighted as a wet blanket.

Richelieu sat amongst the team and Billy continued.

'Leo and George have recently been in contact. George went to visit Leo in remand and we have texts between the two. Leo was worried about his housemate, Jake Freeman. Did Leo think Jake might talk to us about the child abduction slash murder?'

'Pardon, Detective Sergeant,' interrupted Richelieu, 'but what 'as 'appened to this Jake Freeman?' He knew but pretended otherwise.

''We're just back from his funeral,' said Billy.

'Ah, I miss all the good things.'

Muted laughter began. 'Now,' continued Billy, 'Forensics tells us George Little's DNA is in the house where Jake was murdered, and when we had a chat with George, he said nothing. He has no alibi.'

Richelieu continued to play the ignorant detective role. 'So is this Monsieur Little a suspect in the child abduction case?'

'More likely in the murder of Jake Freeman and we have a raid this afternoon. Are you up for it, sir?'

Richelieu looked offended. 'Are the French great lovers?'

More laughter and stirring from the troops, which stopped abruptly when Steele announced, 'With a briefing in one hour.'

He departed and thus ended the meeting.

Meanwhile Jo Best took herself to the Richmond Police Station in Church Street, and arrived just before the change of shift. She was escorted inside where the sergeant introduced her and invited Jo to speak to the troops.

'Thanks Sarge. I'm working in Major Crime on a couple of cases, which may be related. One is the child abduction last month next door in Citizens' Park, and last week there was a homicide in Abbotsford. If anyone was on duty with the homicide, I'd like to have a brief chat, please.' She looked at the sergeant.

The sergeant commanded. 'Okay anyone involved, grab your notebook and brain cells, and walk this way.'

Jo chatted with a few constables. None had anything new or significant to say. She met the last officer and had difficulty pronouncing her name. The constable saw Jo struggling.

'Hi. I'm, Marcelina Sokolowski.'

'Jo Best. Thanks for the pronunciation help. Is it Polish?'

'Well done, spot on.'

'I bet you get a few funny guesses.'

'Mainly from colleagues. "Sock a lot to me" is the current favourite.'

Jo smiled. 'Okay, Marcelina, how were you involved?'

'I went to Foley Street when the homicide was discovered.'

'And what were your duties?'

'Nothing specific. I remember you and your colleagues arriving then leaving. We were asked to keep the rubber necks away.'

'Did you enter the house?'

'No.'

'Have you discussed the homicide with anyone?'

Jo noticed a fleeting hesitation. 'Only my colleagues.'

'And nothing else you can tell me about your time at the property?'

She shook her head. Jo smiled and held out her hand. They shook. 'Thanks for your help.'

Sokolowski went to leave then stopped. 'Have you found the little girl?' Jo shook her head 'Have you got the bastard who took her?

Jo hesitated. 'Not yet, but thanks for your help.'

The constable with the Polish name went to work.

At about the same time, a team of officers prepared to arrest George Little. They had surveyed his rented house in Kensington, and now a number of armed officers were about to make an arrest.

George was a resistance fighter adept at guerrilla warfare with form for not co-operating with police. The Homicide officers hoped he would pop out en route to the local shop but alas no such luck. The police knocked on the front door with a trusty enforcer. The door obliged and officers burst in with their shouting routine in good voice.

George had just finished emptying his bowels. Hearing the raid, he fled hitching up clothing as he ran. He opened the back door where stood three detectives waiting to shout "Surprise". He stormed through them. He was having none of their, "please come quietly, my son," request. He headed for the gate in the back fence.

Half the contents of a mace container zapped the brute. It might as well have been silly string. It barely slowed him. Batons cracked his shins. George's roar was far louder. The officers in the lane released a surge of adrenalin. What the hell is happening in there?

George was happening. He threw open the gate and launched into the night-cart lane. Short of a bazooka, nothing could slow, let alone stop the Little giant.

He kept moving with officers bouncing off him. This was crazy. How could he get past these fit and determined officers? George kept swinging until suddenly he struggled. Fleeing his toilet, George had failed to secure his duds. His trousers fell to his ankles and trying to run caused Mr Little to topple over and roar like a caged beast. In a few seconds, he was wearing bracelets. They weren't his colour.

So George Little was arrested and taken by low-loader—no, not true, he had a paddy wagon all to himself—and ended up at Homicide.

Steele and Hughes got stuck in. The DI hoped that he could crack the homicide and, as a bonus, solve the mystery of the little lady who vanished. As the interview progressed, Steele was certain of George's guilt, with Hughes less so. The facts were telling.

There were damning phone texts with Leo about Jake. George's DNA was in the Foley Street home, and the big lummox didn't have (or wouldn't provide) an alibi for the night of Jake's murder.

'Come on, George,' said Steele. 'Do yourself a favour. Tell us what happened to Jake and the little girl, and make life a lot easier.'

George sneered and adopted the angry-arrested-person technique of saying nowt.

16

JO WAS HOME WHEN HER PHONE RANG. She knew the caller.

'Good evening Doctor Carr.'

'Good evening Detective Senior Constable Best. Wow, that's a mouthful. Couldn't I just call you Officer Best or perhaps the best officer?'

She laughed. 'You could but never in public.'

'How are you? Busy as ever?'

'Yes and no. It looks like the Candy investigation will be taken over by Homicide.'

'Oh,' he sounded sombre. 'Does that mean what I think it means?'

'Not necessarily but we've had no joy and those officers with all the extra bits on their uniform like to see progress.'

'I see. Well good luck with whatever happens.'

'Thanks.'

She paused. He'd rung her and she wondered why.

'Look Jo, I want to ask a favour but seriously, I want you to say no if … well for any reason at all.'

'This sounds serious.'

'It's not. It's just that you've made a real hit with my two little monsters, and they've signed a petition requesting the "nice police lady" to please come and watch them compete in their Little Aths meet tomorrow. Now please, Jo, say no if …'

'I'd love to come.'

That took the wind out of Dr Carr's sails. Then delight filled them.

'Really?'

'Of course. As long as I don't have to compete.'

'That's fantastic. The kids'll be over the moon.'

'But not their father?'

'Oh he'll be doing cartwheels.'

Jo laughed. 'Now that I'd like to see.'

'You're welcome to come back here for lunch. My folks'll be here and we have a Saturday barbie.'

'Thanks, it sounds great. So where and when?'

He told her and she hung up thinking about the call and the situation. *What's going on here? He obviously likes me and I like that.*

Her daydreaming stopped abruptly when her phone rang.

'Hi Mum, how are you?'

'I could be dead for all you know. Why haven't you been to see me? Why haven't you even called?'

'I didn't want to interrupt your love life.'

'Don't be cheeky.'

Shirley sounded annoyed but was secretly glowing.

'So how is Methuselah? I hope you're not making him over-excited.'

'Antony's fine and when are you coming to meet him. You know your sister's been here.'

I bet her husband wasn't there.

'I'm really happy for you, Mum.'

'What did Caitlyn say about Antony?'

The sisters had never spoken about Mum's new boyfriend.

'She said he was very nice.'

'Liar.'

'Look Mum, I'm out your way tomorrow. I could drop in if you're not too busy with your young man.'

'What time?'

'Ah, that's tricky. I'll call you tomorrow.'

'So what's the news on the boyfriend front?'

'Oh, I'm beating them off with a stick.'

'Really? What's his name?'

'*His* name? You mean *their* names?'

'What?' Shirley wanted to know.

'Well there's Pierre the Frenchman who wants to take me to Paris, Jack the widowed doctor with the kids who adore me, Michael the IT whiz who is too shy to kiss me, and finally Alastair the forensic scientist who gets heart palpitations every time we meet.'

'You've learnt your lying skills from your father, Joanna. Call me tomorrow.'

'Yes Mum.'

Mum didn't hear the last two words as she'd already hung up. Having a night in didn't work for Jo as her phone kept ringing. She saw the caller ID and raised her eyebrows. It was Billy Hughes.

'Sarge? I'm not on call and I'm definitely not with Homicide.'

Billy Hughes enjoyed a joke but tonight she wore her serious hat.

'Can you talk?'

'Do you mean is anyone listening, am I in the middle of my TV dinner, or currently copulating?'

There was no response to Jo's attempted jokes. 'I'm worried, Jo. Where is Major Crime on the child abduction?'

'Shouldn't you be speaking to DI Goddard, Sarge?'

'No, I want the truth. Goddard and Steele hate one another and neither will back down or face the truth. Now please answer the question.'

'We're nowhere. One of our suspects got murdered but you know that. The other suspect will probably be released any day. We've been told the case goes to Homicide on Monday and next week, it's all yours, Sarge. But come on, you must know that.'

'And you've charged Leo Smythe with some minor parole violation?'

'We have.'

'And?'

'And I don't think he had anything to do with the abduction.'

'Steele has one of Leo's mates for the murder of Jake Freeman.'

'And you're not sure either?'

'I'm never sure with Steele. And I can't talk to anyone.'

'Anyone?'

'The others never stand up to Steele.'

'DI Richelieu stands up to him.'

'I know but right now he's useless. I think he's in love.'

Jo hesitated then acted shocked. 'What?'

'Someone said he's fallen for a bimbo.'

Jo wanted to laugh but kept up the shock. 'You're kidding?'

'Listen, if you hear anything, please call me immediately.'

'About the bimbo?'

'No, you idiot, about the abduction and murder. Throw in the missing child, and it's now looking like two murders, so we can't have Steele make another cock-up like he did with the double murder in Elsternwick. God I wish you were back at Homicide.'

'Me too,' replied Jo but in a softer voice.

'I'll let you go. But remember, Jo. Hear anything, you call me. Ciao.'

She hung up. Jo spoke aloud in a mock incredulous way. 'He's fallen for some bimbo?'

Then she had a horrible thought. *What if it's true? What if I'm the back-up bird, the lover in reserve? What if I'm his fallback position?*

She smiled then sat at her miniscule kitchen table and started a sort of brainstorming mind map activity, listing anything that popped into her head. She drew rings around words, and linked the ones she thought should be linked.

Relevance didn't apply. If a thought popped into her head, it got listed. Scribble, scribble, scribble. Then, with the page full of words, rings and lines, she sat back and looked at her handiwork. Only one thought jumped out, and that thought kept nagging away in her head.

Saturday morning arrived and she kick-started her day. Jo went running, then showered, shopped and shoe shined. Soon it was time to head out for a social event, a Little Aths meet featuring the offspring of a certain Dr Jack Carr. Just as she grabbed the keys, her phone rang. This time it was a certain Frenchman, the one with whom she recently performed some energetic osculation.

She smiled. *I really am on the boyfriend bandwagon.*

She made an executive decision and sent the call to message bank. *Wow. Did I just snub the wealthy Parisian?*

Driving to Kew, she kept thinking about the phone call from Billy Hughes. If Goddard and Steele both had the wrong suspect in the frame, that meant the real culprit or culprits were still out there and able to abduct or murder again.

She found the playing fields and wandered towards the mass of people engaged in the Little Aths meet. It was hard to recognise anyone. She joined a group of onlookers. Kids ran, jumped, strained, and gained and parents cheered.

A woman beside Jo asked a genuine question. 'Which one's yours?'

'Ah, none. I'm just a friend.'

The woman pointed. 'That's mine. He thinks he's the ant's pants.'

Jo smiled. 'So do the parents help with running the show?'

'They do all of it. Parents, grandparents, everyone. It's great for the kids and good for the adults too.'

'I can see that.'

'I'm a single mum and there are a few blokes I've got my eye on.'

'Oh?' Jo had not considered Little Aths as a pick-up joint.

The woman indicated the long jump area. 'See the guy measuring the jumps.' Jo looked and spotted Dr Jack Carr. 'He's known as the delicious doctor, a widower, and he's available.' She spoke intimately. 'Between you and me, I think he fancies me.'

'Right.' *So much for the athletics.*

Before Jo could say another word, her name was called. She turned to see two young children sprinting towards her. It was a race to see who could hug their favourite copper first. The judges declared it a dead heat so a joint hug it was.

'Look, Jo, said Harry, 'I got two certrifficates.'

'They're certificates,' corrected big sister Grace.

'Well done,' said Jo.

'And I've got a ribbon,' announced Grace.

'That's wonderful, congratulations. Have I missed your events?'

'Yes,' replied Harry without a trace of malice.

'That's okay,' added Grace. 'You can watch us next time.'

'Hello, hello, hello,' said a certain medico making his way towards them. The single mum beside Jo thought all her Christmases had come at once, although her excitement stopped as if shot when Jack walked past her and gave Jo a kiss on the cheek.

'How lovely to see you, officer. As you can see, these athletes are pretty excited you're here.'

'Dad?' asked Harry, busting to ask a question. His father looked at him and the boy knew it was time to wait.

Jack smiled. 'Okay, ask away.'

'Jo, would it be all right if I called you Detective Jo?'

She laughed and Jack and the children loved her response.

'Of course, but you'll have to salute as well.'

Harry thought that sounded terrific without knowing what it involved.

Jo bent and whispered. 'I'll teach you later.' Harry beamed.

Someone called to Jack. 'Gotta go,' he said and pointed. 'Mum's in the canteen. Catch you later. C'mon kids.'

They all departed leaving Jo alone. The single mum gave her a look which was a mix of "You bitch" and "You lucky bitch". Jo headed to the canteen. Peg was busy serving when she spotted Jo.

'Hello Jo. How are you?'

'Fine thanks. I see they've got you working hard.'

She served another customer. 'All for a good cause.' She pointed. 'See that snowy haired old bloke over there sitting at the table.' Jo looked. 'That's my husband, Hugh. He'll be tickled pink to meet you. Would you mind?'

'I'd love to. I'll see you later.'

She approached the gentleman writing results in a large book. She stopped when close and he looked up and smiled.

'Hello. You must be Jo.'

She was surprised. 'How did you know?'

He stood. 'I was told a beautiful woman would appear, and here she is.' He offered his hand. 'I'm Hugh and delighted to meet you Detective Senior Constable Best.'

'Hello, sir, and Jo's fine.'

'My grandchildren have been regaling me with tales about the strawberry picking police officer and here she is.'

A tribe of little athletes arrived.

'But you'll have to excuse me, Jo. No rest for the wicked.' He sat and started writing.

'I'll leave you to it.'

He called as she departed. 'See you at lunch.'

Jo waved and wandered off to watch the races.

Once the meet finished, packing up began in earnest and Jo was attacked by the two Carr siblings.

'Can I come in your car, Jo?' politely asked Grace.

'Me too,' asked Harry with loads of enthusiasm.

'We'll see. Let's ask your Dad. Where is he?'

'We're having sausages,' said Harry, keen to tempt the visitor with his favourite luncheon treat.

'I love snags, and bangers and mash are my favourite,' teased Jo.

'Snags?' Harry was confused.

'What's bangers and mash?' asked Grace.

'Sausages are sometimes called snags or bangers, and mash is mashed potato.'

The kids were tickled pink. Their father arrived.

'Dad,' announced Harry, 'can we please have some mangers and bash?' unwittingly saluting the Reverend Spooner.

Jack and Jo laughed and the children laughed at the laughing adults.

'Are you teaching my children working class English, officer?'

More smiles and laughter as Peg and Hugh arrived.

'Gran,' said Grace, 'do you know what bangers and mash are?'

The grandparents laughed, momentarily exercising their wrinkles.

'My favourite,' said Hugh, licking his lips.

'They're Jo's favourites too, Pa.'

'Then she's got excellent taste,' said the senior.

'Right, homeski you lot. C'mon,' said Jack heading towards the car

Grace grabbed her father's arm. 'Dad, please can we go in Jo's car, please?'

'Please Dad,' added a begging Harry.

'It hasn't got a siren,' said Jo.

Harry thought about that for moment. 'I don't mind,' he said.

Jack looked at Jo who shrugged. 'Do you mind?' he asked.

'Of course not.'

'Okay but make sure you behave.'

'Me or the kids?'

More laughter and the kids were floating on air as they tagged along with Jo. Jack and his parents stood and watched.

'Well?' asked Peg, looking at her husband.

'I think she needs a more mature man.'

His wife slapped him playfully, his son laughed and they headed off to their car.

127

The barbecue was a big success with the highlight being Jo teaching young Harry how to salute. He spent the rest of the day practicing his routine. Even his grandmother had to return his salutes.

Jo apologised and announced her need to depart.

Peg and Hugh kissed her and the whole thing was natural and sincere. The kids gave her a hug and Harry finished with his best salute ever. Jack walked her out to her car with Harry and Grace waving from the front window. Harry continued saluting.

At her car, Jo wanted to make a quick getaway. She wasn't sure why. It might have been because the last man who escorted her like so, took her in his arms and gave her senses a charge of something that felt, well, slightly better than fantastic.

'Thanks for a wonderful day, Jack' she said then worried as he looked serious.

'Jo, I need to tell you something.'

Oh God, he's dying or has another wife or ...

'I'll be blunt. Let me finish and I'll tell what I think at the end.' Jo was hooked, worried and fascinated. 'It's my in-laws.' *His in-laws? And that's a worry?* 'We've never got on. It's a long story and boring. Anyway, the kids told them about you. The in-laws got your name and rank and made some enquiries. My father-in-law knows a number of high-ranking police officers.' Jo was a mixture of fascination and fear. 'Apparently the in-laws reckon you have a charge or something against you re police procedure and they don't want their grandchildren involved with such a person. Now, whatever the situation, I think you're a fabulous girl, a gorgeous, beautiful and clever woman, and funny, and I love the fact that we've met. My kids adore you, and my folks think you're terrific. So as far as my in-laws go, I won't have a bar of them trying to stop you seeing me and my family—but of course only if you want to.'

He stopped. He reckoned he'd said enough, probably too much. Jo wondered what to say.

'They're right, your in-laws.' Jack looked worried. 'I was kicked out of Homicide because I challenged my superiors. I got involved in some criminal activity—it involved scamming a criminal who had stolen my Mum's life savings. I was re-instated when I solved a homicide my colleagues got wrong. Now I've been shunted off to Major Crime trying to find who abducted one of your patients.' She stopped and looked at him. 'And that's about it.'

He paused then smiled. 'Sounds fascinating. It'd make a great movie.'

She smiled and paused. Neither knew what to do. Both wanted to kiss the other. They were about to do just that when a child's voice rang out from afar.

'Detective Jo.' They turned and saw Harry standing on the wall of a garden bed giving the biggest salute he could muster.

Jo and Jack laughed and she took the opportunity to slip into her car. She dropped her window.

'It was a great day,' she said. 'I had a ball.'

She started the engine. He stood back and smiled.

He laughed heartily when she called. 'And give my love to your in-laws.'

17

JO RANG HER MOTHER and told her she was nearby. Jo received an order to attend forthwith. She had spoken to her mother many times since Shirley's life savings were recovered but had never met her new boyfriend. Being filthy rich, he wasn't after Shirley's money. That appeared obvious as a silver late model Merc sat cooling its tyres in the Balwyn North driveway.

Shirley opened the door smiling. What a change. Instead of a reprimand, Jo copped a hug and a welcome. Ah, but was Shirley acting? She was and spoke with a loud voice.

'Come in, daughter number two and meet Mr Antony Carboni. Tony, this is my daughter, Joanna.'

Jo was impressed. The gent wore a dark jacket with cream slacks, and a shirt so white it gleamed. It matched his teeth. He was short, slim and sun-tanned.

'Hello Joanna, I am delighted to meet you. And please, you must call me Tony.'

'Hello Tony. And despite what my mother says I'm Jo.'

'Sit please,' ordered Shirley, 'while I fetch the afternoon tea.' Shirley was laying it on with a trowel. She stopped at the door. 'We're having coffee, Joanna.'

Coffee? What happened to tea and bikkies? And why is she making a formal announcement? Next, she'll be ringing a dinner gong.

Tony remained standing until Jo was seated. She liked his manners but what confused her was his choice of girlfriend.

'Your dear mother tells me you are a police officer.'

'My dear mother is perfectly correct.'

'And you have followed in the footsteps of your grandfather.'

'I think Pop's footsteps are impossible to follow but I'm trying.'

'And am I permitted to ask about your current case? This is partly to make polite conversation and partly because I am a sticky-beak.'

Ah, so you and Mother have something in common. Not so sure about the wit and sense of humour though.

Jo laughed. 'Nothing hush hush, Tony. The case was front-page news and is about a small girl being abducted. Sadly she remains missing.'

'And possibly dead?'

Jo spoke with a softer and solemn voice. 'Yes, I'm afraid so.'

Their conversation was interrupted by Shirley putting on a show for her beau.

'Here we are,' she said entering with a tray. In an instant, Tony was on his feet.

'Shirley, allow me.'

He took the tray and Shirley cleared the coffee table.

'Thank you, Tony. Now, Joanna, no cream for you of course.'

No cream? It's milk, Mother.

Shirley fussed and Jo worried.

Mother, he likes you, there's no need to put on a show. I like him, too, Mother. Just relax and be yourself.

Jo and Tony were willing to chat and discover the other. He'd heard a lot about the police officer, and wanted to get to know her. He wanted Jo to like him, to accept him as a possible stepfather. Shirley kept interrupting the natural flow of things.

'Joanna is my unmarried daughter, Tony, but we live in hope, don't we dear?'

Had Joanna been carrying her firearm, she would have been tempted to discharge same in the general direction of her mater.

'Thank you, Mother. I'm sure Tony is not remotely interested in my marital status.'

He, to his credit, changed the subject without insulting the hostess.

'But Jo, I am curious about the role of women in today's police force. When I was a young man, one very rarely saw a female solving crimes.'

'Big changes today, Tony. Even my boss is a woman.'

Shirley interrupted. 'DI Steele is not a woman.'

Jo was thrown. She hadn't told the family about her second departure from Homicide.

'DS Deborah Hughes, Mother.' A little white lie.

'Oh,' said back-in-her-box Shirley.

'But I know nothing about you, Tony,' said Jo. 'Your car would suggest success in business or perhaps, crime.'

Shirley looked horrified. 'Joanna!'

Tony was on Jo's humour wavelength and knew she was teasing.

'Well if it is crime, Jo, now that I've met you, I am already a reformed character.'

They laughed and Shirley tried to join the party. She failed.

'I'm curious, Tony.'

"Joanna,' interrupted Shirley, 'please behave.'

'How did you meet my mother?'

Shirley retreated—again.

'Ah, now here I could be in trouble with a police officer.' He had both women hooked. 'I am a teacher at our local U3A and your dear mother is one of my students.'

'Ah, so that's why you joined, Mother. You never told me this.'

'You never asked.'

'Well I am delighted.'

'I am learning Italian.'

'That's fantastic. I'm really impressed. Say something, please.'

Shirley paused. 'Comportarsi.' (*It.* behave)

Tony tilted his head and grinned, and even Shirley produced a wry smile.

'I'll take that as a comment, Mother.'

Tony got the story back on track. 'I have heard, Jo, that people in positions of power should not use their influence to, how shall I put this?'

'Don't,' said Shirley.

Tony persisted. 'I worry I may have convinced your mother to have dinner with me because I am the teacher and she is the pupil.'

Jo smiled. She wanted to laugh uproariously but couldn't insult her mother.

'I can give you some advice on this situation, Tony.' He looked at her. Shirley was undecided between crying or dying of embarrassment. 'Go for it.'

Tony laughed and Shirley expelled most of the air in her lungs.

'Grazie Signorina, I will take your advice.'

Shirley joined in. 'More coffee, Tony?'

'Sì,' he said taking his cup to the hostess. When he sat, he spoke to Jo. 'In my country, we have many abductions of children and nearly always it is for money. The parents are wealthy and will pay to have their beloved child returned safely. May I ask if the ransom has been paid in your case?'

'I'm sorry, Tony, I can't speak about it.'

'Of course, forgive me.'

'Abduction?' said Shirley. 'I thought you were in Homicide?'

'It's a joint task force with Major Crime, Mother.' That sounded impressive and Jo left it at that.

Tony persisted. 'In Italy there are only three reasons for an abduction of a child; for money, for sex or for revenge.'

Shirley felt uncomfortable. 'Must we talk about this?'

'Forgive me, Shirley. I was just trying to talk to your daughter about something other than grandchildren and the weather.'

Wow. Shirley got whacked in the face with a handful of duck down. Jo ignored her mother's complaint.

'It's pretty much the same here, Tony. In this case, the parents have little money so ransom is not involved.'

'And you feel the little one is no longer alive.'

'I'm an optimist but even I'm starting to lose hope.'

Shirley changed the subject and both Jo and Tony were happy to do so. For Jo and Tony, the gathering was a huge success. Jo couldn't believe her mother's lucky streak. She regained her life savings, and found a lover (well good friend) who was charming, intelligent and kind and, with a sense of humour.

Tony was impressed with Jo. Having met older sister Caitlyn, Tony was nervous about his new lady friend's offspring. If Jo was as bad as Caitlyn, Tony was in strife. Thank heavens Jo was delightful, smart and displayed a wonderful and cheeky sense of humour. Tutto è buono. (Everything is good).

It was getting dark and Jo made her excuses. It was easy to kiss Tony and they did so in the Italian fashion. Shirley settled for the single peck. Jo waved from her car, hopped in and headed home.

En route, she had plenty to ponder. Jack Carr is a lovely man and his folks and kids are wonderful but what about his in-laws? What did they discover about me? Who told them?

Then there is Monsieur Pierre Richelieu, the wealthy Frenchman with an Honours degree in seduction. And what about my mother's new boyfriend? He's loaded, charming and not a bit like Mum. This is all too much.

It was dark when she arrived back at her flat in Clifton Hill. She parked in her spot behind the building, walked along the path to her front door and was definitely not prepared for what happened.

Two men leapt from the bushes and smashed her against the wall of her building. Pain and fear dominated. The attackers were ready and armed. Judging by the strength of the thugs, they were intent on rape or murder or both.

In the seconds after it began, Jo used her training to fight back. Her right arm was pinned and her left side now throbbed with pain where she collided with the brick wall. She decided to lash out with a foot when she felt something sharp stinging her side.

'Struggle bitch and you die.'

Discretion wasn't the better part of valour, it was the only part.

'All right, all right,' she said going limp.

'Now walk slowly and don't get smart.'

The trio moved towards Jo's front door and froze when they arrived. Both her arms were held fast.

'Open the fucking door.'

'I can't.'

One of her arms was twisted. She gasped in pain.

'Open it.'

'I can't, you're holding my arms.'

Her bag was opened and a bunch of keys produced. A knife pressed against her throat. Her right arm was released. She struggled to choose the key and lean forward without falling. The blade's sharp edge nicked her skin.

She managed to turn the key and one of her attackers kicked the door. It swung open. The trio entered and another kick closed the door.

'Where's the light switch?'

Jo indicated with her head. The flat was lit. She looked at the balaclava-clad invaders.

'Hands behind y'back.'

Jo kept thinking about how she could get out of this situation. Get them talking seemed a good idea.

'Look, I've got money and a few valuables.'

'Shut up.'

'Take them, take the lot. Tie me up and take whatever you want.'

She felt pain and more fear as her head was slapped hard.

'Shut the fuck up, bitch.'

Jo's physical pain was overtaken by her mental anguish.

This is no robbery. This is life threatening. You're in trouble, girl.

With the knife at her throat, and the hand holding the blade shaking, Jo did as ordered, and put her hands behind her back. They were tied, hard and fast and it hurt. The blade was removed, she was shoved into the bedroom and pushed onto the bed. She lay face down.

'Turn around, bitch and you're fucking dead.'

The attackers were the same two thugs who ran at Richelieu last night in East Melbourne and failed. One tripped, one slipped and the Frenchman escaped. Now they were intent on hurting the man they believed had created the web site that ridiculed Darren Sandilands. Their plan was to rape his woman and send him graphic details with a challenge to "Stick this on your fucking web site, arsehole".

Jo's mind kept spinning. What can I say to make them stop? Again she tried to get them talking—it seemed her only option.

'Why are you doing this?'

Darren knelt on the bed and started stroking her bottom.

'Because we can, bitch, because we can.'

Another pair of hands started stroking the inside of her thighs.

'You're gunna love this, babe,' oozed Jordan.

'But why?' she almost cried.

Darren gave her the background story, one she already knew.

'Because your prick of a boyfriend, Joe Best, put up a web site mocking me. Now lucky for him, he got away from a kicking so we've decided to hurt the bastard by fucking his woman. Got that, bitch?'

They removed her shoes and started to pull down her slacks. She wanted to cry. She thought of her mother and that did make her cry. Then she kept talking.

'You do know he's a cop?'

The thugs froze and looked at one another.

'Bullshit,' said Jordan.

'She lying. Get her gear off,' ordered Darren. They resumed the crude undressing.

'He's a detective inspector in Homicide. You do this and you'll have the whole police force in Melbourne hunting you down.'

She sounded convincing. Jordan shed a bit of his enthusiasm. Darren became more aggressive and shouted at her.

'What's your name, bitch?'

Jo froze. If I tell the truth, they'll not only rape me, they'll kill me. Being exposed on what Darren thought was the World Wide Web when it fact it was only on the Dark Web, had sent him into this frenzy. If he discovered Joe Best was really Jo Best, and that he'd been mocked by a woman, God, Darren would explode. Not only had he been ridiculed online, but by a woman.

Actually, it was thanks to IT genius, Michael Chan, but he was acting under express orders of the woman currently lying terrified and bound on her bed in Clifton Hill.

'I said, what's your fucking name?'

'Billy Hughes,' she blurted.

'Billy? That's a fucking man's name. What are you, a dyke?'

Jordan looked nervous. 'Let's do it, man. Fuck her and get out.'

Darren didn't need any encouragement. They tore off her slacks and both removed their jeans. Jordan grabbed her ankles and shoved them apart. Jo's physical pain ramped up. Her mental agony was off the chart.

Darren climbed on the bed and straddled his victim. He grabbed her panties and yanked them to one side. He prepared to penetrate Joanna Best when her doorbell rang.

'Shit,' said Jordan.

'Fuck,' said Darren.

Jo screamed. 'Help. Help me.'

That was all she said as Darren grabbed his knife and put the tip of the blade at the side of her eye. She froze.

'Another sound, bitch, and you lose an eye.'

She worked frantically to remain silent. The silence was loud.

'We wait till they go,' whispered Darren still sitting atop Jo's bare buttocks.

More silence then someone again knocked on the door.

'They're still there,' said Jordan pulling up his strides and instantly losing interest in matters carnal.

'Wait.' Darren leaned into Jo. 'Expecting someone, bitch?'

'No. I don't know who it is.'

Then a voice was heard.

'Mademoiselle, this is your favourite detective inspector.'

Jordan made another bleeding obvious statement. 'It's a cop. She wasn't lying.'

Now Darren tasted fear. He spat at Jo. 'Is Joe Best a cop?'

'Yes.'

He slid off the bed—snakes slide—and dressed. He too lost any interest in sex as his instinct for survival kicked in.

He grabbed Jo's hair and yanked. 'What's another way outa here, bitch? Tell me or I'll cut you now.'

'Through the kitchen. The door goes out to the garden.'

Darren looked at Jordan and indicated with his head. Jordan moved sharpish. The doorbell rang again followed by more knocking.

Darren's ego demanded he have the last word. 'Tell your fucking boyfriend about us and we'll kill you both.' He smacked her head and ran.

Jo lay still. Richelieu called one more time. Jo sucked in air and yelled. 'I'm here, please wait.'

Richelieu heard her and worried. She slid off the bed. Her hands were so well tied she could do nothing about her state of undress. She managed to pick up her keys. The front door was deadlocked.

Her voice sounded strange. 'I'm coming, sir,' she called again.

'Are you okay?' he replied.

'Be patient.'

She held the right key, then with her foot, pushed a chair to the front door and, with difficulty, stood on it. She turned with her back to the door and felt for the lock. She found it and felt to put the key in the lock. She made it and unlocked the door.

'Sir?'

'Oui, I am 'ere, Mademoiselle.'

'When I say, please push the door but slowly. Do you understand?'

'Oui. Slowly.'

She turned the key and called. 'Now.'

The door opened slowly, struck the chair, and Jo toppled forward and fell, unable to use her hands to save herself. She lay crumpled and broken, and wept. Her sounds were horrendous.

Richelieu, worried almost afraid, slowly opened the door, saw Jo and rushed. He closed the door and knelt beside her, cradling her in his arms and kissing her forehead. She wept harder and her tears turned into uncontrollable sobbing.

He did nothing other than offer comfort. He could have asked what had happened, if whoever did this was still present, and more. Instead, he carefully untied her hands then resumed holding her close.

It took some time before they moved. He helped her to sit up. He stood and helped her to stand. He guided her into the lounge and placed her gently on the sofa. He disappeared and returned with a bathrobe. He placed this over her providing dignity. He knelt beside her and held her hand.

'Bonsoir Mademoiselle.' He kissed her hand. She looked a mess and didn't care. Her gratitude knew no bounds. 'I did not 'ear from you, Detective, all day, so I think, maybe she 'as some trouble. And so 'ere I am.'

Jo managed to control her weeping, not completely, but enough to nod and whisper her thanks. 'Merci, Monsieur, merci.' She wept again.

He waited for her to stop weeping then smiled. 'Now, we can go dancing and paint the town red, or we can 'ave a quiet night in with me looking after my favourite senior constable. Which do you prefer?'

She wanted to smile, laugh and share his carefree attitude. She couldn't. The terror of her ordeal lingered.

'Well, whatever you choose, Mon'Amie, I am staying 'ere tonight to guard you and keep you safe.' He patted the sofa. 'This is my bed, and I will respond should you require the smallest of service.' He kissed her hand again, and she felt warm, safe and glad.

He made her some tea and found a bottle of brandy, giving the hot beverage a heart starter. He sat beside her and she nestled into him. He wanted her to start the conversation. Eventually she did.

'I was attacked by the men who attacked you outside in the street the other night.'

'Men? It was only one. But last night, after you 'ad driven away, two men tried to attack me and I escaped.'

'Last night?'

'Oui. After you left my apartment and I walked 'ome in the rain.'

She now knew this was getting out of hand. Each time she and Michael Chan had duped a man or men, they had gone flat out to punish and gain revenge. Darren Sandilands was just another outraged criminal.

'They think you're Joseph Best.' He frowned. 'It's a long story.'

'You want me to make a report and 'ave these animals arrested?'

She thought about it then shook her head. In the past, especially when attending a domestic, she wondered why many women refused to report an assault and why some surveys reckon about 90% of rapes never get reported. Now she had a better understanding. In her case, she attacked Darren so he hit back. She left the assault unreported and tried to explain the Jo and Joe Best situation.

Afterwards, he picked her up and carried her to bed. He wanted to climb in beside her. She wanted him to climb in beside her. Instead, he covered her, kissed her gently then returned to the sofa and spent the night in the room next door. She felt safe, and slept because of his presence.

18

THE COUPLE COUPLED ON THE BACK SEAT. They parked beside the Yarra River not far from its source in the Yarra Valley. He was a married man and playing away from home. She was a work colleague. It was late. The man in the moon switched on a high beam, and once the lovers wiped the steam from the windows, they could see the rushing water. But scenery was not a priority right now.

For him it meant getting rid of her perfume, lipstick and any bodily fluids and aromas his wife might discover. For her it meant getting dressed so not to arouse suspicion from her loving but dull husband.

With adjustments complete, the philanderer returned to the driver's seat and turned on the demister. It wasn't the only thing turned on in this car in the last 20 minutes.

The sex-only secret affair had been going for a few weeks, and tension crept higher. He wanted to end it without consequences. She wanted him to leave his wife. That was never going to happen and the affair's alarm bells got ready for action.

'C'mon, babe, time to go.'

She clambered into the front passenger seat. This was not her vision of true love. She wanted to tell the world about her fella. He explained how much he loved her but now was not the right time to leave the missus. It was the typical have-your-cake-and-eat-it male logic.

He started the engine and as it roared to life, the car's powerful headlights shone on the rushing river. She wiped her side of the windscreen. He put the car into reverse and started to move but jammed on the brakes when she screamed. It was so loud and terrifying, it put the wind right up his recently removed Reg Grundies.

'What the hell!' he exclaimed.

'There,' she cried and pointed at the river.

He looked. 'What?'

'There, in the water, by that fallen tree.'

He looked and saw what looked like the body of a person, snagged on a branch and being buffeted by the current.

'Let's get out of here,' he panicked.

'No,' she yelled and grabbed his arm. He braked.

'What are you doing?'

'What are *you* doing?'

'We can't stay here. This is for the cops. I, we, didn't see anything.'

He went to drive off and she slapped his shoulder hard.

'Stop the car.' He did.

'Babe, it's a dead body, dead. We can't save her. All we can do is get ourselves in a heap of trouble.'

'We have to call the police.'

He got angry with a touch of fear. 'Are you mad? How do we explain finding the body? What were we doing here? Well?'

She looked at him. 'Are you ashamed of me?'

'Of course not. But now's not the time to tell my wife I'm leaving.'

'There never will be a time, will there?'

He looked at her and she saw the truth. She'd been used. She was his bit on the side and would remain so until he dumped her.

'You bastard,' she said and grabbed her phone.

He grabbed her arm. 'What are you doing?'

'What any decent person would do? I'm calling the cops.'

'No.' He grabbed her phone. She hung on to it. They struggled. The struggle got nasty. He pulled the phone towards him. She followed it and yanked it back. He hurt his knee on the gearshift. He pushed it into neutral but went one more. It was in drive. The car started rolling forward. He panicked and hit the brake but missed and stabbed the accelerator. The car lurched forward. They both screamed as the Beamer dived into the river baptising its front wheels.

He recovered and tried reverse. No grip, just heaps of wheel spin.

'You stupid bitch,' he roared. 'Now look want you've done.'

'You'll have to call someone now, my darling. And turn off your headlights. That poor woman's got enough trouble as it is.

He stopped the engine and the body bobbed in the current in the darkness.

'I'll call you a cab' he said, grabbing his phone.

'I'm not leaving till the police get here.'

He pleaded. 'Oh please, babe. Look, I'll stay. I have to. You go. There's no need for you to get involved.'

'I'm staying because I don't believe you'll stay.'

'How can I leave?'

'You'll phone a mate and get a tow and be gone to leave that poor woman alone.'

'Alone? Do you really think she's lonely?'

'She needs some dignity.'

He lost it. 'Oh for Chrissake, she's dead you fat bitch.'

'Pardon?'

'You heard.'

'Wow. I've gone from gorgeous babe to fat bitch in five seconds.'

He fumed. He had no control over her or the situation. How would he explain this to his wife?

'Get out,' he said.

'What?'

'Get out of my car.' He leant across her and opened the door.'

'It's cold, and now it's raining.'

It was too, and windy.

'If you won't go home in a cab, you can bloody well walk. Go on, get out.' He pushed her. She struggled.

'No!'

'Yes! We'll both get out. We'll get a cab. I'll say my car was stolen.'

He got out and went around to her side. She locked the door. He screamed at her and yanked on the handle. He stormed back to his side but she leant across and locked his door too. The keys were still in the ignition. His night went from bad to worse to monumentally awful.

She wouldn't budge. For all he knew she'd already rung the cops. She had.

In a panic he stepped into the river. The man in the moon obliged with maximum brightness. He waded into the icy water.

She saw him and couldn't believe her eyes. She slipped into the driver's seat and switched on the ignition. Up came the brilliant headlights. There he was, up to his waist and approaching the woman, the dead and carefree corpse.

She yelled inside the car. Nobody heard her. He reached the body and snapped the branch which had snagged the dress. The living woman felt a mixture of terror and rage.

He threw the branch into the middle of the river, and the body set off thanks to the current. It headed towards Melbourne, as the crow flies about 50 miles.

He squelched out of the river, his trousers soaked but with traces of his lover's DNA now expunged. His wife wouldn't find any sexual smells but she might be curious as to his midnight swimming routine.

The mistress got out and went for him. 'You bastard. You've killed her.'

He grabbed her flailing arms and shoved her. She fell. He got into his car from her side, closed the door and locked it. Their roles were reversed. He was making things up as he went along.

If she called the cops and they arrive, there's no body. They'll either arrest her for time wasting, or forget everything because I'll deny the lot. She's upset because we've had a fight.

'Look officer, I'm a married man. Nothing happened. Can we please just forget all about it?'

He wasn't confident but he was low on alternatives. He found his phone and rang a mate.

'Pat, I'm in the shit. My car's slipped into the river and I need a tow. Please, buddy, I'm desperate.'

After his mate stopped laughing and noted the location, the call ended and Phil, the philanderer, felt marginally better.

Then his world collapsed as he saw a flashing blue light coming along the road. His lover was off and running, waving and calling.

Phil had no trouble in swearing. He was in deep do-dos.

She told the cops everything including how her brute of a now ex-boyfriend, tried to drown the poor unfortunate woman and then shoved her away downstream.

His story differed significantly. He reckoned he was trying to rescue her and even save her if she was still alive. In trying to unhook her, the current took her body and, in the darkness, she was gone.

The cops didn't know who to believe but either way, the couple's details were recorded and Phil's missus would soon hear the amazing tale of how her heroic hubby tried to save a drowning woman and sadly failed. And all this on top of giving one of his work colleagues a ride home. There was no mention of her having a ride inside the car but that's neither here nor there, and hopefully, Phil and his extramarital shenanigans would remain a secret.

Ha, no chance, Buster.

The gendarmes called in reinforcements and, with powerful torches, they walked along the bank and soon struck gold. The body, released by Phil, was trapped by yet another tree branch a short stroll downstream.

The body was removed from the river and placed on a sheet. It was clothed and appeared to have only been in the water hours and certainly not days. To date there were no reports of a missing person.

The uniformed police gathered around and one of them screamed. A female constable recognised the body.

'That's Karen Galbraith. She knows my sister.'

The sergeant questioned her. 'Are you sure?'

'She's married with twins. Oh God, her family will be devastated.'

'Take it easy, lass,' said the sergeant, who'd seen more dead bodies than the other three cops combined.

'Please don't make me tell her family, Sarge, please.'

He did the job himself.

Phil's mate arrived and helped Phil rescue his wheels. Phil finished up giving the ex-girlfriend a lift home. They didn't kiss goodnight.

At that very moment, Jo Best was sleeping, having been saved by her knight in haute couture armour while he, hero that he was, snored quietly on her sofa.

It wasn't long before DS Hughes from Homicide received a call. It should have been received by DI Richelieu but he was on sick leave. Well, so he said.

The woman in the river was not on sick leave, and declared to be "life extinct" by a local doctor. The locals waited for the big boys (and girls) from town. Homicide had a new case.

19

JO WOKE AND REMEMBERED LAST NIGHT. How could she forget? It was still dark outside and she wondered if she was alone. She slipped out of bed, still in her work clothes and opened her door. A gentle snoring sound drifted from the lounge. She smiled and crept towards the sleeping beauty.

DI Richelieu was a heavy sleeper. He heard or sensed nothing. He had removed his jacket, trousers and shirt, all of which were hung perfectly on chairs or a hanger he found in the second bedroom, currently used as a storeroom and mini gym.

His bare right shoulder and arm lay outside the blanket, which covered his body. She saw the minor wound caused by a gunshot when the two of them were once on duty in Port Melbourne. The bullet missed Jo and nicked the DI. They'd shared an experience or two in her short career and last night's dramatic episode added a new chapter.

She tiptoed to the bathroom and was afraid to flush the loo in case she woke Prince Charming. She waited until the cistern refilled before opening the door. There stood DI Richelieu in his sweatshirt and silk boxers.

'Bonjour Mademoiselle. Did you sleep well?'

She smiled and walked towards him. 'I did. Thanks to you.' She leant up and kissed him then stood back. 'You saved my life, Pierre.'

'It was a pleasure to be of service, Mademoiselle.'

Both wanted to embrace the other yet waited until the other made the move. Last night was not your usual flowers and chocolates date. He knew she'd been through a hell of an experience and didn't want to take advantage of her situation. He thought her gratitude might drive her desire.

'I don't normally look this glamourous first thing in the morning,' she said, tousling her uncombed hair.

'Detective, you would look glamorous in, 'ow you say, a potato sack.'

She moved back to him and they kissed gently. Their arms brought them closer and their kiss even stronger when first his phone rang and then hers a second or two later.

They looked at one another, laughed and moved to their respective phones.

DS Hughes called Richelieu and DI Goddard called Jo. Hughes wanted to know if the DI was able to come back to work. They had a new homicide and needed all hands. Richelieu agreed to return to work although he definitely preferred to stay where he was.

Goddard wanted Jo to accompany her to see Donna and Gavin White to tell the parents that Major Crime would no longer be working on the case. Goddard knew she had to tell the parents in person and had still not figured out a way to explain the case being moved to Homicide. Goddard agreed to collect Jo at noon.

Phone calls ended, and the couple shared their respective news. Their amorous moment had passed and Richelieu knew his colleague's traumatic experience was still fresh in her mind.

Instead of taking the lovely senior constable to bed, the DI dressed and prepared to leave. Jo made coffee and toast, insisting he stay for breakfast.

As they "dined", both felt a new attraction for the other. Of course it was physical but something else began to evolve. Both wanted to get to know the other better.

'I envy you,' said Jo, 'working in Homicide.'

'You will return, ma chérie, and sooner rather than later.'

'You've even taken the case I was working on at Major Crime.'

'And perhaps it is a poisoned chalice.'

'Oh?'

'Two experienced inspectors 'ave failed to solve the case and now it is 'omicide who may do so. And where is the satisfaction in that?' He mimicked a visit to the parents. "Pardon, Madame et Monsieur, but your little girl's body 'as been found". Do you want that job, Joanna?'

He looked at her and she didn't answer. She thought.

Maybe it's better to get out of this case before the inevitable occurs.

They finished breakfast and she walked him to the door. She spoke.

'I'll tell you again, Detective Inspector, you saved my life last night. For that I cannot thank you enough.'

'No need for the thanks. I require only one kiss,' he said.

She stood on tiptoe and kissed him.

'I mean one kiss per day,' he said, smiled and walked away.

After everything that had happened last night, right now she felt quietly excited.

Goddard was on time. Jo was ready and walked to her DI's car. En route, they talked about the case.

'I've broken my golden rule, Jo. I've given the Whites a heads up. I've told them there's no news about the child but news about the way the case is going to proceed.'

'Will you tell them it's going to Homicide?'

'What do you think?'

'Do I think you *will* tell them or *should* tell them?'

'Clever answer. I think the medical profession call it "hanging black crepe".' Jo didn't understand. 'It means being blunt. The diagnosis is bad news so you cut to the chase. No introduction, just spit it out.'

'None of that bit about Grandma climbing on the roof, the wind blowing and ...'

'No, none of that—it's just Grandma's dead.'

'Rather you than me,' said Jo and they drove in silence. Jo resumed the conversation.

'Yesterday I met a gent called Antony, my mother's new boyfriend.'

'And?'

'He was charming, clever and had a delightful sense of humour.'

'I assume your mother is not like that.'

Jo laughed. 'You assume correctly. Antony hails from Italy and asked me about the abduction.'

'Meaning?'

'He told me in his country, abductions were for ransom, sex or revenge.'

'It's probably the same everywhere.'

'We've never considered a ransom. Is that because the Whites don't have that sort of money?'

'True.'

Jo was thinking aloud. 'If the child was taken by a paedophile, we may get a conviction but never locate Candy.'

'Which was why Jake was the key. If he saw or knew something, and told us, we might have cracked the case.'

Jo reluctantly dropped her news. 'I heard Homicide is solid in knowing who killed Jake.'

'Oh yes? From whom?' Jo hesitated. She felt uncomfortable about naming her mole. 'Careful, Constable, you're far too young to be playing office politics.'

'I wondered if we're solid about Leo as Candy's abductor?'

'Don't you start.'

'Ma'am?'

'I'm just as worried as you or anyone. If the child was snatched for sex and Leo's not involved ...'

'Despite the new DNA evidence.'

'Despite the new DNA evidence with both the phony blood splatter and Candy's single hair, then we're stuffed. And if she was taken for revenge then we're worse than stuffed. It's a total disaster and what's worse, Homicide take it tomorrow, and I bet a stroke of luck will see something fall out of the sky, and they'll get all the fucking glory— excuse my French.'

Jo decided the best thing to say was to say nothing.

They arrived at the White house for the last time. All they had to do was tell the parents they would be dealing with detectives who investigate murders. Happy days.

As they approached the front door, the sounds of a party could be heard. They rang the doorbell and got no reply. They knocked with the same result. Then a couple walked up the drive.

'They're round the back,' said the man and the police shrugged and followed the couple.

A BBQ was in full swing. About a dozen people were eating and drinking. It wasn't riotous or even upbeat. Donna saw the officers and moved to them.

'Hello. We've decided to come out of our misery and celebrate Gavin's birthday. Just a few friends, like.'

'That's nice,' said Goddard.

Gavin saw them and came over. He held a barbecue fork which Jo thought could easily be a lethal weapon.

'Well, well, here's a first, a couple of pigs at my birthday. Fancy a turn on the rotisserie, officers?'

Goddard ignored his rudeness. 'Happy birthday, Gavin.'

'Only it's not is it? Thanks to your pathetic police work.'

'Gavin,' reprimanded Donna. 'Not on your birthday. Not in front of your friends.'

The friends were silent and studying the situation. Suddenly Gavin changed tack and put on a mock friendship act.

'Yeah, c'mon, let's all have a drink and forget our troubles. What are you drinking, ladies?'

Goddard wanted to tell the Whites about the switch to Homicide, wish them luck, and get the hell out of the place, but thought to leave now would be churlish. She knew drinking on duty was a no-no but wanted to make the news she was about to deliver less confrontational.

'Thanks, maybe a light beer.'

Gavin looked at Jo. 'And what about you, Constable Best?'

'Thanks, something soft, please.'

With drinks dispensed, people started talking again, and the cops became wallflowers on the shelf.

'Mingle,' said Goddard and, nursing her beer, wandered off to talk to people. Jo stood there like a statue.

Mingle? With whom? These people hate us, abuse us and consider us useless. Why would anyone want to talk to me?

Someone did. 'Hi,' said a woman about Jo's age. 'I'm Julianna.'

'Hi, I'm Jo.'

'Are you one of the cops looking for Candy?'

'I am and sadly, not with much success.'

'Do you reckon she's dead?'

Jo didn't like the question, and coming from someone who presumably knew Donna and Gavin made it worse.

'We continue to hope.'

Julianna disagreed. 'You know there's a little English girl who disappeared in Portugal, and I think the police are still looking for her years after she vanished.'

'The officers may change but the investigation goes on.'

'Is that what's happening to you?'

Jo was cornered. She had to leave that subject to the DI and certainly not tell someone who wasn't a member of the family.

'I can't really say.'

'But you have arrested some pervert. I saw that in the papers.'

'We have made an arrest.'

'And another pervert got what he deserved.'

'I'm sorry, Julianna, but I can't really talk about the details.'

'My husband reckons whoever killed the pervert should get a medal, and that no jury would ever convict whoever it was strangled him.'

Bang! Jo recoiled. *What did she just say?* The murder method was secret. Homicide shared the information but it was never made public.

How did this woman know Jake was strangled? Jake could have been stabbed or shot or anything. Was it a lucky guess?

Jo played it cool. 'So how do you know Donna and Gavin?'

'Ah, my hubby's good mates with Gavin. Steve was in the park on the day Candy was taken.' Jo knew who Steve was but played dumb.

'Was that the footy clinic on the oval?'

'Yeah our son was playing and Steve and Gavin were watching.'

'And you were with Donna in the playground?'

'Nah, I wasn't there. I have a hairdressing business I run from home and that day I was flat chat.'

'That's an interesting name, Julianna. What is it, Italian?'

'No it's Polish.'

'I wouldn't have picked that,' said Jo trying to discover more without sounding nosy.

'My family name's a shocker. People say I married Steve just to change names. Wait for it—Sokolowski.'

Julianna laughed, Jo smiled and her body copped a second shockwave. Jo was desperate to ask if Julianna had a relative who worked for the police, specifically, as a constable stationed at Richmond and who happened to be on duty at the Foley Street house when Homicide detectives attended to investigate the death of one Jake Freeman—i.e. Constable Sokolowski.

Jo couldn't bring herself to ask the question, even in a roundabout way. Then the women were interrupted.

'I'm not sure I like the idea of my wife talking to the filth,' sneered Steve Rumford approaching with beer and fag on the go.

'Pull your head in, babe. Jo, this is my old man, Steve.'

'Hi Steve.'

'Dunno why you lot even show your face around here. What have you done about finding Candy? Fuck all as far I can see.'

'They've arrested one of the perverts, Steve.'

'And what has he told you? Nothin'.'

Steve's aggression grew bolder. He was threatening now.

'We had a bit of bad luck,' said Jo.

'Oh yeah, arrested the wrong pervert have you?'

'No, we had a guy who knew what happened to Candy and he was about to tell us everything when he got murdered.'

Steve looked like he'd been kneed in the nuts. He went red. His sneering hit a brick wall.'

'You all right, babe?' asked Julianna. 'You look shithouse.'

Steve felt his belly. 'Must be them prawns I ate.'

'I'll get you something,' said his wife who went inside.

Jo knew it would be risky to question Steve, here, alone and without permission from her DI. But the iron was hot so she struck.

'Your wife just told me something interesting, Steve.'

'Piss off.'

'She said she knows how one of the so-called perverts got killed.'

'She wouldn't know, just like you.'

'How did your wife know about Jake's murder?'

He looked at Jo and she saw fear. 'Fuck off.' He turned to walk away.

'Is Constable Sokolowski related to your wife?' He turned back and dared her to speak again. She did. 'What's your alibi for the night of the Freeman murder, Steve?' He clenched a fist and growled. 'Was Gavin there? Did he give you one of Candy's hairs to plant in the laundry bag?' More growling. 'Does Gavin know you killed Freeman? Does your wife?'

He hissed. 'Shut the fuck up.'

'Was it an accident? Did you torture him to make him talk? Did the torture go too far?'

'You don't know what you're talking about.'

'And do you know you killed the one person who could tell us what happened to Candy?'

That hurt. If that was true, and Jo had no proof it was, instead of helping his mate, Steve had wrecked the best chance of saving the kid. Steve had messed up big time. His rage was a combination of anger at being sprung, and frustration at having ruined his mate's happiness.

There was a pause and then Steve exploded. He launched himself at Jo. She sidestepped him meaning his momentum saw him crash into an outdoor furniture setting and fall. Furniture went flying. His rage increased. Everyone stopped and turned. Gavin raced to the scene.

Steve was back on his feet and looking for blood. DI Goddard was preparing her "Homicide will take over" speech. She wet herself.

Jo ducked a haymaker from Steve and twisted his arm behind his back. He screamed and swore. Gavin jumped in to help his mate. Julianna rushed out of the house and screamed. Donna panicked. Other guests moved to separate the pugilists.

A neighbour heard the ruckus, took a squiz over the fence then called the cops. He used his phone to start filming.

Goddard was confused. She tried to help Jo but at the same time needed to stop the near riot. Her voice was just one of many.

Jo got Steve in a headlock forcing the raging brute to be less aggressive. He still swore and seethed, and only had his legs as weapons. A sort of uneasy calm settled and Goddard took control.

'Right everybody step back.' Nobody moved. 'Please, move back.' Slowly the partygoers moved away. There was no way Jo was going to release her grip on Steve.

'Okay, Senior Constable, explain.'

Goddard was in despair. The case she'd been drafted into as a last resort had produced nothing. Goddard had failed to find the abducted child. Now, as a public relations and goodwill exercise, she'd come to explain the switch to Homicide, to thank the parents and to assure them the police would continue to search for their missing toddler. Instead of her sympathetic chat, she landed in the middle of a party which turned ugly, courtesy apparently, of her junior officer, a kung-fu expert.

Goddard's reputation and probably her career were in the toilet. She attempted to minimise the damage, and waited for Jo's answer.

'I'm about to make an arrest, ma'am.'

Cries of anger and disbelief arose from the partygoers with Donna, Gavin and Julianna the chief stirrers. Donna stepped forward and gave voice to her weeks of misery and frustration.

'You people are evil. You fail hopelessly to find my baby. You tell us nothing. And now you come into my home and arrest our best friend who has tried harder than anyone to help us. You police are a fucking disgrace.'

The partygoers shared Donna's sentiment.

Goddard saw her career floating off into the distance. Jo looked at her DI. Of leadership came there none. She tightened her grip on Steve and did her best.

Okay, I'm on my own here—thanks for nothing, ma'am.

'Steven Rumford, I'm arresting you on suspicion of the murder of Jake Freeman. You do not ...'

She didn't get any further. Her statement turned the partygoers into an unruly mob. The masses got active, and the revolt kicked off in style. Steve started bucking. Gavin leapt in to help his mate. Goddard finally leapt in to rescue Jo, and Donna and Julianna started slapping Goddard. Others jeered and encouraged the attack on the police. Jo and Goddard felt genuine fear. Steve broke free and turned to attack Jo. She was surrounded and shoved from the front and the back. Steve tried to get in a good kicking. Jo fell. She was at Steve's mercy.

Then a group of uniformed officers burst into the backyard, yelled and grabbed the attackers. More screams and curses with plenty wanting to deliver a coward's punch at the cops. The police went for those in the thick of the fighting—Steve, Gavin, and a certain duo of plain-clothed cops. Oh dear.

It was one cop for each of the brawlers. They were "escorted" off the property to the jeers of the mob with the wives calling their support to Gavin and Steve.

Goddard immediately tried to explain who they were and what they were doing.

'Save it for the station, madam,' interrupted the male constable beside her. Jo looked at her escort, a young female constable and whispered. 'We're cops. You're making a big mistake.'

It was hard to see the arresting officer's eyes behind her military-style glasses but Jo sensed a change in the young woman's attitude. She said nothing. They reached the first of two paddy wagons, double-parked outside the White house.

Gavin and Steve were struggling and abusing the cops. Goddard's officer ordered his female partner to help the other two constables. Goddard and Jo were alone with one constable. He opened the rear door of the paddy wagon.

Goddard made another attempt to stop this lunacy. 'We're police officers, Constable. We're on duty. Let me show you my ID.'

'Been drinking have we madam?' asked the constable.

Goddard wanted to scream. She'd sipped a light beer in order to break down any barriers between "them and us" before advising the parents about the Homicide takeover.

'Inside madam,' ordered the constable. Goddard hesitated. 'Don't make me force you, madam,' he said threatening Goddard.

Jo saved the situation by entering the paddy wagon. Goddard took another hard look at the arresting officer then followed Jo. The door closed.

Inside, in steerage class, the arrested cops looked at one another and Jo reckoned Goddard wanted to break the sixth Commandment—Thou shalt not kill. The vehicle took off and Jo took some initiative.

'I'm sorry, ma'am.'

Goddard ignored her. They travelled in silence. Both women had a vision of their respective careers. Goddard wondered what early retirement would be like. Jo wondered if anyone had ever been sacked from both Homicide and Major Crime.

20

JO ENTERED THE RICHMOND POLICE STATION for the second time in two days. Nobody knew her, there being a different shift. Gavin and Steve were already being processed. They complained and muttered to one another. Goddard and Jo stood back with their arresting constables either side.

Wearing plain clothes, Marcelina Sokolowski entered and headed to the locker room. She glanced at Jo and stopped.

'Hello Senior, back again?'

The female constable standing beside Jo felt sick. Then Marcelina saw her brother-in-law and she too felt queasy. Jo beckoned with her head. Marcelina approached adding confusion to her queasiness.

Jo spoke quietly but loud enough for the two constables to hear.

'Constable Sokolowski, the woman standing beside me is Detective Inspector Trish Goddard from Major Crime. Would you please inform your sergeant that your colleagues here have arrested two serving police officers, who were on duty, having refused to inspect our ID.' Marcelina hesitated. 'Now, Constable.'

She hurried out of the room. Steve saw her and called. She ignored him. Goddard saw another side to Jo's ability. The male constable standing beside Goddard needed the toilet urgently.

A sergeant appeared and moved to Jo and Goddard. He recognized the DI.

'Detective Inspector Goddard, I'm Senior Sergeant Rossi. I believe there's been an misunderstanding. Please come into my office.' He gestured and Goddard and Jo walked out of the room.

The two constables who had arrested them received a look which would have stripped paint from a wall.

In his office, the sergeant apologised profusely, explaining that his constables were either letter-of-the-law maniacs or fresh out of the academy.

Goddard chose not to explain the situation or reprimand the constables involved. She did, however, request a lift back to her car. This was arranged without hesitation. Being a mean bastard, the senior sergeant assigned the two arresting constables to drive Goddard and Jo back to the so-called crime scene. No discussion took place and when the police car arrived, both constables flew out of the vehicle and opened the respective back doors for their senior colleagues.

Goddard's response was to say nothing. She walked to her car. Jo looked at the ashen-faced constables, remembered how she was one of them not long ago, and how she too had fallen foul of her superiors.

'Good luck,' she said and followed her DI.

Jo had to wait at the passenger door. Goddard kept her waiting. Jo gently tapped. The door was unlocked and Jo slid in not knowing what to expect.

'Right, madam, chapter and verse, and don't you dare lie or leave out anything. Go.'

Jo remembered the time when she and Detective Senior Constable Charlie Baldwin got in a car and he lost it, blaming Jo for wrecking his career. This seemed like Groundhog Day.

Jo explained everything about the Polish sisters, one being married to Steve Rumford, one being a constable stationed at Richmond, once on duty at Foley Street, and how one, possibly both the sisters knew the method of Jake's murder. She described Steve's responses and reactions to her questions.

'That's the lot, ma'am.'

'And DI Steele has arrested some paedo for Jake's murder.'

Jo couldn't believe it. No praise for her detection. No thanks for probably solving the murder. All DI Goddard could do was gloat over a possible wrongful arrest by DI Steele.

If he's the Pope, she's bloody Joan of Arc.

Goddard drove Jo home. En route Jo's phone rang. She recognised the number but was afraid to say the name of the caller, at least not with DI Goddard within earshot.

'Hello.'

'Senior Constable Best, it's AC John Crowley speaking.'

'Good afternoon, sir.'

'Are you well? Not on duty I presume.'

'I'm well, thank you, and just out driving.'

'On speaker phone of course.'

'Of course, sir.' *What does he want?*

'I'm checking to see if you're okay with your speaking engagement at Cheltenham tomorrow.'

God. That was hardly in my thoughts having just been arrested.

'Absolutely, sir.'

'I understand there may be some parents and grandparents in attendance. But I suggest you pitch your talk at those bright young things who might be thinking about a career in the force.'

'I'll do my best, sir.'

'Is that a pun, young lady?'

'Sir?'

He laughed. 'Never mind. I'll see you in church. Bye.'

'Goodbye, sir.'

Jo hung up and waited for Goddard's remarks. She said nothing. After a while Jo asked.

'What do you think we should do about arresting Steve Rumford, ma'am?'

'I'm tempted to do nothing.'

'Ma'am?'

'I'm tempted to wait until DI Steele makes public his arrest of his man and then we trump him.'

'But what if Rumford is guilty? We can't leave him on the streets to kill again or to intimidate witnesses or destroy evidence.'

'I'm joking, Detective. Of course we expedite Rumford's arrest. Good work there. And just then I was indulging in my rare serve of schadenfreude.' Jo looked puzzled. 'Look it up.'

'I will.'

'Now you must know I can't have you involved in the arrest.'

Jo was disappointed and confused.

'Ma'am?'

'You're a witness, Detective,' said Goddard. 'Your evidence could be crucial in securing a conviction. I'll give Colin and Ben the background then have them drop in on Steve as soon as he's released.'

'Yes, ma'am.' They reached Jo's flat. 'Thanks, ma'am, and again, I'm sorry about today.'

'I never did get to tell Donna and Gavin today's our last day. I'll leave that to Homicide.' Jo started to get out of the car but stopped when Goddard spoke. 'So you think you've solved Jake's murder?'

Jo closed the door. Goddard wanted to talk.

'Not at all, ma'am, although he and his sister-in-law certainly have some questions to answer.'

'I agree.'

'But how is Jake's murder related to finding the abductor?'

'I don't think it is, ma'am.'

'Go on.'

'I don't think Jake or Leo had anything to with Candy's abduction.'

'So Homicide and Major Crime have both arrested the wrong man?'

Jo hesitated. 'The blood we can discount but the hair may point to the killer.'

'Rumford?'

'Possibly, although I don't think we can rule out a paedophile and if so, then we're dealing with an unknown perpetrator.

'And if so we've got bugger all.'

'Agreed.'

'Or?'

'Or it could be revenge and, if so, that would almost certainly involve someone who's had dealings with Donna or Gavin or both.'

'Revenge for what?'

Jo shrugged. 'Could be money, a bad relationship, family grudge—anything. And worse, it could be someone we haven't met. The event which triggered the revenge might have happened years ago, and Donna or Gavin may not even know they caused it.'

'Any thoughts?'

'Nothing concrete, ma'am.'

Neither spoke. Their brief partnership was about to end.

'It's been nice working with you, Jo. Recap in the morning and then off we go to who knows where?'

Jo didn't know what to say. She grimaced. 'Ma'am,' she said and got out of the car. Goddard drove off and Jo's eyes darted about looking for any rapists lurking in the bushes.

Next morning the Major Crime team met in the Incident Room. Goddard was fuming. Footage of the brawl at the White's BBQ, involving two police officers, was doing the rounds on social media. When Jo saw it, she feared the worst.

Goddard's response was to ignore it, and had DS Gregory report.

'We arrested Steve Rumford last night on suspicion of the murder of Jake Freeman. We've advised Homicide.'

Goddard took over. 'Colin, I want you and Ben to meet with Jo and get any details you don't already know. Let's give Homicide a complete report.'

'Ma'am.'

'And Ben, what happened with the uniformed constable?'

'Cathy Bryant and I interviewed Marcelina Sokolowski under caution last night. She made a statement in relation to the Foley Street homicide, and has been suspended pending further enquiries.'

'Excellent work everyone and especially Senior Constable Best.' A brief round of applause broke out. 'Look I reckon we're finishing on a high. We didn't solve the abduction and that I regret more than anything.' The mood was sombre. 'And as soon as I hear about future duties, I'll let you know. Jo, have that final chat with Colin and Ben. The rest of you, tie up any loose ends so that Homicide has everything to crack the case. Thanks again and when we knock off, the drinks are on me.'

Team members muttered and got to work. Jo told Gregory and Grimes everything she knew about Steve and his sister-in-law.

She returned to her desk not knowing what to do. Would she return to Homicide? Would Steele cool down and agree to her return to Homicide? She was about to find out.

Her phone rang. 'Bonjour Mademoiselle,' said Richelieu. 'I believe congratulations are in order—again.'

'Hello, sir.'

'Pierre, please, we are friends are we not?'

'We are.'

'I am afraid, Mademoiselle, I 'ave bad news.'

Jo groaned. 'Oh?'

'News of your arrest for the Foley Street murder 'as reached the ears of DI Steele and 'e 'as, 'ow you say, blown a gasket.'

Jo died inside. 'No chance of a return to Homicide then.'

Richelieu mused. 'Maybe all is not lost, Mon'Amie. But let me take you to lunch to celebrate your latest triumph, s'il vous plaît.'

'Thank you, Pierre, but I have a speaking engagement later today and I need to prepare.'

'But I did not know this. You 'ave not told me anything.'

'Oh, so now you are my keeper as well.'

He smiled. 'I would like that.' So would she. 'So please, what is this engagement?'

She told him.

'I am impressed, Mademoiselle. Good luck with your performance. We will talk soon, n'est-ce par?'

'Of course.'

'Au revoir.'

She hung up feeling a scary type of happiness. The butterflies in her stomach seemed to be bumping into one another.

She knocked on Goddard's open door. 'I'll be off, ma'am. It's that talk I told you about, telling young gels about the joys of policing.'

'Good luck,' said Goddard, 'and thanks again, Jo. I hope this is not the end of our working relationship.'

Jo left thinking good thoughts. Then a vision of DI Steele reacting to the news that Jo had again found another suspect for the murder Steele thought he'd solved. She shuddered remembering his blistering voice and demeaning language.

She arrived at Cheltenham Girls' Grammar School and was met by two senior students, delighted to have a young woman as guest speaker.

Jo met the teachers and entered the room where the students were waiting. Speaking to teenage girls about the police was not covered in her training. She was thinking about the abduction and not concentrating on her speech but focused instantly when the audience began to clap.

The teacher indicated the lectern and Jo looked at the expectant faces in front of her. *Will I be interesting?*

She spoke about what she knew—job opportunities, especially for women, in today's police force. She thought the students seemed interested. Questions followed and the first was about her training to become a police officer.

'I finished Year 12 and studied Law. My parents thought I would become a lawyer but instead I went to the Police Academy and became a constable on the beat. I won promotion to Senior Constable, and then I was lucky to be accepted by the Homicide Squad which, as you can imagine, investigates cases involving murder.'

All was plain sailing until someone threw a curve ball.

'Officer Best, as a detective, have you ever made a mistake?'

A murmur filled the room. Jo waited.

'Many I'm afraid. A police officer must follow rules about procedure, and should be sensitive when dealing with the public. Sadly I've not always followed the rules or behaved in a sensitive manner. And if you want me to give you an example, well if I told you, I'd have to arrest you.'

That set off a lively response. When the hubbub settled, another hand appeared. Jo acknowledged the student.

'Senior Constable Best, do the police ever break the law?'

The murmuring began again and teachers exchanged glances. This was no Dorothy Dixer, and in fact, seemed just the opposite, a when-did-you-stop-beating-your-wife type of question.

The teacher in charge stood, preparing to disallow the question but stopped when Jo gently raised a hand.

'It's fine, I'm happy to answer.' She paused and the students had never been so attentive.

'Police officers are human, just like lawyers, doctors, even teachers. Sometimes in life you face a difficult situation. Let's say someone has been robbed online, scammed. I'm sure you've heard about computer fraud. Well catching criminals can be difficult. I won't say impossible but there are some people who break the law and get away with it. For them, crime really *does* pay. So, if I discovered an injustice and knew the authorities would not or could not help the victim, then yes, I would certainly consider breaking the law to see that justice was done.'

That triggered a reaction which almost exploded when the student called out above the noise.

'And have you?'

That was too much for the staff. They stood to rule the question out of order but Jo got in first and when she spoke you could have heard a hairpin hit the floor.

'Again I could tell you but rather than arrest you, this time I would have to bump you off.'

A huge reaction erupted followed by excited chatter. The teacher in charge decided enough was enough. She moved to the microphone and called the students to order.

She thanked Jo for her most interesting talk and the students agreed giving the speaker a splendid and prolonged round of applause. The students departed with Jo escorted to a smaller room where refreshments were provided.

Members of staff were there, some parents and grandparents, and the two senior girls who had met Jo when she first arrived. Almost everyone wanted to speak to the visitor.

Jo was busy being told things rather than being asked things, which is typical behavior from so many in today's society. A voice from behind interrupted proceedings.

'Congratulations, Detective Senior Constable Best. People stopped talking. Jo turned to see a smiling Assistant Commissioner Crowley. He held out his hand and Jo shook it.

'Thank you, sir. I didn't know you were here.'

'I had to be. My daughter ordered me to attend.' He beckoned to the students who had escorted Jo into the school. 'I believe you've already met Bo and my daughter Katrina.'

'Hello again,' said Jo and they all shook hands.

'Thank you for a very interesting speech,' said the Chinese student.

'You made the police service sound really exciting,' said the AC's daughter.

'Oh and I don't,' sounded her wounded father. That provoked laughter. More chat ensued before the girls departed.

The AC beckoned to an older couple. 'Jo, I'd like you to meet some friends of mine, whose granddaughter is a student here. Myles and Celia Hopkins, Detective Senior Constable Joanna Best.'

Hand shaking all round and offers of gratitude and congratulations followed. The AC asked to be excused and wandered off to chat to others.

'We have something in common,' said Celia, and Jo was intrigued. 'We believe you know two of our grandchildren.' It was as if she was teasing, seeing if Jo knew who Celia was talking about.

'Oh?'

'Grace and Harry Carr,' said their grandfather. The penny dropped.

These are the infamous in-laws, the ones who warned their son-in-law, the lovely GP, about the crooked cop he had befriended.

'Oh, hello,' said Jo, churning inside yet smiling and being charming on the outside. 'They're delightful children. You must be so proud of them.'

'We are,' said Celia making a statement which seemed more of a warning.

'We're good friends with AC Crowley and he speaks very highly of you. He told us about an adventure you and he got up to at a certain railway station.'

Jo was uncertain. *How will this end? Where is this going?*

'Yes, he was a great sport and helped catch a conman.'

'Not to mention a few of your colleagues,' added a smiling Myles.

Jo was seriously confused. *Are they joking or serious?*

Before Jo could reply, a man approached. 'Pardon Madame et Monsieur, but may I 'ave a word with the detective, s'il vous plaît?'

Myles and Celia acquiesced, thanking Jo and bidding farewell. Jo looked at the Inspector and whispered. 'What are you doing here?'

He shrugged. 'I 'ad to 'ear the famous detective make 'er speech. It was magnifique, Mademoiselle, especially the part about breaking the law. Congratulations.'

'Does the AC know you're here?'

'Why? Is there something wrong with supporting a colleague?'

Jo relaxed. 'Of course not. And thank you, Pierre.' He lifted her hand and kissed it, smiled and departed.

Members of staff approached and again thanked her. She thought they were a bit over the top but their praise seemed genuine. The two senior girls stood ready to escort her back to her car. She waved to the AC as she left. He smiled and gave a mini thumbs up. She felt great.

The girls were bubbling at having met the now super popular detective and walked Jo to her car, chatting nine to the dozen.

'It really was a terrific talk, Detective Best,' said Katrina.

'Yes, you were inspiring,' added Bo.

'Thanks girls. And good luck with whatever you do.'

'Bye,' they chorused and Jo was alone. She opened her door but stopped when she heard a familiar voice.

'Pardon Mademoiselle, but may I take you to dinner?'

DI Richelieu smiled, and that in itself was worth a long look.

'Thank you, Pierre, but I have some loose ends with the abduction. Homicide may now have the case but I'd like to tidy up a few things before I hand it over.'

'You mean you would like to solve it.'

She shrugged. 'That too.'

He moved in close. 'I can wait, Mon'Amie. I will be sad and lonely but I can wait.'

He looked into her eyes, paused, then leant in and kissed her gently. He smiled. 'Au revoir,' he said and walked away. Jo tingled. She would have felt less excited had she known who was watching. Myles and Celia Hopkins saw the romantic interlude as they were about to get into their car. The dreaded in-laws saw it all.

21

THE POPE LAUGHED. That in itself was unusual with a smirk his preferred expression. When he heard that Goddard and Best were arrested for affray, he laughed aloud with gusto. When he was shown the backyard footage, he had trouble containing his glee.

Sadly, for him, the laughter was short-lived. The next news kick started his rage. Major Crime, thanks to a certain senior constable, had arrested and charged a man with the murder of Jake Freeman. Were there two murderers? Homicide Squad had arrested someone else—George Little, a pal of Leo Smythe. The police discovered George visited Leo in prison, George's DNA was in the murder house, and George and Leo had exchanged texts re Jake. To top it off, George had no alibi for the murder. Now bloody Best and Goddard had charged someone who knew the parents of the abducted child.

Shit.

Steele addressed Homicide detectives the day after Steve's arrest.

'No doubt you've heard that just as we take over the child abduction case, Major Crime refuse to let go and charge someone for the Foley Street murder.'

'I heard their case is strong, sir,' said Billy Hughes.

'So is ours,' snapped Steele.

'Why don't we take their evidence and see how it flies?' asked Fleming.

Richelieu was back in harness. 'We already 'ave the body from the river and now the abducted and probably murdered child.'

Steele was worried. It showed in his face and fidgety movements. Some months ago, he approved the arrest of the wrong suspect for a double homicide only for that upstart Best to pinpoint the real killers.

Another mistake would turn his previous embarrassment into ridicule. He announced decisions.

'DI Richelieu, will run the woman in the Yarra case. Choose your team.' Richelieu nodded. 'DS Hughes, take the Major Crime arrest and test it against George Little. If their arrest pans out, release Little— quietly.'

'Sir,' said Billy.

'Take whoever is not working with DI Richelieu.'

'What about the abducted child, sir?' asked Fleming.

'I'll run that with you and DSC Payne. All right?'

Squad members muttered assent and met to plan their approach.

At home that night, Jo looked again at her Mind Map with its comments, doodles, arrows and random words. She needed someone to share it with, to test it and to challenge her thinking; preferably someone who knew little if anything about the case, who is smart and not afraid to speak their mind. She rang that person.

'Michael Chan speaking.'

'Joanna Best speaking.'

He almost sparkled. Jo sensed a happiness in his voice, a mood of excitement.

'Good evening Detective. Are you well?'

'I am and you?'

'Fine thank you. How is your bully with his special web site?'

There was a slight pause. Michael sensed something was wrong. Jo recovered.'

'I'll tell you when I see you.'

'Oh, and when will that be?'

'In 20 minutes?'

He laughed. 'I'll tell Alan.' The call ended.

She worried about having to talk about that horrendous night. He worried that she had something sad or bad to relate.

As Jo arrived at Michael's warehouse, Myles and Celia Hopkins headed to their son-in-law's home in Mont Albert. They rang just beforehand to warn the GP of their impending arrival.

Jack never enjoyed their visits and wanted his children bathed, bedded and asleep before they arrived. But whatever he thought of his late wife's family, he went out of his way to allow his kids to see all their grandparents.

He went into Grace's room and whispered. 'Darling, are you awake.'

'Yes, Dad, why?'

'Grandma and Grandpa are coming to see me and I thought you might like to say hello.'

'Do you want me too?'

'I want you to do what you want to do.'

'Okay. I'll get my dressing gown.'

Jack went to check on his son who beat him to it.

'What's happening?' he said yawning.

'Grandma and Grandpa are coming to talk to me.'

'What about?'

'I don't know. Grown-up things.'

'You can stay here, old man. Grace is coming down but … '

'If Grace is going then I want to go.'

Jack smiled in the dim light. The doorbell sounded, the kids scampered to find their dressing gowns, and Jack headed downstairs. He opened the door.

'Good evening Celia, Myles.'

'Good evening,' they chorused and entered. Two small adults appeared in pyjamas, slippers and dressing gowns.

Grandma was unimpressed. 'What are you children doing out of bed. It's after 8 o'clock.'

Despite the reprimand, and lack of greeting, the kids stood their ground.

'We just wanted to say hello, Grandma,' said Grace.

Instead of a hug and welcome, one pair of their grandparents maintained their status as strict, solemn and sourpuss-ian.

Everyone went into the lounge. Celia and Myles sat with Jack standing, an arm around each of his children.

'Okay, you two, say goodnight and then off to bed.'

Each child went to kiss each grandparent, which was as formal a greeting as a monarch welcoming a foreign dignitary they couldn't abide. This was love minus the love, and friendship like revenge—best served cold.

The children departed and Jack sat facing his in-laws.

'To what do I owe this unexpected pleasure?'

'We went to Annabelle's school today.'

'Oh?' said Jack.

'Tell him, Myles.'

He opened his mouth but lost out to his wife—again.

'The speaker was that policewoman you know.'

Jack was all ears. 'Really? Did she speak well?'

Jack knew additional criticism was on its way so when Celia replied, the GP was gobsmacked.

'Very well, didn't she Myles?'

'She did, very well indeed.'

Jack recovered. 'I'm pleased.'

'Assistant Commissioner Crowley was there,' added Myles throwing in his golf club membership and snobbery in one fell swoop.

Celia took over. 'Apparently he was joking when he told us she'd been engaged in criminal behavior and in fact, she really is a most successful detective.'

Why am I not surprised? thought Jack.

'That's good to hear,' said Jack, 'but forgive me because I don't understand why you've come here in person just to tell me that.'

Myles was bubbling. 'We heard in her first Homicide case, she arrested four suspects—four.'

'On her own,' added Celia.

Jack felt he was a mere member of the Jo Best fan club. 'That sounds impressive.'

'She's a very impressive young woman,' said Myles.

'Does this mean you've removed your objection to my children having anything to do with the Senior Constable?'

'Don't be petty, Jack,' retorted his mother-in-law.

Me? Petty? Hello Missus Black Pot.

'We have no objection whatsoever,' said Myles, 'but we think there is something you should know.'

Jack's emotional rollercoaster started a downward plunge. Celia was busting to deliver her news.

'Of course your private life is your own, Jack,' she said. 'We wouldn't dream of interfering.'

'Wouldn't dream of it,' supported the vice-captain.

Don't make me laugh, thought Jack.

'However, we feel obligated to share something with you.'

At this point, Jack was ready to kill or be killed. 'Is there a problem?'

'Of course we couldn't help but see what we saw.'

'Couldn't help it,' said Celia's assistant.

'And it was only a kiss,' continued the mother-in-law. Jack's stomach muscles tightened and stayed tight. 'Although it was definitely not a peck,' continued Celia.

'Much more than a peck,' added Myles.

Jack couldn't stand their beating around the bush. 'Are you trying to tell me something?'

His question came out with a touch of anger. Celia stiffened. Myles remembered he was on her team and added a look of outrage.

'We thought you ought to know that your police officer friend has an admirer and with whom she shared a romantic kiss,' smiled Celia.

She smiles as she delivers the dart.

'In the school grounds,' added Myles, 'in public.'

Jack couldn't diagnose himself, and even if he could, science was yet to create a cure for heartache.

Celia slipped back into her version of morality. 'We wouldn't want our grandchildren becoming friendly with a woman who ...'

She struggled not wanting to use the word *tart.* Jack helped her.

'Do you mean a woman who kisses her lover in a school car park?'

Whack. Celia copped it between the eyes. Had Myles been smarter, he would have reacted to Jack's rebuke. Celia was already on her feet.

'Well if that's your attitude, there's nothing more to be said.'

She took off. Myles got the message and followed. Jack let them go. He was torn between sadness and anger. He wanted them to leave with no apology or any attempt to placate his snobbish in-laws. He followed then stepped forward and opened the door.

'Thank you, for coming,' he said as the Pharisees departed. 'Goodnight,' added Jack. Celia said nothing and kept moving.

Myles said, 'Goodnight,' before realising that wasn't protocol.

Jack closed the door. He turned and saw Grace sitting on the stairs.

'What are you doing there, young lady? Off to bed.'

Arm in arm they climbed the stairs. She hopped into bed. He kissed her and turned out the light. She spoke in the darkness.

'Dad?'

'Yes Grace Margaret Carr?'

'Do you still miss Mummy?'

He paused. Her comment hurt. 'Of course, every day.'

'So do I.'

'Time for sleep, young lady.' He went to close the door.

'Dad?'

'I'm not here.'

'Will you ever get married again?'

That hit hard, damn hard. 'Only one question a night. Now go to sleep.' As he closed the door he heard her voice.

'Goodnight Doctor Carr.'

Jo showed Michael her mind map. 'I did some brainstorming and came up with this.'

'Are you sure this wasn't drawn by Google Maps on drugs?'

'How about I tell you what I reckon and you tell me if I'm wrong.'

'You're wrong.'

'Ha ha.

'Okay, but I've got a dental appointment on Tuesday week.

'Shut up and listen.'

'Is this your most difficult case?

'Yes and no.'

'Oh, so you speak Irish too.'

'It's tricky but it's no longer my case.' He looked at her seeking an explanation. 'The case has been given to another squad. I'm no longer working on it.'

He absorbed that fact. 'So I'm helping you solve a case which is not your case?' She nodded. 'Okay, I'm game. Fire away.'

Jo explained the three possible aspects of the abduction—ransom, rape and revenge. She discounted the first two although if it involved rape by an unknown predator, she had nothing.

'So you're stuck on revenge?'

'I am.'

She explained Gavin's teenage son, Gavin's sleazy stepfather, Donna's best friend and Donna's former lover. She dismissed the first two as improbable and impractical.

'Those two men wouldn't hurt a child and even if they wanted to, don't have the nous and resources to pull off a kidnap.'

'The field narrows,' said Michael.

'You haven't challenged me yet,' replied Jo.

'I'm reserving my judgement, officer.'

Jo explained about Kylie being Donna's best friend, and how Lawrence was once Donna's lover. 'And that's where I'm at. What do you think?'

He said what he didn't want to say. 'I think you haven't told me what happened with your bully and the revenge porn site.'

That flattened Jo. She'd been concentrating on her child abduction case, and Michael's question came out of the blue. She struggled.

'Not now,' she said and had difficulty breathing.

He knew he'd said the wrong thing. 'I'm sorry. Forgive me.'

Jo had pushed the attack in her apartment to the back of her mind. She kept working on *not* thinking about it. Suddenly it leapt up and roared. She looked at Michael and tears appeared.

He moved to her and took her hands in his. Neither spoke. He was sensitive and knew the best thing to say was nothing, certainly not about whatever had caused her breakdown.

Alan wandered over and Jo became distracted by the cat.

'I'll make coffee,' said Michael, and went to the kitchen. When he returned, Jo was receiving and giving plenty of feline love. Coffee arrived and Michael let Jo lead the conversation.

'The bully and his mate bashed me at my flat.' Michael felt pain. 'I was about to be raped. A colleague arrived and saved me.'

Lots of silence. Finally Michael spoke.

'I think it's about time you gave up the criminal life, Jo Best.' She gave a sealed lips grin. 'I'm serious,' he added.

Always up for an argument, a recharged Jo hit back.

'Well if I followed your advice Mr Chan, my mother and your parents would be broke, and a young abused woman might have self-harmed or worse.'

He didn't have an answer. 'You know I removed that web site about the lovely Darren.'

'I do, and thanks.'

He went for a complete change of subject. 'So, re the case you are no longer investigating, whodunit?'

She appreciated his attitude and especially his question. 'I'd love to speak to the girlfriend's mother.'

'Kylie?'

'Her mother Brenda gave Kylie an alibi for the day of the abduction, and my colleagues were satisfied it was genuine.'

'But you're not?'

'I came late to the case and never met the mother and now she's disappeared. Kylie said her mother went to the country.'

'Did she say where?'

'No.'

'Did you ask her?'

'I was afraid. I had this feeling I'd spook her. I'd love to find Kylie's mother and arrive unannounced. My current DI likes surprise arrivals.'

'So, will you spring a surprise visit?'

'Yes.' She looked at him. 'Will you come with me?'

He felt sorry for her. He liked her. He wanted to help.

'Sure. When?'

'Tomorrow?'

'Okay.'

She smiled and felt heaps better.

'You do know,' he said, that the "country" is a big place.'

'I can describe the house.'

He thought she was mad. He remembered a story about an old Englishman who met an American pilot in London in WW2.

"I had a mate who went to America a few years back," said the Pom. "Name of Tommy Jones. Have you ever come across him?"

But Michael knew Jo's madness included an eagle-eyed memory.

'In Kylie's home there was a photo on the wall of an elderly couple, I guess her grandparents. Kylie said her mother had gone to stay with her parents. I can describe that house in detail and behind it was this really tall chimney.'

'How tall?'

'Oh, 20 metres, hard to tell.'

'Describe the chimney.'

'Well it wasn't round, it had corners.

'You mean like a statue or a monument, something on a grave?'

'It seemed too tall for a statue.'

'An obelisk?'

'A what?'

'They're tall, rectangular and taper towards the top.'

'That could be it.'

'Could you see any writing on this chimney?'

'No, the people were in front of the house and the ... what is it?'

'An obelisk.'

'The obelisk was in the background.'

He clicked on one of his computer keyboards and typed. 'Obelisks Victoria, regional cities.'

'Not Ballarat.'

'Not Ballarat.' He watched the screen. 'Describe the house.'

Jo explored her memory. 'Weatherboard, white, tin roof, biggish garden.'

Michael flicked through different screens. Jo watched. Many of the obelisks were not near houses and were easily dismissed.

'I can tell you what the old couple were wearing.'

Michael kept flicking. 'Good. And what did they have for breakfast?'

She liked his sense of humour. More images. Then Jo shrieked.

'That's it. That's the house. That one.' He made the image larger. 'You've found it. Michael Chan you are a star.'

He explored. 'It's the Burke and Wills obelisk in Castlemaine.'

'That house is the one on the wall in Kylie's house, and you can see part of that monument in the background.'

'You've been reading too many Sherlock stories, Detective,' he said.

'I'm going to Castlemaine first thing in the morning. Do you still want to come?'

'I said I would. What time?'

'I'll pick you up at 6.'

'6 am!'

She leant in and kissed his cheek. Alan and his master purred.

22

JACK SAT IN THE DARK. He wasn't much of a drinker but held a glass of single malt. It was more than two years since his wife died, thanks to that bastard, breast cancer. He blamed himself for not encouraging her more often to have a scan. She died quickly and left a void in his life. He hoped their kids would recover better than he had.

Marriage was not front and centre in his mind. His mother was a brilliant female role model. She gave the kids love in spades. But something changed not long ago. A woman came to his surgery, not for any medical need but information.

Detective Senior Constable Joanna Best caught his eye, heart and imagination. He wasn't religious but he thought the gods were on his side when they met by chance at Puffing Billy. From that day he knew she was special. When his kids almost adopted her, he dared to dream.

He thought about any number of possible situations—all except one. He didn't consider she was spoken for.

He couldn't believe how dumb he was. He couldn't believe how sad he felt. She gave no indication she was in a relationship. Getting the news of Jo's romantic tryst was bad enough. Getting said news from his in-laws was the absolute pits.

He sipped the whisky. It didn't help. What would he tell his kids? What if they asked about their favourite detective? Should he tell them the truth? Now his pain would be their pain.

Bugger.

Jo was up and about at 0500 hours. It was hunch time again. In her previous Homicide cases, apart from examining the evidence, she found herself dreaming or thinking or imagining the guilty person being so and so. She called it her hunch approach, a feeling in her gut.

Thanks yet again to the brilliant Michael Chan, she was sure she'd found a house in Castlemaine, a photo of which hung on Kylie's living room wall. The elderly couple in the photo had to be her grandparents.

So what? Did they have anything to do with the abducted Candy White? Was Kylie's mother, Brenda living there? Probably not. But what other lead did Jo have? The investigation was now with Homicide. Talk about last throw of the dice.

She made coffee and toast, gobbled muesli, then headed off to visit Castlemaine, 2 hours and 120 clicks north-west of Melbourne. She went via Northcote to collect a certain IT expert, a Mr Michael Chan.

An hour or so later, Jack Carr made breakfast for his kids. They came downstairs dressed for school. Grace was immaculate and Jack not quite. His shirttail hung free, his tie was skewwhiff, his hair uncombed, and his shoelaces were on holiday.

The kids got started on their breakfast, both talking at cross-purposes. Jack had become a househusband of the first water. He could have his kids fed, washed and watered, and off to school with an almost military routine.

He didn't sleep well. The news about his favourite cop smooching with her boyfriend played on Jack's mind. He tried to concentrate on other things until his children ruined his day.

'Dad,' piped up Harry while eating, 'when is Jo coming to see us?'

Jack squirmed. 'Well she's a busy person. Police officers have a difficult job which takes up a lot of time.'

'She said she would come and see us run at the next Little Aths day,' said Grace.

'She did,' added Harry.

'Can you please ask her, Dad?' pleaded Grace.

Jack struggled. 'Okay, I'll try.'

'Promise?' asked Grace.

'I promise,' replied her father.

Harry had an idea. 'You could take me to the police station, Dad, and I could go inside and ask her to come to our house.'

Oh boy. This sure ain't easy, folks.

175

Michael was ready to roll. 'Good morning,' he said carrying his backpack to her car. 'Should you make me a deputy or something?'

Jo imitated an American police officer from the Deep South.

'Well gollee, if it ain't Deputy Sherriff, Michael Chan. Howdy partner.'

'Don't give up your day job.'

They set off.

Both were anxious with Jo desperate for a break in the case she had already left and Michael unsure if she liked him as much as he liked her.

'So what's the plan, Detective?'

'We find Castlemaine. We find the obelisk. We find the house. We play it by ear.'

'I notice you keep using the plural personal pronoun. Would that be the Royal we?'

She laughed. 'We've been a terrific team so far, Michael. When you're on a good thing, ...'

'Yes, okay, got the message.' He paused. He wanted to bring up the traumatic event which upset her last night. He wanted to be sure she didn't get into dangerous situations ever again.

'You weren't on a good thing when those men attacked you.' She fell silent. He paused then spoke slowly. 'I don't want you to get hurt, Jo.' Another pause. 'I care about you.'

The penny dropped and Jo twigged.

Oh no, he means he fancies me. For crying out loud, that's three boyfriends. They're like bloody trams. You wait for ages and then three arrive together.

Jack delivered his kids to school with lots of waving and calling. He headed to work. Half way there, he pulled over and took out his phone. The pressure was enormous. He wanted to contact Jo. His kids wanted him to contact Jo.

Damn it, I'll contact Jo.

He rang her number. It rang in a car cruising along the Calder Highway. She hadn't connected it to her hands-free device.

'Michael, can you get that please?'

He reached for the phone. 'Oh, so now I'm your gopher.' He answered the phone.

'Detective Senior Constable Best's phone.'

Jack was thrown. Who was speaking? Is this the carpark kisser?

'Oh hello. Is Detective Best available? It's Jack Carr speaking.'

'Jack Carr,' said Michael to Jo.

'Can you put it on speaker? Bottom right.'

Michael looked at her. He was an IT genius being told how to work a mobile phone. She grinned. He pushed the button. She spoke.

'Good morning, Dr Carr.'

Jack felt a flood of emotion. 'Oh hi Jo, is this a bad time?'

'I'm on the road, Jack, driving to Castlemaine.'

'Okay, well, the kids asked me to call you and ...'

'That's lovely. Say hi to them from me. Are you all well?'

Jack struggled. He wanted to speak to her and he didn't want to speak to her.

'We are, thanks. And you drive carefully.'

'I'm having a day in the country with my friend, Michael.'

'Sounds great. Look, I won't interrupt. I'll call you later. Bye.'

He ended the call. He felt far worse than before he rang.

She's off on a romantic jaunt with her boyfriend. I've made a complete fool of myself. I can recover. But what will I tell the kids?

The would-be boyfriend on the phone felt flat. The would-be boyfriend in the car felt flat. Jo thought about her love life.

And I've got that offer of a trip to Paris as well. My mother won't believe me. Hi Mum, I still haven't got a boyfriend, I've got three.

They reached the outskirts of Castlemaine. Michael had the Rolls Royce of GPS systems and gave clear directions. They headed up a hill. He saw it first.

'There's your obelisk, Jo.' She saw it and got excited. 'Listen,' said Michael, 'I don't want to be a wet blanket but perhaps you should set your expectations at low and that way, if things don't work out, you'll not be so disappointed.'

She thought about it. 'You're right.'

They drove higher. The obelisk got closer.

'This road goes up to the obelisk. If you park near the house, you'll lose your surprise arrival.'

She pulled over. 'You definitely should have been a detective, Mr Chan. I need a partner like you, Mister Methodical.'

Just not Mister Desirable, he thought.

Jo pulled over about 50 metres before the house. Michael broke the silence.

'What's the plan, Chief?'

'Don't take this the wrong way, Michael, but I'm going in alone.'

'Was it something I said?'

'The fewer strangers the better, and a woman alone is much less of a threat.'

'I've got a dress in my backpack if that helps.' She smiled. 'Gotcha. I'll stay here and eat my apple.'

She touched his hand, and got out of the car. He watched her walk up the hill and stop beside the house she'd seen in the photo.

Her mind was racing. She'd planned her approach, what she would say but right now, felt shaky. Her nerves got busy. She took a deep breath and walked onto the property.

She walked along the drive, onto the verandah, and up to the front door. She could hear voices. *Someone's home.*

She used the doorknocker. The voices inside stopped as if shot. Then Jo heard the voice of an adult female. Footsteps. Jo heard someone approaching. She heard two sets of footsteps with the second ones being softer and quicker.

Jo strained to hear. A small child was speaking. It sounded female and happy. Well, at least not in distress. Jo froze.

She couldn't believe her luck. This hunch, this shot in the dark had come up trumps. Jo had found the abducted child who was alive!

The door opened but the fly wire door made it difficult to see.

'Yes? What do you want?' asked an elderly woman.

Jo stared through the wire door. She thought she recognised the woman but she sure as hell didn't recognise the little girl. All the disguise tricks in the world couldn't hide the fact that Candy White wasn't black.

23

JUDGE RANALD SLIGHT was, at the time of his appointment, the youngest person ever appointed to the Supreme Court in the state of Victoria. He was a brilliant jurist and knew the Law and then some. He was also the youngest Supreme Court judge to die, aged 47.

It was a strange death. In leafy South Yarra, Judge Slight set off for work but never made it past his front gate. His car alarm sounded and didn't stop. Some neighbours were annoyed, others worried.

The incessant piercing sound attracted the police and two uniformed officers arrived. They couldn't open the gate—it too was alarmed—and one gave the other a bunk up. Once inside, the cop couldn't open the gate without the code. Keys are so passé these days.

Having explained the situation to his colleague in the street, the officer on the property walked down the steep driveway to the Bentley with its alarm firing on all cylinders.

'Hello,' called the constable. If the judge had been nearby, he wouldn't have heard the cry thanks to the foghorn on his motor.

The car faced the closed garage door. The officer looked inside the vehicle and saw nothing or no one. He pulled the driver's door handle. The door opened. The keys were in the ignition and the cop then realized the motor was running.

A combination of an expensive car and a loud alarm buried the sound. The officer turned the keys and the engine and alarm stopped. This was a coincidence. The alarm had run its course. Silence roared. Neighbours sighed.

'What's happening?' called the constable out in the street.

'Nothing,' replied his mate, who closed the car door and walked to the front of the Bentley. Then he found the judge.

It was ugly. His worship's head was squashed between the bumper and the solid garage door. Constable Woodley threw up. He recovered and spoke to his Worship.

'Hello, sir? Can you hear me?'

Being dead, his Worship was deaf. The constable veered towards panic. He'd seen road fatalities before but this was his first on a driveway. He hurried back up the drive, and told his colleague.

'Should I move the car?'

'Are you sure he's dead?'

'He's not moving or speaking and his face is real mess.'

'I'll call the station.'

Soon the neighbours had plenty to stare out as police vehicles, an ambulance, a fire engine and homicide squad officers arrived. Piccadilly Circus took root in whisper-quiet South Yarra.

Last to turn up was Dr Gabrielle Strange, self-described pathetic pathologist, and whose voice could match the switched-off car alarm.

'You don't expect me to walk down that.' She froze at the top of the slope. Billy Hughes saw her and climbed the "hill".

'Good morning, Doctor Strange. As they say in the movies, "Walk this way".'

The pathologist understood the gag, and followed Billy to steps and descended with care. They made it to the Bentley and the body.

The medico looked around. 'This is out my price range, Sergeant. I couldn't even afford the rates.'

Richelieu was the senior officer. 'Bonjour, Docteur. We are not sure if this is a 'omicide. We await your opinion, s'il vous plaît.'

Strange inspected the body, still in its horrific state and position.

'Well I'm not getting under the bloody car even if it is a Bentley. You'll have to move it. The car, not the body.'

They did—slowly. A tent was placed over the body to thwart nosy neighbours, and the paparazzi in choppers or using drones.

'Jesus wept,' said Strange once she dressed for the occasion.

Billy Hughes spoke quietly to the pathologist. 'The victim's a judge, Doctor. Please be careful what you say.'

The pathologist looked at the detective. 'Well it looks normal for the death of a lawyer, Sergeant—there are no skid marks.'

While the gag-cracking pathologist went to work, Jo Best played her hunch in Castlemaine.

'Hello. I'm looking for Kylie's mum, Brenda. Can you help me?'

'She's not well. Are you from Centrelink?'

'No, no, nothing like that. No, I just wanted to drop off some things from Kylie.'

The little aboriginal girl tugged at the old woman's dress. Jo went for the friendly touch.

'And what's your name little girl? I bet I can guess.' The child went all shy. 'Is it Susie Swizzle Sticks?' The child smiled but shook her head. 'I know, it's Penelope Pinkpants.'

More smiles and head shaking. Having declared her friendly nature and love of children, Jo switched back to the woman.

'I've got some things from Kylie for her Mum. I can drop them off at the farm on my way back to Melbourne.'

The woman wavered. 'She didn't say anything to me.'

'She wouldn't. That girl would forget her head if it wasn't screwed on. But I know she wants these clothes.'

'Okay, I suppose it'll be all right.'

'Trouble is she said she'd be here or at the farm and she didn't give me directions.'

Kylie's grandmother pointed. 'Go back into town, take the Muckleford Road and after the creek it's on your right. The farm's called *Wattle Glen.*'

'That's lovely, thanks for your help. You're Kylie's grandmother. I recognised you from the photos.'

Grandma smiled and relaxed. Jo bent and teased the little girl one more time.

'Bye bye Betty Bloomers.'

More shy smiles from the child and Jo waved as she left the property. Michael saw her hurrying towards him.

'Your body language suggests success,' he said as she opened her door, hopped in and clicked her seatbelt.

'We take the Muckleford Road and, after the creek, the farm's *Wattle Glen* on your right.'

'Is that my right or your right?'

She smiled and felt her pulse quicken. He used his fancy GPS and they were on their way.

'So what's the verdict, Doctor?' Billy Hughes wanted to know.

'Well it's either a very elaborate murder or the most ridiculous suicide I've ever seen.' Hughes and Richelieu looked at one another. 'I can tell you more, perhaps much more, once the good judge and I become more intimately acquainted.' She struggled with her gloves and Teflon suit.

'Permettez-moi, Madame,' said Richelieu, helping the pathologist.

'Merci, Monsieur. And tell me, what's happened to the lovely young Senior Constable Best?'

'Ah she is 'elping Major Crime on a special assignment.'

'Well after what she did for you, I would have thought she'd be your star player.'

Being French, Richelieu was unfazed by what was said. The others were curious and Billy was all ears.

Jo drove too fast. She wanted to get to this farm and test her hunch. Would the mother give Kylie an alibi? Would Kylie be in the clear?

'That could be it,' said Michael, pointing.

Jo slowed, stopped and they looked at the property. The house was set well back from the road.

'What's the plan, Detective? Should I hide in the boot?'

'I think we drive in, both hop out, and then play it by ear.'

'I've only known you a few months, Jo Best, but in that time I've had several death-defying adventures.'

She looked at him. 'And your point is?'

He smiled one the biggest smiles she'd even seen. 'Let's go.'

She pulled into the property, and drove along the dirt driveway for 100 metres or more. Jo watched the potholes while Michael watched the house. There were plenty of potholes but no people. If someone was home, they must have known they had visitors.

Jo pulled up in the space beside the house. The place looked deserted with no cars in sight. Jo and Michael got out. They looked at the house and at one another. The silence was scary.

The result of the breeze caught Jo's eye. In the back yard, the washing flapped.

'Someone's living here,' she said softly, indicating the laundry.

Michael wanted to speak but didn't. *Kid's clothes on the line.*

Jo decided. 'We're in the bush. Let's go in the back way.'

They moved to the rear and approached the back door. Jo hesitated then knocked. 'Hello,' she called. The only sound was the flapping of the washing.

'Nobody's home,' said Michael who now knew he wasn't cut out for going on police raids. 'Let's go.'

Jo ignored him and turned the door handle. The unlocked door opened. Of course it did. In the bush, locks are for keeping out honest folk. She called louder.

'Hello? Anyone home?' Again no reply so she entered the kitchen.

'Jo,' called Michael with a voice tinged with fear. He followed.

She was almost through the kitchen when another voice was heard. 'Stop or I'll shoot.'

The rifle was pointed at Jo but Michael felt he was in the firing line.

Jo turned and appeared calm. 'Hello, you must be Brenda.'

'Get over there, by the stove, both of you.'

Michael had further to travel but did so in rapid time.

'I'm Jo and this is Michael. We wondered if Kylie was home.'

'Why?'

'Because we wanted to ask her a couple of questions.'

Michael wasn't keen on the personal pronoun.

'What sort of questions?'

'Is she here?'

'Who are you?'

'I've just told you our names?'

'You're the police.'

'I'm not,' said Michael in a flash.

'It's true, I'm a police officer but Michael is a friend.'

Some friend, he thought.

The woman raised the gun. 'I want you to leave. Kylie's done nothing wrong.' She indicated with the gun. 'Now get out and don't come back.' Jo hesitated. Michael went to move and Jo held his arm. 'Move,' shouted the woman. 'Move or I'll shoot.'

'No you won't,' said Jo.

The woman pointed the gun and then shifted her aim to Michael's chest.

'Jo,' he almost squeaked.

'That's enough Mum.' Kylie entered the kitchen from the hallway. Her mother turned angry. 'They want to take you away. I won't let them.'

Mother and daughter looked at one another. Jo stepped forward and took hold of the firing end of the rifle. Michael thought her bravery sheer stupidity. It wasn't. Jo saw the gun's firing mechanism had been removed, and the weapon was only good for clubbing.

'Why don't we all sit down,' said Jo and they did. The kitchen table sat four with ease.

Jo sounded like a loving parent worried about a naughty child. 'Where did you put the wig, Kylie?'

She looked surprised. 'I chucked it.'

'How did you know about the Foley Street house?'

That puzzled her. Michael too was confused.

Surely the first thing to ask would be about the child!

'Why did you take her, Kylie?'

Again, nothing about the whereabouts of the child. Why?

Jo remembered DI Goddard's tip about not mentioning the name of the victim thus taking the emotion out of the subject. And Jo worked hard at avoiding confrontation and accusation. The mantra being, "Become her friend". As a result, Kylie wanted to explain. She was glad to tell someone.

'It wasn't fair. When I was with Gavin, I lost my baby. She died before my time.' Tears appeared. Kylie let it all out. Her mother rubbed her daughter's arm. 'Then Donna stole Gavin. He didn't leave me, she took him. How can a friend do that? We were besties. We trusted one another and she stabbed me in the back.'

'The bitch,' said Brenda.

'And then my so-called friend got pregnant and had her baby. Mine died and hers lived. It wasn't fair. Candy should have been my baby.'

Michael marvelled at the way Jo got Kylie to open up and confess. The one thing he couldn't understand was the missing direct question, "Where is the child now"?

'I bet you take good care of Candy,' said Jo.

Now the change to using the child's name—the personal touch.

'Of course,' snapped Kylie. 'I love her. She's mine. She wants to be with me. She knows I love her.'

Jo paused and let the passion fade even if a little. She spoke softly.

'Will you take me to see her, please Kylie?'

Anger flared immediately. 'No, you want to take her away. I won't let you.'

Again Jo paused. Now she wanted to know about Candy but still asked in a roundabout way.

'Is Candy happy?' Kylie didn't answer. 'Does she ask about her Mummy and Daddy?'

Kylie spoke the truth. 'At first she did but not now. Now she has a new family, a new Mummy and a new Daddy.'

Slap! Jo and Michael copped a smack in the face. *A new Daddy?*

'I'll feel a lot happier, Kylie, if you just let me see Candy. I promise I won't hurt her or scare her. If you like, I won't even let her see me. I'll stay out of sight and just have a little look.' She paused. 'Please?'

Kylie looked at her mother who nodded.

'Okay,' said Kylie, 'but you must promise not to frighten her.'

'I promise,' said Jo. 'You lead the way.' Jo and Kylie stood.

'Not him,' said Kylie pointing at Michael who'd been watching everything with a mix of disbelief, and admiration for Jo.

Jo agreed. 'Okay.' She addressed Michael. 'Please stay here and look after Brenda.' Michael nodded. What else could he do?

'Where's Candy now?' asked Jo.

'In the shed. Whenever someone comes to the farm, we take her to the shed. Mum does everything when we're not here.' She stopped. 'How did you find us?'

Jo didn't want to frighten the horses. 'You told me, Kylie.'

She screwed her face. 'No I didn't.'

'In your flat, you told me about your grandparents.'

Kylie had to think about that. She didn't remember naming any address but didn't argue. She moved to the back door then suddenly panicked. A loud racket exploded. It was a backfiring engine. Kylie screamed and bolted out the door.

She screamed. 'No!' her voice trailed on and on as she ran from the house. Jo was after her in a flash. Brenda picked up the rifle and Michael panicked.

Kylie ran to the driveway shouting. Jo caught up to her. All they could see was dust as a motorcycle sped away towards the road.

'He's taken her. He's taken Candy.' Kylie was hysterical.

'Who,' yelled Jo. 'Who's taken her?'

Kylie howled. 'He promised he'd never take her, never.'

Michael arrived. 'What's happening?'

Jo grabbed Kylie. 'Tell me, Kylie, please.'

Kylie had lost her dream, her life was over. Her mother joined them and spoke to Jo.

'That's Lawrence. He thinks Candy has a terrible father, and he could do a much better job.'

'Where will he go?'

Brenda shrugged. 'He works for the tourist railway on weekends.'

'Which way is that?'

Brenda comforted her inconsolable daughter as Jo took off. She sprinted to her car with Michael racing to catch up. He climbed in holding the rifle.'

'Dump it, it's useless,' yelled Jo staring her car.

'What?'

'Dump it,' she yelled doing a three-point turn.

Michael tossed the rifle and nearly fell out of the car as it swerved and headed along the potholed drive. He managed to close his door and attach his belt. They stirred up a cloud of dust, and reached the end of the drive.

'Which way?' cried Jo.

Michael looked at the skid marks in the gravel. 'Right.'

Jo accelerated. The road was clear as they headed away from Castlemaine.

24

'IS THIS WHEN YOU CALL FOR BACK-UP?' asked Michael.

'Once we locate them, yes.'

'Are we dealing with a couple of nutters?'

'We don't use that sort of language, Michael, but yes, you're right. Having sirens and a chopper turn up might tip him over the edge. We do all we can to keep them safe and then we call for back up.'

'There's a lot of "we" going on here, Detective.'

'This is the other side of policing. And please keep your eyes peeled.'

He wanted to say, "Give me the IT department any day" but didn't.

They raced along hoping to find the motorcyclist and, more importantly, its precious cargo—its passenger. Jo didn't want to think about finally solving the mystery of the little lady who vanished for it to end in tragedy. They saw nothing of their quarry.

They came to an intersection. A car had stopped at a stop sign. Jo wound down her window and yelled.

'Have you seen a motorbike with a man and a child?'

The driver couldn't hear. Jo drove closer and yelled. 'We're looking for a motorbike.'

The driver pointed. 'One went flying past that way.'

'Thanks,' said Jo reversing then accelerating in that direction.

'Brilliant job, Detective, in finding the little girl.'

'Finding and saving are not the same, Michael. Please keep looking.'

Jo lost her ability to laugh and smile. They sped along seeing or hearing nothing.

Michael pointed. 'Over there, what's that?'

Jo looked. 'Dust. We'll take it.'

She turned into Muckleford-Walmer Road. The dust was on their right but settling.

'If that's the bike, he's stopped,' said Michael.

They slowed and looked. There were railway trucks resting in a siding and buildings.

'Brenda said he worked for the tourist railway,' said Michael.

They drove over the railway tracks and along a dirt road. That was the source of the dust. Jo drove carefully towards the Muckleford Railway Station. It was part of an old branch line to Maldon. The line closed in 1976 but 20 years later was restored as a tourist railway.

Jo stopped a fair way from the main station building.

'What's the plan?' asked the deputy.

'Good question. How about I approach the station and you hang out in those trees. Keep out of sight. If I yell, dial triple zero and get the world here asap.'

'And where's here?'

'You mean the man with the world's latest Satnav device is lost?'

'Just testing,' he replied and they got out of the car, closing doors as quietly as possible.

They parted company. Jo walked softly towards the Muckleford Station as Michael went to hide in the trees. He had a view of the rear of the building.

'Pssst,' he called. She looked at him as he indicated and mimed, "Motorbike". She gave a thumbs up sign.

It wasn't hot but Jo sweated. She thought her footsteps sounded loud. She didn't have a plan other than to go softly and slowly. She reached the front of the station. The door seemed locked and secured.

She took the plunge and spoke without shouting.

'Hello, Lawrence. It's Jo Best. Remember me? How are you?' Nothing. Jo thought she heard a whimper but wasn't sure. 'I just want a quick word, Lawrence, then I'll be on my way.'

Another pause before a man's voice was heard. 'Go away.' It was calm but definite.

Jo felt an enormous sigh of relief. Contact at least. 'I've got a message from Donna.'

More silence but this time there was no "go away". 'What message?'

Jo paced her replies. 'She wants to tell you that she's very sorry.'

'And?'

'She didn't mean to say those hurtful things and wants to ask for your forgiveness.' Jo was winging it. Would it work?

'It's too late.'

'No, Lawrence, please, it's never too late.'

Suddenly a child's cry rang out.

'I want my Mummy.' Jo died inside. She moved back so Michael could see her. She beckoned him to come to her but put a finger to her lips requesting silence. If things got physical, Jo wanted back up.

She called to the people inside. 'Hello Candy. My name's Jo.'

Soft voices came from inside the station. Michael joined Jo and whispered. 'What now?'

Jo shrugged. Her priority was the safety of the "passengers" inside the station. 'Lawrence,' called Jo. I have something for Candy. May I give it to her?'

'Go away.'

Michael whispered. 'Is this the time for back-up?'

Jo agreed. She took out her phone when a terrible scream came from inside the little building. Jo and Michael rushed towards the door. The screaming was from the child and the raised voice was from Lawrence. Jo knocked on the door.

'Lawrence. Please open the door. I have a first-aid kit. Please let me help.'

More horrific sounds came from inside with more calling and knocking from outside. Suddenly a sound as the door was unlocked. Jo and Michael had no control over their heart rates. The door opened a fraction. Jo pushed it and she and Michael entered.

Jo's mind was in freefall. All this time, all this way, all this searching, and it had to end like this.

It took a few seconds to adjust to the light. Lawrence was crouched in a corner, his head between his knees, sobbing. Candy was against the wall, lying on the floor.

Jo and Michael knelt beside the child. She had a look of horror on her face. Jo tried to help her up.

'I'll get her,' said Michael and scooped up the child.

They took her outside, ignoring Lawrence. Jo's basic first-aid training seemed woeful. Michael held Candy and Jo tried to communicate.

'It's okay, Candy, it's okay. Where does it hurt, darling? Where's the pain?'

The little girl's index finger pointed back at the station. 'Spider.'

There was a coating of fear in her speech but it brought a surge of happiness to Jo and Michael.

'It's gone, Candy. The spider's gone. You're okay,' said Jo who started to cry. This surprised the child. Who was this lady and why was she crying?

'This is Michael and I'm Jo. We're going to take you home. Would you like that?'

The child nodded. Jo stroked her arm. Michael will take you to the car and I'll be with you in just a minute. Okay?'

Candy nodded again. Jo looked at Michael and her eyes gave instructions. He carried Candy to the car.

Jo called the local police and asked for two cars; one for Lawrence and the other for Kylie and Brenda. Then she rang a Melbourne number. Donna answered.

Jo had never made a call like this. She found her mouth going dry. Having to tell Donna her child was dead would have been terrible. But strangely, having good news was pretty darn nerve-racking.

'Hello,' said Donna.

'Donna, it's Detective Jo Best.' Jo thought she heard Donna go cold. Jo wanted to get the good news out instantly. 'Donna, Candy's alive and well.' Jo heard a shriek and couldn't tell what Donna had done. 'Are you there, Donna?'

'Is it true? Please, is it true?' Donna was begging.

'It's true Donna. We found her in the country. She's been well looked after and she wants to come home.'

More shrieking from Donna. Gavin came into the room and snatched the phone.

'Hello. Who is this?'

'Gavin, it's Jo Best. We've found Candy and she's okay. She's alive, Gavin and we'll bring her home as soon as we can.'

The once loudmouthed and abusive husband fell silent. Jo could hear Donna crying. Gavin helped his wife then spoke again.

'Where are you?'

'We're in the country, Gavin, about two hours from Melbourne.'

'Who took her?'

Jo hesitated. She sensed he was intent on retribution. Telling Gavin and Donna that their friends, their lovers, people they knew were involved, and that paedophiles had nothing to do with the abduction seemed like a bad idea.

'Who took her?' he screamed.

Donna tried to remonstrate with her husband.

Jo lied. 'We're still investigating, Gavin but your little girl is safe and well and we'll bring her home as soon as we can.'

'When? Where are you? We'll come and get her.'

'Please Gavin. We need to have her checked out by a doctor and then we'll bring her to Melbourne and to you and Donna.'

'I want to see her now.'

Donna pleaded with her husband. 'Gavin, let the police do their job. Give me the phone. I want to ring Mum.'

Donna came on the line. 'Thank you. I don't know what to say. And Candy's okay? Are you sure?'

'Is she scared of spiders?'

'Oh God, she's terrified of spiders. What's happened?'

'She was crying when we found her, and we thought she was hurt but it turned out she was scared by a spider.'

Donna poured out her thanks. Jo promised to ring her in the next half hour, and managed to end the call.

She looked at Michael. He'd lifted Candy and placed her on the car. Jo called. 'Five minutes.' Michael waved. Jo waved then headed into the Muckleford Station.

Lawrence was still on the floor, weeping.

'Hello again, Lawrence.' He looked at Jo. His face spoke volumes. Jo sat beside him. 'You did the right thing, Lawrence. You were brave and right to let us help Candy.'

Between his tears he muttered, 'That's easy for you to say.' His middle name was Despair.

Jo tried to encourage him. 'You really loved Donna, didn't you?' He wailed. She let him sob.

Eventually he recovered. 'She told me she loved me. She did.'

'And I know you loved her.'

191

That set him off again. 'I still do and I told her. But she's trapped. She doesn't love that bastard. She hates him. She and Candy could be so much happier with *me*.' He was distraught. His dream was dead.

Jo believed he was sincere and might even be correct. But life can be tough and when deception takes hold, tangled webs are everywhere.

She placed a hand on his arm. 'Thank you for taking such good care of Candy.' He broke down again. She even felt sorry for him. Then she heard a car approaching. 'Lawrence,' she spoke quietly. 'It's time to go.'

He wiped the snot and tears on his sleeve and nodded. 'I know.'

'I'm going to have to arrest you, Lawrence.' He said nothing. 'Do you understand?' He nodded.

Two uniformed police officers arrived. They entered ready to tackle a dangerous criminal. Jo raised a hand stopping them in their tracks. She held up her ID and identified herself. The police officers were impressed with the young woman who had things so obviously under control. She turned to her prisoner.

'Lawrence Blair, I'm arresting you for the kidnap of Candy White. You do not have to say anything but anything you do say may be taken down and used in evidence against you. Do you understand?'

He took his time but then nodded. He knew his life would never be the same. He'd blown his chance of a life with Donna and Candy. The real possibility of going to jail loomed large. Kylie and her mother too would face a custodial sentence.

Jo stood. 'You'll have to go with these officers, Lawrence.' She put her hand under his arm and helped him to stand. 'What do you want me to do with the keys to the station?'

That tipped him off. Being in an unrequited love relationship and having done something dreadful in abducting a child he loved were bad enough. But now he had to give up the tourist railway, his favourite pastime. The railway authority would never employ him again.

He handed Jo the keys to the station and the keys to his motorbike. She looked at the officers who stepped forward and took Lawrence away. Pathetic was a good word to describe this broken man.

She told the police she'd come to the Castlemaine station (police not railway) as soon as possible. She locked the door of the Muckleford Station, and walked over to Michael and his new little friend. He and

Candy were watching a cartoon on a tablet Michael had produced from his backpack.

They had no child seat in the car but secured her as well as they could and headed back to Castlemaine. On the back seat, Candy seemed happy with her cartoon.

Michael looked at Jo. 'Well done, Detective Senior Constable Joanna Best. You've done it again.'

She looked at him. 'And well done you, Michael Chan.'

25

DI GODDARD FELT LOUSY. She failed to find the abducted child. She failed to charge anyone with the abduction. She lost the case to her rival, DI Steele, in Homicide. True, her bright young senior constable had solved the murder of Jake Freeman, but that arrest was the only bright spot in the case. Goddard still felt lousy. Then her phone rang and life became wonderful. The caller spoke from the Castlemaine Hospital.

'Ma'am, it's Jo. Are you sitting down?'

'What's happened?'

'I'm in Castlemaine. We've found Candy and she's alive and well.'

Goddard fought hard to suppress some colourful language. She had a list of questions and Jo's answers gave her great joy.

'That's amazing, Jo, bloody fantastic. Who have you told?'

'Only Donna and Gavin. Once the Castlemaine Hospital give Candy the all-clear, we'll head back to Melbourne.'

'In your car?'

'Yes, my friend Michael has gone to have a child car seat fitted. Don't tell anyone or they'll think I'm pregnant.'

Serious laughter broke free. 'I'll tell everyone.'

'With the all clear from the medicos, we'll drive straight to the White house, and I assume you'll want to be there.'

'Tricky. It's gone to Homicide.'

'But why? They don't handle lost kids who turn up alive and well.'

Goddard relished the development. 'You're right. I'll inform DI Steele of the changed situation.'

'Be gentle, Ma'am.'

'Homicide won't mind. They've got a dead judge to sort out.'

Jo knew nothing about Rupert Slight and his unfortunate death by Bentley accident. Goddard explained and Jo tingled. What a case.

'Gotta go, Ma'am. My taxi's here.'

'Brilliant job, Detective. You can work on my team any time.'

'Thanks ma'am, I'll call when we hit town.'

Michael arrived smiling. Jo had never seen him smile so often and so enthusiastically. He even cracked a gag.

'Baby-seat fitted and I've already tested it. Car's out the front.'

That now proved to be a problem. Some enthusiastic hospital cleaner discovered the identity of the little girl and rang the local TV station. They were hot to trot and told their parent company in Melbourne. The world and its mother soon knew Candy White was alive and well in Central Victoria. This was lead story material.

The local police got busy. The senior officer approached Jo and explained the situation. 'You've got the media here, Detective. You've put Castlemaine on the map. One TV station has offered to fly you back to Melbourne.'

'For an exclusive no doubt,' said Jo. 'I don't have the authority to make that decision, sir.'

'Then I suggest you call your boss.'

Jo nodded. She looked at Michael. His eyes turned sad. He'd run around to get the child seat for their two-hour journey back to town, and now he'd be driving Jo's car back on his own, the child seat empty.

Jo took Michael aside. 'I'm not happy about this, Michael.'

'What about the police chopper instead?'

'Look, if the doctors say she's fine, let's finish our day in the country as we planned it.'

He shrugged. 'You're the boss, boss.' Inside, he purred.

'Drive the car around the back and avoid the media.'

'Are you sure about this?'

'We could have a sing-song in the car. Do you know any songs by The Wiggles?'

'All of them. My sister's kids love The Wiggles.'

'Right, Deputy Chan, move the car—ah, please.'

Jo went to the senior officer and explained the plan. He grinned. 'Brave move, Detective. I'm good at police-speak. How about I make a nothingness statement while you leave town on the quiet?'

She thanked him, handed over the keys to the Muckleford Station and to Lawrence's motorbike and the escape plan went into action.

Little Candy and her two new friends were well on their way to Melbourne by the time the police statement was delivered. The media remained in place waiting for Candy's appearance. They waited in vain. Some journos could well be described as pissed off.

The phone rang in Homicide. 'DI Steele.'

'DI Goddard.'

The Pope froze. He disliked his colleague, no, he loathed and mistrusted her. She was a rival in his scramble up the promotion pole. His voice expressed his feelings.

'What can I do for you, Inspector?'

'Just a courtesy call to let you know the child abduction case we handed over to you has been sorted.'

This was difficult for the head of Homicide. Someone else had solved his case, stolen more like.

'Meaning?'

'The abducted child is abducted no more. She's alive and well so, if you like, we can tidy up the loose ends and let you get on with all those the murders on your plate.'

'What happened?'

'Nothing special, just a bit of old-fashioned police work.'

'That's not what I asked.'

'Look, Grant, let it go. We had a weak lead which involved a trip to the bush. I let a team member go touring and they struck gold. End of story. The abductors are locked up, the kid's being returned to her parents, and you'll see it all on the news tonight.'

Steele experienced a sinking feeling in his stomach. He didn't want to ask but couldn't resist not doing so.

'Who was the arresting officer?'

'Your smartest detective, Inspector, the best of the best.'

Goddard heard the phone go click.

Grannie Carr (Peg) was getting tea. Her son, GP Jack Carr, worked late most days and his two kids were collected from school by Pa (Hugh). He waited for his grandchildren by the school gate at the back of Mont

Albert Primary School and then walked them home. Harry couldn't stop talking and Grace struggled to announce her news thanks to baby brother the chatterbox. When they arrived, Peg had already fed Rags the dog and made a start on preparing the family's evening meal.

Being a widower and a busy GP, Jack would have struggled to raise his family, and his parents were a godsend. It was a win-win situation. Peg and Hugh lived nearby, loved being with the kids who loved Gran and Pa. The kids were not so keen on their deceased mother's folks, Grandma and Grandpa aka Misery Guts and Mr Floppy.

Once home, Grace and Harry were hanging out for an after-school snack freshly baked by Gran. Then it was walkies with Rags followed by a bath before tea. With a bit of luck, Dad might be home soon.

Before tea, Grace was reading while Harry played with Rags. Peg and Hugh were having a pre-dinner sherry and watching the news which was interrupted by a breaking story.

Hugh spotted it and called his wife who had slipped into the kitchen to check on the pot roast.

'Peg, they've found that little girl.'

She came into the sitting-room and looked at the telly.

'Really? And she's alive?'

'That's what they're saying,' said Hugh, pointing.

The trip back to Melbourne was joyous with lots of singing. Candy seemed normal. It was as if the last few weeks had been a holiday. Jo was thrilled about the girl's health but worried about the reaction of Candy's parents. Would Donna and Gavin's raw emotions frighten their daughter?

Jo pulled over about an hour from the CBD, got out of the car and called DI Goddard.

'We've dodged the media, ma'am. But chances are they'll be waiting at the family home.'

'They sure will. It's all over the news, front page on every web site and news bulletin.'

'Should we meet at a secret location? Avoid the media?'

'I've spoken to Donna, and she wants her daughter back in her own home, in her own bedroom, and nowhere else.'

'Okay, ETA one hour.'

'I'll meet you there. Drive carefully.'

She did, and told Michael of what might happen with the media throng once they got Candy back to her parents.

'Would you like me to drop you at home en route?' she asked.

'What, and miss all the fun?'

'That doesn't sound like you.' She glanced at him. 'You've turned your home into a fortress, Michael Chan. You're Mr Privacy.'

'There's a first time for everything, Detective. Maybe I should get out and mix with the great unwashed.'

Jo laughed. He was a brilliant IT specialist, and a kind and gentle man. But she had the feeling he wanted more from their relationship than she was prepared to give. That troubled her conscience. Unrequited love can hurt.

Does he really want a new and public persona? Or is trying to impress me?

They hit the suburbs of Melbourne which seemed to expand as you looked at them.

'How's the passenger?' asked Jo.

Michael looked. 'Sound asleep.'

'I'm worried about the media outside her home, and the way her parents will react.'

'Can you drive into the property and dodge the paparazzi?'

'There's a carport but if the mob are blocking the drive we'll finish up in the street, and have to run the gauntlet. All those cameras and lights, and her parents going nuts could terrify the kid.'

'I could announce a train derailment or terrorist attack in the next suburb.'

'A bit of fake news, you mean?'

'Just say the word.'

'The scary thing, Michael, is I know you could do that. You are, in some ways, the smartest and the most dangerous man I know.'

'But I could never solve cases like you, Jo Best. And the best part about this one is it has a happy ending.'

She smiled at him. He wasn't smiling but serious and that caused Jo to worry. This sounded like some undercover chat-up line.

They got closer to the White house. This one didn't have the Secret Service guarding it but it did have a scoop of journos, photographers and TV crews camped in the street. Neighbours were there in droves. Anyone with a hot dog stand could have made a killing.

Donna and Gavin were so worried they rang the local police and just before Jo and her precious cargo arrived, a couple of coppers turned up. Goddard had already thought of that and had all of her Major Crime officers in the street on the job.

'Dad's home,' called Harry as the doctor's car rolled down the drive. Rags barked, Grace kept reading—it was a really exciting bit—and her father came in via the kitchen.

'Evening all.' He kissed his mother, and gave Harry a hug. 'Something smells good.'

'We're having pot roast,' announced Harry.

Jack wandered into the sitting room. 'G'day Dad. Hello favourite daughter.'

Grace gave a wave as in "do not disturb".

Hugh asked his son a question. 'Did you hear about that little girl?'

'What little girl?'

'The one who's your patient.'

Jack was stunned. 'Candy White? What's happened?'

Peg came into the room. 'She's alive and well. They found her in Castlemaine.'

Jack's mind started spinning. *Castlemaine?* He rang Jo Best this morning to discover she was on the road and heading to Castlemaine. Finding Candy in that town was either an amazing co-incidence or else that particular senior constable had solved the mystery. What a woman.

'Dad?' asked Harry.

Jack was distracted. 'Yes, Grace.'

'It's me,' said Harry indignant at being called a girl's name.

'Sorry mate. What's up?'

'When is Detective Jo coming to our house again?'

The grandparents looked at their son. They had talked about the police officer and how she related so brilliantly to their grandchildren.

They saw how their son looked at Jo Best, and knew he was keen, if not besotted.

'Well, old man, she's busy. Police officers work at night as well, and we must let her do her important job.'

'I've been practising my salute. Look.'

Harry gave his sharpest salute and everyone, including his sister, was impressed. Gran and Pa added a smattering of applause.

Jo's car drew ever closer. They turned into the White's street and she spoke softly.

'Oh shit.'

There were cars, TV vans, people, many dogs on and off-lead, Major Crime detectives and five uniformed police officers. The original two had called for back-up.

Michael's jaw dropped. 'My Mum'll kill me for not wearing a tie.'

'How's the leading lady?'

Michael checked. 'Still asleep.'

'Bless her. If only she stays that way till she's inside.'

Jo slowed, as much worried about hitting a dog or one of the little kids who thought it was great being outside with half the world for company. Somebody pointed to Jo's car. Nobody knew what they looking for but this was not a through road and any car could be the one. This one was.

Goddard knew Jo's car and signalled to the uniformed officers. They cleared the driveway. TV crews jockeyed for position. It was like herding cats. One crew would be moved back only to be replaced by another. Steady boys.

Suddenly Jo was driving between lines of excited people. They clapped, cheered, waved and yelled.

'Should I give the Royal wave?' asked Michael.

'This noise'll wake Candy.' Jo pressed the central door lock.

Michael looked. 'She's still sleeping.'

Jo spotted Goddard. She became a traffic cop pointing to the White driveway, and giving camera crews a hard time. The car slowed a few metres from the driveway. People surged forward.

'They'll terrify the child,' gasped Jo.

Then the car was surrounded.

'Don't get out,' snapped Jo. Michael began shaking. Jo had to stop. Donna and Gavin pushed through the throng. They went to the driver side not knowing the child seat was behind the passenger.

The parents then had to push through the media throng to get close to their baby. Camera lights flashed and shone. What a nightmare. After weeks thinking their child was dead, she suddenly appears and, when delivered to their house, the parents can't get to their darling because of the press of the press.

Donna's teary face pressed against the back window. Candy stirred. Michael reported. 'She's waking up.'

Jo decided. She placed a police light on her dashboard and turned it on. No sound just the flashing light. Then she gave her horn a decent blast. It had the desired effect. People stood back a little and Jo drove forward. She hit the beginning of the driveway when a cameraman twigged he was on the wrong side to photograph the child. He raced across in front of her.

Whack. Jo's car hit him and down he went.

Polite swearing filled the car. Jo was stuck with people rushing around the now stalled vehicle. From out of the throng, Gavin White appeared. He disappeared below Jo and Michael's vision then stood grasping the victim who didn't appear injured although the shove he got from Gavin certainly left its mark.

The driveway was momentarily cleared and Jo drove into the carport. Then everything became a blur. Donna and Gavin were beating on the glass. Candy awoke and cried. Jo released the door lock and the parents and their daughter were reunited. A few daring photographers sneaked onto the property with exploding flashlights. Police pushed and the Whites were escorted inside.

It was over. They did it. Jo looked at Michael. She held up her hand and they high-fived. Flashlights meant the couple's salute was captured in living colour.

In the Carr household, Hugh interrupted the family discussion. He pointed to the TV. Live footage appeared from outside the White house. A reporter spoke to camera. She had to shout and ward off people who pushed past and into her. Cheering neighbours got on TV.

The Carr family stared at the screen. Even Grace gave up her book reading. The reporter told the viewers what they knew. Candy White was alive and well and back in the bosom of her family.

Then the cameras turned on a woman who spoke.

'My name is Detective Inspector Trish Goddard from the Major Crime Squad.'

'I think that's Jo's boss,' said Jack.

In his office, DI Steele watched the screen and uttered a non-Sunday School word.

Goddard continued. 'Candy White, the little girl who was abducted from a park in Richmond almost six weeks ago, has been found safe and well, and been returned to her family.'

'Who took her?'

'Where was she?'

Goddard ignored the questions. 'We will not be answering questions at this time but a press statement will be issued in due course. I will, however, tell you that the success of the operation was due to the outstanding work of a member of the Major Crime team, Detective Senior Constable Joanna Best.' Goddard turned to indicate Jo who stood a little behind her DI.

Flashlights went crazy.

'That's Jo,' yelled Harry. 'Dad, that's Jo on TV.' He gabbled and hopped. Grace was excited. Gran and Pa were impressed, and Jack had a burning feeling in his chest. Physician, heal thyself.

'Thank you, ladies and gentlemen,' said Goddard. 'The family will greatly appreciate being left alone at this important time. Please leave the area safely and quietly.'

The TV reporter came back on the screen. Footage of the recent events was screened including shots of a certain senior constable.

Harry kept hopping, his excitement overflowing. 'I saw Jo, Dad.'

'Yes, Harry, we all saw her.'

'She solved that case,' said Hugh. 'The Inspector said Jo was the one who cracked the case.'

'What does "cracked the case" mean?' asked Grace.

There were explanations aplenty and the pot roast, as good as it always was, hardly got a mention as the hot topic around the table that night was Jo Best.

Jack was in two minds. How could he deny his children who wanted to contact their hero? How could he try to get to know her better when she already had a boyfriend? Tricky.

Darren Sandilands dropped his beer and his pizza. 'What the fuck!?' He was watching the news—no, it was on while he ate his junk food meal—and there, as large as life, was the woman he and his mate Jordan attempted to bash and rape. She was on the fucking telly.

But wait, it got worse, much worse. The bitch is a cop and, wait for it, she's a she. The bitch is a bitch. Joe Best is Jo Best. WTF!

Jordan answered his phone. 'Yeah?'

'That bitch is a cop.'

Jordan was used to Darren sounding off and starting stories in the middle of the second chapter but this was far too cryptic.

'What bitch?'

'The one we tried to screw the other night.'

'She's a cop?'

'Yeah and she's Jo Best.'

Jordan couldn't complete Easy Crosswords so a super-tricky cryptic was way above his pay grade. 'You mean Joe Best's bitch is a cop?'

'Yes and she's Jo Best.'

Jordan knew what a homo was but a homonym had him beat.

'You're talking, crap, mate.'

Darren started losing it. 'Jo Best is a woman and she's the person who set up that web site calling me a prick.'

'Joe Best is a woman?'

Darren screamed. 'Yes, that's what I'm trying to tell you.'

'Well who's the other Joe Best?'

'I just told you.'

'So the bloke called Joe Best is sleeping with a woman called Joe Best? That's weird, man.'

'Shut up and get planning. Tell me how we can get Jo Best.'

'Which Joe Best?'

'I've never killed anyone but this bitch is gunna be the first.'

26

JO AND MICHAEL SAT IN HER CAR. They were not game to get out as TV crews continued to hang around.

'I think you're famous, Jo Best,' he said.

'Whoopee,' she replied without any enthusiasm.

'Your family'll be proud. And your grandfather'll be over the moon.'

Jo hadn't told Pop she'd been transferred out of Homicide—again.

Goddard came out of the house and to Jo's window. 'The family wants to see you.'

'Ma'am, did you meet Michael?'

'Yes, hello again,' said Goddard. 'Now come on, both of you. That's an order.' She went back inside.

Jo looked at Michael. He made a face. 'She can't order me,' he said, 'I'll wait here.'

Jo mocked him. 'Maybe I should get out and mix with the great unwashed.'

He got the point, and they went inside where Goddard nodded to them. Candy was on her father's knee with Donna sitting beside them. When Donna saw Jo, the mother was on her feet, embracing the officer. Donna's passion was full on. She wept and blurted her thanks.

'Thank you, thank you, thank you,' she said with tears aplenty.

Gavin came towards them holding Candy. It became a sort of group hug. But Gavin's restrained gratitude soon became full-on questions.

He wanted to know who took his daughter, where they were now, and when they'd be charged. Goddard steered the gathering towards the rescued child.

'We'll come and have a session with you both in the next day or so. All you need to do now is rejoice that Candy is home, safe and well.'

That stalled Gavin's desire for revenge. Michael was introduced and took the opportunity to say as little as possible. Then he and the police left. At the door, Gavin didn't know the meaning of subtle.

'How much should we charge the media for an exclusive interview?'

Goddard looked at him. 'We'll give you a call.' Outside with Jo and Michael, she expressed her feelings.

'Can you believe that guy? His daughter's just been found and returned safe and well, and all he's thinking about is money.'

Jo didn't like him. 'I'd rather not come back here, ma'am.'

'Coward,' said Goddard but knew Jo's thinking.

'Gavin won't like the truth,' said Jo. 'I think he knows his best mate murdered someone who had nothing to do with the abduction. He doesn't know his mate's sister-in-law could lose her job, or that his ex-girlfriend and his wife's former lover abducted his daughter.'

'Bring on the tabloids,' said Michael.

'Right you two,' said Goddard leading them to their cars. 'Drinks and nibbles at my place. It's time to salute the superstars.'

Jo and Michael hesitated. She was tired and he was shy.

'Ah, ma'am, thanks but we're both knackered.'

She unlocked her car and called as she got in. '24 Montgomery, Hawthorn. Be there.'

She drove off leaving Jo and Michael looking at each other.

'Just the one,' said Jo unlocking her car. 'This is the start of your new social life, Mr Chan.'

Darren waited for Jordan to bring the drinks. Darren never bought the first round. Jordan placed the beers on the table.

'You can't be serious, mate,' he said.

'That bitch made a fool outa me and now she's gunna pay.'

'But the web site's gone. They removed it.'

'I don't give a flying fuck. She mocked me and, nobody does that to me and gets away with it. And especially not some fucking slag.'

'We can break into her flat and trash the joint, set fire to her car, anything but you can't kill her, mate—she's a cop.'

'She has to pay.' Darren drew on his beer. Certain things made him angry. That dancer bird dumped him. Then his reputation was trashed online, and a woman stitched him up—a fucking woman. But he knew

Jordan was right. Killing a cop would bring him a whole lot of grief but he had to hurt that bitch and get his revenge.

'Why don't you just wreck her career?'

Darren looked at Jordan. 'What?'

'Stitch her up. Frame her. She's a cop. Just think how she'll suffer if she gets arrested, kicked out of the police, and sent to jail.'

Darren's thinking got busy. The few intelligent brain cells he did possess worked hard. 'Not bad,' he said. 'Tell me more.'

'We could plant drugs in her flat or dump some stolen gear. We wait till she gets home then tip off the cops.'

'And we can get in through that door to the laundry.'

'It's a piece of piss.'

Another draw on his beer sparked Darren's imagination. 'What would be best though would be murder.'

Jordan lost it. 'Jesus Darren, listen to me. You can't kill a cop.'

'We don't kill her. We get a dead body and place the stiff in her flat.'

'What?'

'Forget drugs. We set her up for murder.'

Jo and Michael found Goddard's little pad. There were a few cars in the street, spread apart. The residents in this upmarket suburb had off-street parking for multiple motors.

Michael looked at the Goddard pile. 'Is your DI corrupt?'

'I think her old man's a lawyer.'

'I'm in the wrong game.'

They walked up the drive. It took a while even at a reasonable clip. The garden had suburbs. The doorbell was architect-designed. They looked at one another while waiting for the door to be opened.

The butler was a silver-haired, corporate lawyer. He grinned.

'Ah, *See, the Conqu'ring Hero Comes!*'

'Hi, I'm Jo and this is Michael.'

'I'm Giles,' he said then turned back into the house and called. 'They're here.'

Jo and Michael had been reluctant to start with, and were now mildly scared.

'Come in, come in,' said Giles closing the door behind his guests.

Goddard appeared in the hallway. 'What kept you?'

She disappeared inside and Giles led them in that direction. He stood back and indicated Jo and Michael should enter. They did and died.

Bright lights came on and the 20 or so quiet people inside all broke into applause and cheers. Everyone from Major Crime was there plus most of Homicide. Not the Pope. It was party time, time to celebrate.

Billy Hughes was the first to come forward. She embraced Jo and a startled Michael. 'Brilliant job, both of you.'

Others joined the congratulations. Richelieu was at the end of the handshake, kiss and/or hug conga line. He congratulated Michael then concentrated of the female component of the team.

'Superbe, Mademoiselle. You are beautiful, talented and now heroic. Magnifique.' He embraced her and she reciprocated but with reserve. The embrace lingered until he was "tapped" from behind.

As on a dance floor, someone wanted to "cut in". But it wasn't a bloke—a woman did the tapping. 'Piss off, Froggie.' Richelieu stepped back, and Gabrielle Strange embraced the detective.

'Hello, Deranged Detective.'

'Hello, Pathetic Pathologist.'

'Bloody well done, Missy.'

Jo enjoyed the hug. They chatted as intimates.

Then Goddard tapped a glass, called for order, and proposed a toast. It was heartfelt and fulsome. She finished with, 'To Jo and Michael,' and the crowd repeated the toast with gusto.

'Speech,' called someone and Jo had no choice.

'Wow, I wasn't expecting this. Thanks for your kind words, ma'am.' She placed an emphasis on *ma'am* which evoked a loud "oooo" from the crowd.

'I couldn't have done it without my friend, Michael. He found the country town, and the house, and his Sat Nav is the best in the world.'

Someone shouted. 'Oooo, cheeky.' Laughter followed.

Then another called, 'Show us your Sat Nav, Michael.'

More hearty laughter and Michael Chan smiled the biggest smile of his life. Maybe there really was life outside the cave.

Jo looked at Michael and their eyes locked. Jo finished her speech and it scored a solid round of applause. People chatted in groups. More pizzas appeared and drinks flowed. Michael became a focus of attention. He began to enjoy a public life.

Jo chatted as much with her former colleagues at Homicide as she did with her current colleagues. Time went on and people started leaving. Michael approached Jo.

'I'm going, Jo.'

'God, I'm sorry, Michael.

'It's okay, I've got a lift.'

'Oh?'

'I'm fine. Connie lives in Northcote.'

Jo looked at a smiling DSC Connie Bryant and nodded. Jo wanted to say, "Be careful, Michael, she'll have you for breakfast," but instead thanked him again. 'I'll call you.'

The stragglers drifted away. Richelieu approached but stopped a metre or two away. He blew her a kiss and left. Jo saw she was alone with Goddard, her husband Giles, and Billy Hughes. They drank coffee.

'Have you heard about our recent homicides?' asked Billy.

'Ah, yes. Was one a judge?'

'And the other a mother and supermarket worker in the Yarra Valley at Warburton.'

'Right,' said Jo. 'And you're telling me this because?'

'Because you need to get back to Homicide, Senior, and the sooner the better. Murder's your bag, Jo, you're a natural.'

Jo looked at the two women. They were friends and had obviously been discussing Jo's future.

'Don't look at me,' said Giles Goddard. 'I'm just the barman.'

That quip added a touch of levity but Jo knew the score.

'I'd love to come back, Sarge, but we both know the situation. DI Steele doesn't rate me and until he changes, I'm better off elsewhere.'

'What if Detective Inspector Steele's antipathy disappeared?'

Jo's mind worked overtime. 'Disappeared?'

Goddard spoke. 'You know the drill here, Detective. If you repeat what we now tell you, we'll have to kill you.'

'Not me,' said Giles. 'I'm strictly no violence.' He wandered around collecting glasses and plates.

Jo didn't say a thing. She didn't have to. There was a long pause.

'There's a rumour at Homicide,' said Billy, 'that DI Steele is off to greener pastures.'

They waited for Jo's response. 'Rumours are often just that.'

'We heard he's been interviewed for a role in counter-terrorism at the ever-expanding Department of Home Affairs.'

'He has contacts in the AFP,' said Goddard.

Jo wondered how they knew that.

I think it's called Friends in High Places.

'So-o,' said Billy, 'if the Pope does abdicate, then as soon as we get some white smoke from the Vatican chimney, I'll get DI Richelieu to recommend your return.'

Goddard looked at Jo. 'Do you think DI Richelieu would want you back in Homicide?'

She knows, thought Jo.

'Possibly.'

Liar, thought the other women.

'Well, that sounds terrific but to quote the world's greatest sceptic, "I'll believe it when I see it".'

They finished their coffee, and Jo thanked all three and left. Giles walked her to the door.

'Lovely to meet you, Jo. And if you ever need a half-decent barrister, give me a call.' He handed her a business card.

'No wills and conveyancing then?'

He laughed. 'Far too complicated for me. I'm addicted to crime.'

She thanked him and left. Sitting in her car in the now empty street, her mind was racing. She'd switched off her phone ages ago, and had forgotten it. She switched it on.

There was a text from her mother, father, grandfather and a Dr Jack Carr. She opened it.

> *Dear Detective Jo. We saw you on TV tonight. They said you found a little girl. We think you are the best detective in the whole world. Love from Grace and Harry. P.S. I have been practising my salute. Harry.*

She sat there and smiled. She really liked those kids. And their old man wasn't too shabby either.

So where to now, Missy? And with whom?

It was late when she got home. She'd driven over 300 clicks in a single day, been through more emotions than a shark-jumping daytime soap, and felt seriously pooped.

She parked at the back of her building and locked her car. The brutal attack by thugs made her wary. She walked out into the street and along the well-lit road before turning hard left to her front door.

It was locked. It felt strong. Once inside, she closed the door adding a security chain. The place looked normal, like it always did. She wandered through her flat checking windows and the back door. She wasn't sure but the rear entrance seemed even stronger than before.

It was stronger thanks to her recent visitors. They'd removed her back door and re-set it making it easier to access in the future.

They spent time checking out her flat. Plumber Darren and builder's labourer Jordan were planning a little revenge attack on Detective Joanna Best. All the thugs needed was a corpse.

To be continued

The Detective Joanna Best Mysteries

www.cenfoxbooks.com

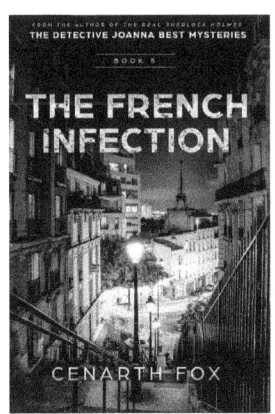

www.ingramcontent.com/pod-product-compliance
Lightning Source LLC
Chambersburg PA
CBHW071108100726
47908CB00008B/2308